UNIT 416

UNIT 416

J. LEON PRIDGEN II

and

A. JOHN VINCI

ST. MARTIN'S GRIFFIN

NEW YORK

UNIT 416. Copyright © 2017 by J. Leon Pridgen II and A. John Vinci. All rights reserved. Printed in the United States of America. For information, address St. Martin's Press, 175 Fifth Avenue, New York, N.Y. 10010.

www.stmartins.com

Designed by Omar Chapa

The Library of Congress Cataloging-in-Publication Data is available upon request.

ISBN 978-1-250-08997-7 (trade paperback)
ISBN 978-1-250-08998-4 (e-book)

Our books may be purchased in bulk for promotional, educational, or business use. Please contact your local bookseller or the Macmillan Corporate and Premium Sales Department at 1-800-221-7945, extension 5442, or by e-mail at MacmillanSpecialMarkets@macmillan.com.

First Edition: July 2017

10 9 8 7 6 5 4 3 2 1

Dedicated to the men and women who I have had the distinct honor and pleasure to serve with and all of the soldiers serving or who have served our country in lands near or far. Thank you for your service.

—J. LEON PRIDGEN II

For H.

This book is dedicated to all who serve our country in places and ways they cannot talk about.

—A. JOHN VINCI

ACKNOWLEDGMENTS

There was a time in my life that I was a soldier. I am proud of my service to this country and of being a member of the 82nd Airborne Division, and I loved getting my "Knees in the Breeze." It has given me friends that I still have to this day. Thank you to all the women and men who have proudly worn the uniform and served this country.

UNIT 416 is a work of fiction and a collaborative effort. I would like to thank God with whom I had a lot of conversations during the writing of this novel. A big thank-you to A. John Vinci for bringing the treatment forward and creating this opportunity. To the team that has made this dream possible—Brendan Deneen, Monique Patterson, and Alexandra Sehulster, I cannot thank you enough for your support of this effort. The conversations, pushes and pulls have challenged me and I am better for it. I am forever grateful.

To my literary agent, Sara Camilli, who brought this project to my attention, I want to thank you for your continuous support of my efforts, belief in my vision, a mind that is open, an ear that always hears, and a shoulder when it was necessary. You have once again walked page by page with me through this book and this process. I am humbled and Blessed to have you representing me and my work. More than anything, I cannot thank you enough for caring more about me as a person than as an author. Your representation is grounded in love, and thanks for this home.

To my mother, Mamie Sue Mitchell Pridgen, and father, Timothy Garfield Pridgen Jr., without whom there would be no me. Thank you for the great gift of life, and I am good. My mother's love has sustained me during times of want and plenty. From her I know what the term unconditional love means. God rest your souls, be at peace, I love you both.

To my wife, Gail, my parents have given me life but the life we share continues to give me purpose. You are the most incredible woman in my life and I thank you for accepting me as I am. With you I have transformed from a young man into a husband and a father. You are my rock and the foundation of our family. I will never be able to thank you enough for your support and for the two special gifts that we call our children. Leondra and Leon Jr. are adults now and the best of whatever I have been and will be. We have been Blessed with children who have constantly amazed us with their goodness and love for family and friends. You, Gail, are an amazing woman who makes that all possible. Thank you for giving me that day that was the best day—The Day I Met You!

—J. Leon Pridgen

I'd like to thank Brendan Deneen at Tor Books for immediately seeing the promise of *Unit 416* and helping in every way with this project; Leon Pridgen for being such a great author to work with; and Monique Patterson and Alexandra Sehulster for help-ing to make this happen. I'd also like to thank Mary for continu-ing to support me in everything I do.

—A. John Vinci

1

OCTOBER

Why did they have to send a newbie just when they were ready to wind down in Afghanistan? Keeble had tuned out the new guy, Whales. He was focused on finding his target. They were close to finding Anemah Maasiq, a man they had hunted for nearly two years, and he knew it was better not to talk when they were on patrol. He wanted to be alert to the surroundings. A change in tone brought Keeble back to the conversation in the Hummer.

"You guys married?" Whales asked.

The driver tensed for a split second. "Yeah, to this shit right here."

"Right. I married my high school sweetheart while I was on leave before I shipped over."

"Shut the fuck up, Whales!!" Keeble erupted from the backseat.

"Sergeant?"

"Shut it, Whales. This is not the place for a trip down memory fucking lane." Keeble's voice was low and intense.

"I was just . . ."

"You were just dying, son."

"What?" Whales responded weakly, completely flustered.

"Home is home, and we ain't there. You don't take this shit back there and you sure as hell don't bring that shit out here. You fucking got me?"

"Yeah, Sarge."

"There are men out here who need you to be with them. If your mind is floating back home at any time while you're out here, you might as well get fitted for a pine box. Roger that, Whales?" Keeble waited. "Fucking roger that?"

"Roger, Sarge."

"We take care of us and everything else takes care of itself. Now shut your hole."

"Roger that."

Keeble pushed his night vision goggles up on his helmet and stared holes into the back of Whales's head. Whales could feel the stare and did not utter another word. Keeble pulled the goggles back down and checked his map.

"Everybody, I need you to lock it down in two klicks." Keeble spoke into his headset. "Recon shows a clear path into this rough but then it gets a little dicey. Need all eyes and ears locked in."

"Roger," came back to him from the drivers of the other vehicles in his contingent.

Before the radio communication went silent, there was a loud explosion that struck the first Hummer. It buckled the vehicle on the right side and almost tilted it over onto its left.

"What the hell!?" Whales was rattled.

"IED got 'em. There was nothing coming from up top." Keeble was quickly assessing the situation. "Rollins, get up and flank them on the left; we got them covered on the right." Keeble listened for gunfire, but there was none. "Move quickly. They're not firing yet, but they're close. I can feel it. We gotta get the boys out of that vehicle and set a perimeter in the valley. Taylor, how bad is it?" he asked over the radio.

"I'm good. Wells is a little woozy. I can't tell with Schmitz; he's out. He took the brunt of it in the passenger seat, but he's breathing."

"I got him; you and Wells get in with Johnson, and grab your shit. Everybody else set up for suppressive fire."

In these moments of chaos, Keeble was at his best. He knew what needed to be done and where everyone needed to be. The drivers flanked the damaged Hummer. Keeble used hand signals to direct everyone into position. Still no enemy fire and they all scanned the tree line for movement. All eyes were on Keeble as he counted down with his fingers—three, two, one. They sprang into action. Taylor and Wells moved into Johnson's Hummer, banged up and cut, but not too much the worse for the wear. When Keeble reached Schmitz, though, that was a different story. The IED had exploded under the right tire and into the floorboard, which was peeled back like a can of sardines. Schmitz's legs were shredded in the process. Keeble didn't flinch at the sight; he unbuckled Schmitz and pulled what was left of him out of the wreckage.

"Wells," Keeble called to the Hummer on the left. "Are you good?"

"Yeah, Sarge."

"Change of plans. I need you in here with us."

"Fuck . . ." Whales uttered as he caught a glimpse of Schmitz.

"Keep your eye on that horizon for movement. Schmitz, I got you; you're going to be okay," Keeble said calmly, but Schmitz was still out. He got him to the back of the Hummer and laid him down there. "Let's get into that valley and set the perimeter; take it slow and keep those eyes three-sixty."

Each Hummer pulled slowly away from the damaged vehicle.

It was thirty yards to the tree line of the valley on the left. The drivers made a straight line in that direction, one behind the other. Keeble worked quickly in the back of the Hummer to stop as much of Schmitz's bleeding as possible and stuck him with an EpiPen. The shot of adrenaline revived him. Schmitz's eyes opened; a gasp of breath as he struggled for words, but there were none. Keeble locked eyes with him.

"I got you; rest easy," Keeble whispered.

Schmitz nodded his head, slowly drawing in his breath and never closing his eyes. Hearing the words from Sarge was good enough for him. He gathered his strength to speak and he motioned for Keeble to lean closer to him. As Keeble leaned in, the night erupted with the sounds of a rocket launcher.

"Incoming!" someone shouted.

The vehicles split right and left and the rocket narrowly missed both vehicles, striking the tree line in the valley. Johnson's Hummer absorbed the brunt of the reverberating impact and careened into a tree. Their driver pulled closer to the trees so the passenger side faced the east ridge.

"Where was that from?" Keeble barked.

"About three hundred yards to our east, from the ridge," Whales responded.

"Start laying fire at anything that moves. They weren't set up for us; they would've had something on us when we hit that IED if they had been. Johnson, how are your boys?"

As Keeble waited for a response, semiautomatic weapons began to pepper their position from the ridge to the east. Keeble knew immediately from the sound that the enemy was armed with AK-47s. He scrambled out the back and dragged Schmitz with him. Whales, Wells, Taylor, and the driver covered him while he got Schmitz into some of the heavier brush. The gunfire coming at them was picking up in intensity, more guns gathering at the position on the ridge, but the boys were handling their own.

"Start to fall back into the tree line. Whales, grab my SCAR and ruck," Keeble said on the headset as he low crawled to Johnson's vehicle.

Johnson and the rest of the fellas were already gathering their equipment and preparing to get to the tree line when Keeble got to them.

"Thought you fellas were gonna skip the party?" Keeble asked.

"Hell, nah." Johnson was keeping an eye on the ridge. "I make about eighteen of them so far; nothing from the west. How's Schmitz?"

"Alive when I left him. He doesn't have long out here."

Just as the men exited the vehicle and made their way into the tree line, a rocket struck the vehicle, causing an explosion. The men ducked as shrapnel flew all around them.

"Fuck me!" Taylor yelled. "My back."

A piece of shrapnel was wedged into his right shoulder blade.

"Everybody, keep it quiet. We need to move farther into the trees. Nobody shoots. And get Taylor patched up. Johnson counts roughly eighteen of 'em. Probably a couple more will be joining them. Take a few minutes and then we're going after 'em," Keeble ordered. "I got Schmitz."

Before another word could be uttered, the whistle of a mortar shell was heard; it landed near the Hummer Keeble had ridden in. A bloodcurdling scream told Schmitz's brothers-in-arms that his life had come to an agonizing end. Sounds of laughing and celebration over the successful strike could be heard from the ridge.

"Fuck these raghead motherfuckers. Spread out. And, Rivers, I need you and Ellis on three-sixty. If you get a lock on any of 'em, burn 'em!" Keeble ordered over the headset.

Keeble found Whales and grabbed his Special Forces Compact Automatic Rifle and ruck. The movement of the Taliban was ever so slight but a number of them had already given up their position to Keeble with their celebratory laughter. Once his men were set, Keeble fired two shots in that direction. When shots were fired back, they were from about two hundred yards away. Keeble was waiting with a shot that landed on its mark and a Taliban soldier was down. They received more gunfire from the Taliban, and Keeble and his men shifted their positions on his orders as they prepped two M203 grenade launchers for two hundred yards. The strike took down several soldiers, but forced more gunfire back at the grenade launchers' position. Whales was one of the launchers and he was subsequently struck by the enemy. Keeble saw the shot that felled him; it caught Whales in his Kevlar helmet. Keeble stood with his weapon still locked, loaded, and firing as he moved to Whales's position. When a Taliban soldier adjusted to shoot at him, he exposed himself to Keeble, who felled him with a shot, center mass. He picked off two more as he neared Whales. Sixty yards away, one of his men yelled, "grenade" and they all took cover. Keeble jumped on top of Whales as the grenade detonated.

"Whales?" Keeble said, while on top of him.

"I'm okay; just can't see a thing," Whales answered. His Kevlar helmet had been shattered by the bullet that struck it; it saved Whales's life. His forehead and eyes were bruised, but he was alive.

Keeble's men let another four rounds of grenades off on the Taliban soldiers while Keeble resumed picking them off, one by one. As the fire from the enemy slowed and they began their retreat, it was the right time for Keeble to move Whales. He hauled him up in a fireman's carry to move him. He heard a crack as he stepped on something. Keeble never realized the grenade's explosion caused a compound fracture to the lower part of his right shin. He just kept going.

"Taylor, radio air support to clear this area and get us a Black Hawk. And keep laying down fire until that bird is here," Keeble ordered.

"What happened to your leg, Sarge?" Whales's vision was beginning to come back. He thought he was seeing things when he saw part of Keeble's bone sticking out near his boot.

Before Keeble could see what Whales was looking at, a shot rang out. Keeble could hear it as clear as a bell. It's been said in military folklore that if a bullet has your name on it, no one hears it quite the way you do. It struck Keeble in the back and pierced through his Kevlar vest. The burning sensation turned into an inferno in his back. The pain caused him to lose his grip on Whales. Keeble dropped him as the pain caused him to collapse. Keeble could taste the blood filling his lungs. As unconsciousness began to lay its heavy hand on him, Keeble's last thought was, *I heard it. Is this how it comes to a close?*

2

COMPTON, CA

Neighborhood Pride Day had taken over Kelly Park on the east side of Compton. There were smiles, laughter, and children at play. The thoughts of a brighter tomorrow with better schools and motivated educators filled the atmosphere. But it was only for the day. Tomorrow the park would be back in the hands of the Kelly Park Hustlers. The bangin' and drive-by shootings would return and this day would be little more than a distant memory.

Mike Winston was twenty-four years old, wearing Beats headphones that played old-school NWA, and the clothes he wore, although not completely thugged out, left little doubt as to where he came from. He'd helped sponsor the event for the day, bought all the food, shook all the hands, and even kissed a few babies. He spoke with pride about the direction his neighborhood was taking. He was the guy handing out turkeys in the neighborhood on Thanksgiving. A person just looking in would think he was running for mayor.

But as he stood by his tricked-out El Camino, he sensed

there were quite a few people on both sides of the law who knew today was just another collection day for him. What Mike was unaware of was that elements of both sides were working together; today was the day that was planned to get him off the street one way or another.

The two African-American undercover officers in a blue, sixty-nine Nova watched from a quarter mile away as their mark made his way to Winston. Winston and the mark greeted each other with the familiarity of old friends. There were a couple of smiles and words exchanged, all of which was being recorded for testimony to be used at a later date. The mark then attempted to hand a package to Winston, which he refused, nodding toward the passenger seat of the El Camino. The awkward moment passed as the mark placed the package in the car. He then gave Winston some dap and patted him on the back, two times. Almost as quickly as he came, he was gone.

Instead of getting into the El Camino, Winston began walking away from it. Not at all what the officers expected. They watched as his casual pace began to pick up speed. The undercover officers hit the blue lights and blasted the sirens signaling the foot officers that the chase was on. The siren might as well have been a starter pistol because as soon as Winston heard the noise, he sprinted toward the flow of traffic.

The noise startled quite a few people, but none more so than a young boy. Maybe five or six years old, he lost his bearings and stumbled toward the oncoming traffic. Winston saw the boy headed toward the cars; he also saw his opportunity for an escape. The shrill voice of a woman screaming for her child caused Winston a split second of indecision. His instinct took over and he darted toward the boy, catching the tail end of his shirt as he dove after him and snatched him away from the traffic. Winston rolled to a stop and saw the boy was safely out of harm's way. But before Winston could scramble to his feet, he was forced back to the ground by several officers. The cuffs were on him before the little boy was back on his feet.

TERRELL, TX

Levern "Lev" Smith was about as big as they come in Texas. At six feet eight inches and two hundred and forty pounds of pure muscle, the natural assumption was that the twenty-two-year-old would someday be playing thirty-five miles down the road for the Dallas Cowboys. But a couple of NCAA violations at A&M and a prominent booster who didn't take too kindly to his beautiful, blond-haired, blue-eyed, apple of his eye baby girl tomcattin' around with the big ole' black tight end who couldn't stay out of trouble, had him off the team and back in Terrell, Texas, before he could say Aggies ten times.

These days all he was catching was hell from the farmers who were expecting their repairs to be done the day before yesterday. The people who used to cheer his name under the Friday night lights now just called him "boy" or "that lazy rascal down at the garage." Occasionally he might have to remind an antsy farmer that he could work on his tractor faster if he didn't have to stop and talk with him for long periods of time. Whether it was the disarming smile or the biceps and forearms that flexed as he squeezed the wrench that convinced them to let him get back at his work, he wasn't sure, but it always seemed to work.

As Lev quietly worked to repair the same John Deere tractor for the third time in the last two months, he heard a car skidding to a stop outside the garage. If that was Mr. Butler back to check on his tractor again, he was going to get a heck of a lot more than a happy-go-lucky smile and a few squeezes of the wrench today. He heard arguing and knew immediately that it wasn't Butler. Lev lifted his head up from the tractor to get a peek out the window and he saw a man yelling at a pleading woman.

As she got out of the car, Lev took in the beauty of the young Hispanic woman. She was crying and apparently moving away from him in fear. Lev got outside in time to see that the man was already out of the car and snatching her arm.

As she struggled to free herself from his grip, he backhanded her across the face and yanked her by her hair. "Bitch, get your ass back in the car!!"

"Hey! Sir! That's not necessary. There is no need to hit her."

The man turned his attention toward Lev and paused for a second as he took in the size of this big man, but in his fit of rage he didn't give a damn about this man's size. "Fuck off, coon! I'm talking to my wife."

"What you're doing doesn't look like talking to me," Lev shot back.

"Wait a minute. I know you." He pushed his wife down and kicked at her. "You're that big, dumb, fucking nigger that got kicked out of A&M for raping white bitches!"

Before the man could utter another word, Lev's fists were already swinging and connecting. The man made a futile attempt to fight back. But the problem with men beating on women is that they forget how to fight men. In Lev's fit of rage, he pummeled the man and it was only the pleading of the man's wife that pulled him out of that moment.

She called 911. When the ambulance and the police arrived, it was Lev who was arrested for assault and battery. The husband cooked up a story of stopping in to check on pricing for tractor repairs when a disagreement on pricing led to him and his wife being assaulted by Lev. The wife, with a fresh bruise on her face and day-old bruises on her body, corroborated his story. There was no opportunity for Lev to explain, just some nice, new, shiny silver bracelets for his wrists.

CHICAGO, IL

Darrell Jones attracted a crowd to join him at the corner of Michigan Avenue and Monroe Boulevard. The nineteen-year-old African-American whiz kid computer geek had a dynamic gift of gab and the ability to multitask. He was beating some schmoo for fifty bucks at speed chess while pontificating to his captive audience about the ills of domestic violence.

"When we take time to examine domestic violence, particularly as it relates to culture, then we get a better understanding, a deeper understanding as to why we continue to push such negative behavior onto our women. No, son! You don't want to do that. Check!" Jones made his next chess move. "In the black culture, can you blame a brother for the violence he perpetrates against his woman?"

A number of people nodded and said yes. A few were very adamant in their affirmations. Just what Jones loved, a captive and engaged audience. It was akin to being a talk-show host, a repartee of give and take. The more they talked, the longer they stayed.

"I would argue that you cannot." That response drew moans and hisses from the crowd. "Give me a moment and I'll clarify. Checkmate!" The schmoo was so wrapped up in Jones's oratory, he'd lost sight of the game. He ponied up his fifty bucks and the next victim sat down. "These brothers who have survived a history of oppression, societal ills, and let us not forget slavery, have not developed the coping skills to properly address their frustrations. These frustrations manifest in many forms of expression. Be it self-inflicted, self-medicated, or be it transferred to the next person or thing closest to them."

As Jones continued his diatribe, an extremely nerdy white guy, complete with pocket protector, stood there, transfixed. What the participants didn't know, or never even suspected, was that their fast-talking, chess-playing sidewalk host was stealing their identities.

Jones had stolen a local Wi-Fi password, rewired his cell phone, set up a bogus free mobile hotspot, linked the two systems together, and he was in business. The passwords, PIN numbers, and credit card info of unsuspecting passersby was downloading to his rewired cell phone. These folks would spend the next year trying to recover their identity and untangle their new financial history.

As his audience dwindled and there were no more schmooes to hustle, Jones closed up shop. He pulled out the rewired cell phone. It was still syphoning off data wherever it could gather it. He powered the phone down and put it away. Walking south on Michigan Avenue toward Jackson Boulevard, he spotted the nerdy white guy waiting for him. Darrell gave him a wink and a nod. The nerd returned the smile and Darrell read his amazement at what he'd just witnessed.

"It's that easy, bro. I can do it every day if you need me to," Darrell boasted as he pulled out the cell phone and cautiously waited for the nerd to produce the money.

"I don't think I can afford to do this every day." As he pulled the envelope out, he could see Jones grin. "Oh, I have a little something extra for you." The nerd reached back into his pocket but this time he pulled out a badge. "U.S. Department of the Treasury; you're under arrest."

LITTLE ROCK, AR

Five weeks ago, Tyrin Turner was looking at the concrete walls in a ten-by-ten cell vowing never to return. His conviction was overturned on a technicality. The judge overseeing the appeal found irrefutable proof that the prosecutors forged, coerced, and manufactured evidence and witness testimony to convict Turner of the attempted murder of a rival gang member. Now, driving around Little Rock with a gun in his hand and a directive from his gang to carry out the same hit five years later, he knew it was only a matter of time before he would be back in that same cell despite any vow he made.

For the five years that he sat in that cell, there were no visits from any members of his gang, his so-called family. They cut ties with him and left him on his own. The only person who visited him faithfully was his mother. She constantly pleaded with him to take the opportunity to turn to his faith and turn his life around. When Tyrin made her aware of his impending release, he confided to her that his walk of faith and her belief in him had delivered him from his circumstances. He pledged to her that this time would be different. He was tired of looking into her saddened eyes every Sunday afternoon when she came to visit. But at this moment, like so many of the promises he'd made before, the one he had made to his mother was empty.

Even though his charges were dismissed, it felt to him like everyone in Little Rock knew more about the case than he did. There was little doubt in his mind that the court of public opinion had him guilty as charged. People who knew him before he went to prison were well aware that he was hell on the streets when he was banging. Five years wasn't long enough to erase those memories.

Just five short weeks of life as a free man proved that no one in Little Rock would open their door to welcome him in, to give him a second chance at life. No one, that is, except his old gang family. In the last week, they had shown him more love than they ever did during his five years on the yard and possibly his entire life. He had never drunk as much liquor, smoked as much weed, or fucked as many women as he had this week. This is what his gang family called a welcome home. He felt that he was truly being welcomed, until he was given the proposition. If he completed the execution, the gang family and this life were his.

"What the fuck am I doing?" Tyrin reasoned with himself. These motherfuckers had five years to handle this themselves, and nobody in the family stepped up. And now they had given him two weeks to get the job done or the gang that called themselves his family would be closed to him as well.

As he drove through downtown Little Rock, he contemplated and ran different scenarios in his mind. There was so much running through his head; his mind started spinning in confusion. He pulled the car into a parking space to unwind from the dizziness. Settling there and letting his mind clear, he took a deep breath and looked up to see where he'd parked. He was at an army recruiting station. Some things happen for a reason.

BRONX, NY

The old lady was reluctant to take his hand. The first thing about him to catch her eye was the ungodly number of tattoos running up his forearms and disappearing into his T-shirt. But the warm and inviting smile the skinny young man possessed disarmed her reluctance.

"H-H-H-Hello, I s-s-s-saw you w-were h-h-having a little trouble in crossing? It would be a p-p-p-pleasure if I could assist you," Jack Daisy offered with sincere humbleness and a stutter.

"Thank you," the elderly woman replied.

Jack made sure to steady her before moving forward into the intersection. He took care of her the way he would his own grandmother. Once on the other side of the intersection, she gestured to pay him something for his time. Jack shook his head, bowed to her, and flashed his quirky charming smile before heading off about his business.

Jack Daisy had a name that had never belonged in the Bronx, and the face he showed the lovely elderly woman didn't belong there either. But when he saw some of his boys as he approached the Pelham Parkway, his demeanor changed to match the menacing company he was about to keep. The menacing look was part of the image they all displayed to go with their rap mogul future. These boys were all about being the next Jay Z or Lil Wayne.

A battle of rap lyrics was already underway and Jack was anxious to join in. Although he had a stuttering problem, his rapping skills were impeccable. In this hood, he was widely regarded as the second coming of Marshall Mathers. Jack had some new lyrics he was dying to spit out.

He and Rotund Fun—everyone called him Ro for short— had been going head-to-head the last couple of weeks, and the skinny kid with the tattoos and stutter had been getting the better of him. Today was no different. If it was a boxing match, Daisy would have been hitting him with a jab that was wicked, combinations that were brutal, followed by a series of body blows before finishing him off with an uppercut. Daisy's lyrics cut through Ro like a knife.

Instead of throwing in the towel and uttering *"no mas,"* Ro opted to tap out the only way he knew how, by talking shit.

"Fuck this skinny, stuttering motherfucker!!! Let's have a goddamn talking contest. I'll fuck this skinny nigger up then!" Ro shouted.

Ro roared with laughter, but few others found the humor in his words. Least of all Jack. Before Ro could inhale for his next breath of laughter, Jack was all over him, punching, yelling, spitting, and cursing Ro, his mama, and anybody who looked like him. The group soon realized Jack's ability to curse was like his ability to rap; it was stutter free. It was evident that Ro was more suited for the rap game than the scrap game. It was unclear whether he was able to land a blow in defense before he fell into a state of unconsciousness.

Police did not miss a beat and were on the scene within seconds. As they pulled little Jack Daisy off of Ro, he was still kicking, swinging, and cussing. Handcuffed and shoved into the back of the squad car, Jack was still letting Ro have it.

3

APRIL—EIGHTEEN MONTHS LATER

Colonel Lawrence Jameson was on a short list to be promoted to Brigadier General. He stood in his office up on the hill, with his back to the door, staring out the window at division headquarters. Fort Bragg had been his home for the last twelve years with a few temporary duty assignments in between. He was six foot two and weighed one hundred and ninety-six pounds. He was a dark-skinned African-American with penetrating eyes. He moved with the agility and grace of a cat and his nickname was Panther. This day was one that was long in the making, and he was glad that it was finally here.

Jameson was an excellent military mind who had pulled two tours in Iraq. He had completed Ranger School eleven years ago and served with them for four years. The last seven years, he'd served the military as a Special Operations Consultant, which was a fancy way of saying he was an orchestrator of military personnel.

He was up this morning before the crack of dawn reviewing for the umpteenth time the files of the men he had handpicked as he prepared to meet with two of his oldest friends. These were friends that went back to his childhood in Moncks Corner, South Carolina. The last thirty-plus years had taken them to different parts of the world, with many accomplishments to each of their names. But because of their chosen paths, they always had a way of coming back together.

The door to his office opened quietly as Jameson waited for the sun to rise. He never moved a muscle as the two men crept into the room and eased their way toward him.

"Why don't you make yourselves at home?" Jameson said as he continued to stare out the window.

"We had you," Marv Goldberg said.

"Not even on your best day. Have a seat," Jameson replied. He turned to his friends as they each took a seat at his desk.

Seated in front of him was Marv Goldberg, Central Intelligence Agency chief of field operations for South Asia, and Erick Harlow, chief of field operations for Central Asia. Although all three were approaching their fifties, physically, they could easily be mistaken for men in their midthirties.

"Good to see you both. Been way too long. How are the families?" Jameson said as he reached across his desk to grab Goldberg's hand.

"All is well on the home front. The nest is finally empty—" Goldberg started.

"Cut the bullshit," Harlow interrupted.

"Screw him. Wife number four just bailed on him. He's not interested in discussing anything family related."

"The twenty-five-year-old with the great tits? She's gone? Say it isn't so," Jameson said to Harlow.

"I thought we were here to take care of something!" Harlow snapped at the two of them.

"Just like when we were kids; next thing you know, he'll be

grabbing his ball and going home." Goldberg took one last jab at Harlow before letting it go. The look Harlow gave him let him know it was time to move on.

"Marv's right, it's time to get to work; we can catch up later," Jameson said. "On the desk in front of you are profiles on each of the men that I have selected based on what you have told me that you're looking for." Jameson paused for a few seconds as they began to glance at their files. Harlow stopped almost as soon as he started.

"This guy is damaged goods. And he is the guy that you have to lead them?" The file in Harlow's hand was Keeble's.

"It's the background that you want. This man has served his country honorably, a decorated hero who almost lost his career in defense of this country. I've had eyes on him since he returned to Bragg. He was close to losing his military career but he hung on and fought his way back."

"So, he's in?" Goldberg asked.

Jameson paused and the slight hesitation answered the question for him. "Not yet. I have a meeting with him this morning at oh-nine-hundred. But don't worry; he'll be jumping at the chance to be a part of this."

Goldberg turned the page on Keeble's file and saw a picture of Keeble's surgically repaired lower right leg. It would have drawn a reaction from a man who hadn't seen as much death and carnage as he had over the last thirty years. Instead, he just said flatly, "I don't know how much jumping he's going to be doing on that."

"You would be surprised. This man is a beast that wants to rejoin Special Forces; medically, he won't ever meet those military standards. This operation is so far off the military radar, it will be perfect for him."

Harlow riffled through some of the other files. The more he

read about each one of the men, the more his dissatisfaction grew. "This is some kind of a joke, right? These can't be the guys that you came up with. These guys are criminals and, well, I mean . . ."

"And all but one of them is black," Jameson finished his thought.

"I didn't say that." Harlow tried to cover his ass.

"You wanted to, but you just couldn't. Look, you guys have been losing people in the field and haven't been able to successfully disrupt the arms cartel. That's why you came to me and you knew what I would bring back. At least Marv did. What you need are legitimate criminals to blend in with the cartel, people who can associate with the Taliban rebels. That's what I have."

"We need the best of the best that you have to go in there to root these people out," Harlow resisted.

"No, we don't. If we got the best of the best, they wouldn't take this 'off the record' high-risk mission." Goldberg understood the bigger picture.

"These guys have some problems with authority and discipline, and are a little rough around the edges, but they have an undying will to survive. Keeble has the ability to get these men to succeed and he can separate the ones who can't. You might not be able to see it now, but these are special men. I have monitored their progress in the army as closely as I have watched Keeble. As unique as these other men are, they can't hold a candle to Keeble. And without him, all the other files, all of these other men, are useless."

4

Dawn approaches, but the sunrise and sunset and most of the hours of daylight and darkness between have lost their meaning to the highly decorated Master Sergeant Miles Keeble. He lives by his military motto: Duty, Honor, Country—This We'll Defend. The only hours of importance to him are the hours within which his mission is to be completed.

The last year and a half of his existence had been a stark contrast from the previous nine years of his mission-oriented military career. The six foot, one hundred and eighty-eight pound, shaved-head sergeant had been spending his time on recovery from the wounds he suffered in Afghanistan. There were so many nights where the events leading up to his injuries would replay in his head. In the midst of all the chaos, he was composed. It was in those moments that he felt the most at peace and truly understood his purpose. He saw himself taking out threat after threat with precision shots. He would recall the intense focus that overrode the sharp pain in his lower right leg. His brain would relive the horror of seeing members of his nine-man Special Forces team injured in the firefight, re-live grabbing his brothers and pulling them to safety. The one thing he could never remember was the shrapnel that rendered him unconscious. Keeble could not remember being pulled to safety by Jeremiah Johnson, his brother from Jasper, Texas, who surrendered his life in the effort to save him. These thoughts and visions would permeate his mind as he fought day and night to get back to his team.

Keeble had little regard for the steel rod that was placed in his shin to stabilize his fractured leg. The pain he felt on the field of battle was caused by a bullet. He often was told he was fortunate to have been struck by shrapnel and knocked unconscious. A number of his team members would recount the severity of the compound fracture that would not slow Keeble down. The harder he worked to save his team members, the more pronounced the fracture became. If not for the shot that forced him off his feet, the leg would have likely had to be amputated due to the damage he suffered.

As the sunlight crept through his windowpane and illuminated his humble quarters, Keeble adjusted his eyes to it. He searched his walls for the familiar pictures of his team. The brothers he trained with, fought with, and had been willing to die with. A piece of him died with them in Afghanistan. Keeble entered the military as an infantryman with an Airborne Package Platoon designated for the 82nd Airborne Division, but Keeble was destined to join an even more elite fighting group in the Special Operations Forces—the men he was now disconnected from. They were his brothers, closer to him than any family had been for the last ten years. They were the reason he battled so hard with his recovery. If he could get back to the team, it would help him put to rest some of the thoughts that wreaked havoc on so many hours of his daily life. He cursed the name Anemah Maasiq for forcing him into this position.

It was almost 0630. Reveille. The official beginning to each military day was about to begin. Keeble did not need a clock to remind him of the time. At six thirty a.m., his body and mind were conditioned to respond. Keeble assumed his customary position at the window where he would observe the flag being raised. He positioned himself in parade rest and watched as the American flag was being placed on the flagstaff. As the first note of "The Star Spangled Banner" was heard, Keeble snapped to attention and saluted the flag as it was raised. He smiled a bit to himself as he realized that the pain in his surgically repaired right leg was bearable. It was a sign of the positive day that lay ahead for him.

At 0900 hours, Keeble would be meeting with Colonel Lawrence Jameson. He was the man who held the key to Keeble's military future and the man who would help mend his military past. He was a hard-nosed, tough-as-nails, by-the-book military man. He was Keeble's kind of officer, a hard ass like himself who understood the military way. Jameson would understand Keeble's need to defend his country, the need serve with his team. Keeble's attitude was "damn what everybody else thinks; damn what the army protocol is regarding injuries to military service people." Today would mark a day in history. It would be the day in which Keeble became the first serviceman to make his way back from the near loss of a limb to return to his Special Forces team. Keeble was a few hurdles away from stepping back on the battlefield and participating in active combat.

Anticipation shifted Keeble's thoughts as the national anthem came to a close. He snapped his salute back to his side and assumed the position of parade rest. There was a time in his military career when he stood side by side with other soldiers as reveille came to an end. Gone were the days of falling into formation with the other troops for physical training, which the army simply termed PT. PT for Keeble now stood for physical therapy. Gone too, were the days when he reported to the doctors on base for physical therapy. Keeble felt they were preparing him for a life outside of the military while his goal was to be prepared to stay in. He never missed the opportunity to tell the therapists that they were too soft for what he needed. Keeble went as far as telling one of the physical therapists that "If he wanted to sit in the lap of luxury, he'd call on the PT's lazy, breastfeeding heifer of a wife." These days, his physical therapy was self-administered. He would document his work and report it back to them once every two weeks. They marveled at what he would put himself through, but they had their doubts, especially Major Watson. At least until the major took it upon himself to challenge Keeble at one of his alleged workouts. The major spent a couple of weeks in physical therapy attempting to recover from his unwise decision.

Keeble quickly dressed in his running shorts and T-shirt. Today his target was a run of six miles at a pace of six and a half minutes. And by his calculations, the run would be completed in thirty-nine minutes. Not the thirty-six-minute total time he used to take on his casual runs. But to Keeble, it was all relative. The thirty-six-minute time was before there was a titanium rod stabilizing his shin to his ankle, and before he had changed his gait to minimize the pain he experienced. In his mind, there was no doubt that in due time, he would have his pace down to what he considered normal.

As Keeble started out for his six-mile run, he noticed his familiar spectator again. Major Watson stared at him in utter disbelief. If he didn't have his own bird's-eye view, he would not have been able to fathom the level of activity the wounded warrior put his body and mind through.

"Good morning, Major Watson. Care to join me?"

"How far are you going?" the major replied, knowing damn well he wasn't running anywhere with this maniac.

"Six miles; need to be done in thirty-nine minutes." Keeble was daring him.

"Nah, taking a different route today."

"Airborne, sir," Keeble replied, but he might as well have said "bullshit, sir," because that certainly was his intent.

The major's eyes were transfixed on Keeble's right lower extremity. The shape was disproportionate to the well-developed left leg and the scarring was obvious to any onlooker. Keeble felt the stare, and kicked the leg up a little higher with his first stride, raising the major's eye level. He gave a nod to the major.

"My best to the missus," Keeble offered.

Whether it was a genuine peace offering or a comment from a smart-ass war hero, Watson's look of astonishment quickly left his face. Keeble could see the wheels turning in Watson's head, recalling Keeble's previous parting shots about Watson's wife. Keeble was successful at diverting the major's attention away from his extremity. The major never noticed the slight wince Keeble gave with the first couple of steps of his stride. It was now part of a customary habit that Keeble's will had given in to.

Today's run was designed to be an extremely grueling one. Area J was a wooded tract of land off of Bastogne Drive, some of the most difficult terrain to navigate. The area was used for combat training activities, but it was now fertile ground for Keeble to recapture the man he used to be. A normal man would be commended for taking on the six-mile trek in forty-eight minutes. Anything faster than that was a push. But a six-and-a-half-minute mile pace would be nearing the insane pace and standard set by the elite fighting forces of the black beret–wearing Rangers or the green berets of the Special Forces. But that is who Keeble was and who he still believed himself to be.

Breathing was solid and the nagging pain in the shin subsided as he struck dirt on the ground that had become a sanctuary for him. He was careful of his footing, sprinting up the slight inclines and coasting on the winding, downhill slopes.

Two miles into the run, his body had heated up and the chill in the air did not exist to him as his body settled quickly into its second wind. As his body flowed, doing what his mind required, his mind was able to settle into its own peaceful place. It was as if his body was running free and he was watching it from above, merely guiding it through Area J. Keeble felt a twinge in his shin as he came out of Area J. There was one mile left but the twinge was becoming a pain. Something wasn't quite right. Keeble hesitated to look at his shin. It was still stable and he knew it was just pain from pushing so hard today. The quick glance revealed no sign of blood; everything was good.

Completing the run in the thirty-nine minutes he'd allotted himself was his validation; the pain in his shin was part of the sacrifice for his success. He would spend the next few minutes in a state of near exhaustion and nirvana. His physical body, although not in the shape it was in before his combat-related injury, had been pushed beyond its current limits. He was ready. It was time for him to go back to the team, back to the friends who had become his family. It was time for Keeble to go home.

5

A fresh pot of coffee was brewing and the aromatic scent wafted throughout his office. Jameson glided purposefully over to the maker and poured a cup into his favorite mug. It was an 82nd Airborne Division mug. On it was a rendering of a set of jump wings and under it, a caption read DEATH FROM ABOVE. No cream, no sugar. The coffee was as dark as his skin. Coffee in hand, Jameson sat down at his desk, attempting to relax into his chair and enjoy his java. He would try as best he could to just let the 0900 hour approach.

"Colonel?" his aide's voice came over the intercom.

"Yes?" Jameson sat up.

"I believe we have Sergeant Keeble approaching. I just picked him up on the monitor."

"Good; let him in and have him take a seat. I'll be with him in five minutes." *Just like dating*, Jameson thought; *don't want to appear too excited.* He reached for a newspaper on the side of his desk. Reading one article should fill up the time. Jameson, however, struggled to read any article as nothing else at the moment could grab and maintain his attention. After two minutes of skimming his way through a couple of articles, he'd had enough. He punched a code on his phone, which prompted his aide to call him back. A routine they'd worked out a long time ago.

"Sir, Master Sergeant Keeble is here to see you."

"Thank you, Corporal. Please show him in." Jameson stood behind his desk.

Keeble was led to Jameson's door. The aide tapped on the door twice, then opened it for Keeble. The aide nodded at Keeble, granting him access to enter. Keeble carried a file in his left hand. As he entered, he took a quick visual of the room to analyze his surroundings. Not that he expected to find anything unusual; it was just his way, a habit that had become second nature to him. Jameson took heed of his approach and liked it. Keeble stopped three feet in front of the desk. He snapped to attention; brought his right hand to a salute, holding it there. Jameson then came to attention and returned the salute, allowing Keeble to lower his right hand.

"Master Sergeant, welcome," Jameson offered.

"Thank you, sir."

"Please, have a seat." It was not an order, but it was no request either.

"Again, thank you, sir." Keeble chose to sit in the chair to his left, always left over right.

"Master Sergeant Miles Keeble. It is my pleasure to meet with you. You may not be aware, but I have kept a watchful eye on you. News of your heroism reached this base long before you returned to it."

"Begging your pardon, sir, but the privilege is mine," Keeble replied.

"On that point, I think we should agree to disagree," Jameson offered with a hint of a smile and Keeble returned one ever so slightly as well.

An awkward moment passed between the two. There wasn't much to size up here. Both men knew their reason for sitting in front of each other; only Keeble operated under the assumption that Jameson's agenda matched his own. Jameson waited, letting Keeble twist in the wind a little bit.

"Permission to speak freely, sir?" Keeble cracked, giving up control of the situation. But he already knew who held all the cards here. He was just ready to have them dealt.

"Of course, Sergeant. That's why we are here."

Keeble's agenda was not a hidden one. This was not the enemy. It was an officer who, beyond the shadow of a doubt, understood the military and its men. Jameson was a career soldier just like him. They shared a kinship and a brotherhood.

"I am a soldier," Keeble began. "It is what I do. I don't know anything else, nor do I care to. *De oppresso liber.* To free from oppression. As you know, that is the motto of the United States Special Forces. That is the code I lived by daily until these past eighteen months. I'm sure I don't have to tell you what happened to me in Afghanistan; that file sitting in the middle of your desk with my name on it tells you that. Likely, it also tells you all the reasons why I am not the soldier I used to be. It will tell you about the severity of the injury I suffered to my right leg. It gives you all the logical explanations about why I am not fit to serve in the same capacity, what the army regulations are, and what the history has been. It does not tell you that I begged for them to save my leg on the field that day. It does not tell you that before they put me under and there was only a small chance for me to keep my leg, I begged and pleaded with God to step in. I made a deal with him that day. I vowed to make it back, not just recover, but make it back to my unit. This file charts my documented progress on my rehabilitation." Keeble set his personal file in front of Jameson. "I want you to pay attention to my recent physical readiness test and my psychological evaluation. When you compare this information to the data compiled before I joined SF, the information is virtually interchangeable. That means I exceed the basic criteria to be back where I belong. All your files, documents, and this injury have me pinned in your crosshairs, trapped in limbo, and I don't have the ability to move forward without you, sir. I am caught; I am oppressed. *De oppresso liber* actually means from a caught man to a free man." Keeble paused for a second to let the thought register, and then said, "*De oppresso liber*, sir." Keeble stopped short of begging.

Jameson hung on every word of the impassioned plea. He would like nothing more than to send him back to his unit today. Everything reported, everything he'd heard, and everything Jameson had seen was completely accurate. Keeble was beyond the real deal.

"Sergeant, it has been reported to me that you want to be assigned back to your SF team. It saddens me to tell you that it will not happen. Due to the extent of your injury and rehab, your team has moved on."

"Another team then? Another group then?"

"It wouldn't make any difference. I've looked at this every way imaginable; it's just not going to happen. As long as that titanium is in your leg, Special Forces is out; regular army, for you, I am sorry to say, is also out." There was no easy way for Jameson to cut it.

Stunned silence. Keeble was done. Life as he knew it was over. He had nothing outside of the military. No children, no connection with family, no significant other, an ex-wife who was long gone and one woman that got away. Eighteen months committed to getting back to what he loved. And now the only love in his life had no place for him. Keeble, although sitting still, was disappearing in front of Jameson.

"There is something, though." Jameson pounced on the moment of vulnerability. "You are too valuable an asset to be left sitting on the sidelines."

Keeble was distraught but listening. Grasping at any straw was better than having no straw at all to choose from. Soldier up; pick up the pieces and move on.

"Sir?" Keeble mustered, but had little else to offer.

"I have a mission for you. It's a way to keep you connected to the military, but it will be in conjunction with the Central Intelligence Agency."

"The CIA?"

"That's right, the CIA." Jameson nodded. "This is preparation for groundwork in Central Asia."

"And I fit into this how? In case you haven't noticed, I'm not fucking Asian." Keeble's bravado was creeping back.

"Nor do we want you to be," Jameson shot back. "This is a mission that has been a year in the planning by the CIA. You are a cog in the wheel, a very valuable cog, but you are still a cog. Are we clear on that?"

Jameson and Keeble eyed each other. No exchange from Keeble, but there was an understanding. Keeble knew to keep his mouth shut.

"I have put together a group of soldiers—twelve to be exact. We will be assembling them down at Fort Benning. They have risen from a group of forty-five and find themselves in a precarious position that they are not fully aware of. These soldiers come from some very troubled backgrounds. The specifics on each one vary, but suffice it to say that if these people weren't in Uncle Sam's army, they would be in some state's penitentiary.

One or two of them are on the edge of going back. They are not much to look at and they all have less than two years of active service, but they offer some intangibles that we believe you can mold to help the army, the CIA, and your country."

"Why me?"

"The army is not willing to let your skill set go to waste. The skills you have acquired since enlisting in the army and the skill set you left behind when you joined the military."

This was a surprise to Keeble; his past had not even been a fleeting thought over the past fourteen years. "Uh-huh."

"You are being asked to train them, find out where their loyalties are, and prepare them for a mission that could cost them their lives. I can't go too deep into specifics right now, but if you take this assignment, I will brief you at Fort Benning."

"Are they committed? Why them?"

"That's what we need you to find out. And why them? It's because they are expendable, and a couple of them are on their way out of the army if they don't get their act together." Jameson paused to let his words hover over Keeble before he slowly continued. "These men, all of them, were criminals. The army was their last choice; it was either this or a long stretch in a penal institution. The fact is, if they don't come back, who's going to miss them?"

"That's fucking heartwarming . . . sir." Keeble pondered the thought. "And what happens to me if I decide not to take on this assignment?"

"I'm not sure if the army has a place for you. Maybe some menial jobs for you to do until you retire or you could be medically discharged. Knowing what I do about you, those aren't options for you. You could opt out now, satisfied with your accomplishments thus far. Or you could man up, take this challenge head-on, and continue to serve your country with the pride and dignity you have always shown. Master Sergeant Miles Keeble, the choice is yours to make. But know this, we are talking about saving American lives, soldiers that need your service."

"There is no choice for me to make here. My choice is to be back with Special Forces." Keeble stood from the chair, came to attention, and raised his right hand to salute.

Jameson rose to return the salute. Keeble dropped his salute, took a step to the right, did an about-face, and left the room without looking back. He was leaving the colonel's office on his own terms. Or was he?

6

The red clay of Fort Benning, Georgia, had been the training ground to millions of infantry soldiers since its establishment as Camp Benning in October of 1918. Never before in its extraordinary history had it been the home of such an eclectic group as the one now standing on its hallowed ground.

The group of twelve ragtag, urban misfits had been identified for a unique task force that would be known as the Army Special Missions Unit 416—Unit 416 for short. Twenty minutes earlier, these men had been told to report to MacArthur Field and stand at attention, an order that stood as long as the NCO, Sergeant Berg, was in sight. Once he was gone, so was their military discipline, or what little they possessed. Turner was the only one who wasn't sloppily dressed, and the worst offender of the dress code was Jack Daisy. Spit-shined boots and well-pressed fatigues were not terms to be mentioned with this bunch. Rough around the edges was putting it mildly.

Most disgusted by the people standing next to him was Mike Winston. He stood in the middle of the front row of six people.

He had his head on a swivel, slowly turning from his left to his right, taking in what was now his peer group. Peer group? The mere thought that he was lumped in with this group damn near turned his stomach. This is what it had come to? He'd set the obstacle course record for infantry trainees at Fort Benning. Should have been thriving in the military because of his potential, was what he heard constantly. He had a penchant for standing his ground, and always looking for a fight had presumably landed him in this so-called Unit 416. Eighteen months ago, he was the man owning the streets of Compton, California. A moment of weakness, what others would call compassion, cost him his place there and landed him here. In the misguided perception of his mind, Winston believed he controlled his destiny. He understood the game, how it was played, and the pitfalls that lay ahead. But he let compassion—no, weakness—snatch the reins of power from his unfaltering grip. Scanning the group again, he did notice one individual: Tyrin Turner, standing at attention, sharp and crisp as a military man should be.

That butt-licker Turner, Winston thought to himself. He'd just met him a few minutes ago and had him pegged as the brown-noser of the bunch.

Winston was so engrossed in thoughts of self-pity that he paid little attention to the Humvee pulling up behind them. But the arrival of the vehicle did little in the way of motivating these men to straighten up. Turner, a young man released from prison, who viewed the military as a way for him to finally find some direction and purpose for his life, was the only one who continued to stay at attention, and the only one aware that the vehicle approached.

Riding in the passenger's seat of the Hummer was Keeble. The military driver pulled to the shoulder of the road on the right side of the street and turned the vehicle off. MacArthur Field was to their immediate left and full of activity. A military band was four hundred meters to the northeast of the field, marching and rehearsing. A thousand meters to the northwest were several companies being put through the paces of a pass and review. But the group commanding Keeble's attention was the one that stood at some semblance of attention fifty meters across from where the Hummer was now parked.

"Here we are, Sergeant Keeble." The military driver was a motivated young soldier, no more than eighteen or nineteen. His rigid jawline did little to hide his acne.

A knot turned in Keeble's stomach as he hoped to see another twelve men somewhere else on this field.

"The fuck am I doin' here?" Keeble uttered.

"Not the kind of men you get with SF, huh?"

"Who told you I was Special Forces?"

"The combat patch is a dead giveaway. Sergeant Keeble, you're a legend. The Bronze Star that you were awarded hit the wire for the *Army Times*. I couldn't wait to pick you up. When they told me you were coming, I jumped in line and volunteered for double duty to drive you. I was scared to say anything before. The boys said to let you speak first 'cause they know I talk a lot and—"

"Damn, son!" Keeble cut him off. "These are the men."

"Yes, that's them. I hear they don't look like much, but they are supposed to be something else."

Keeble eyed the driver, then the men, and looked back to the driver. "You're right. They don't look like much." Keeble weighed his options. For the first time that he could recall, running was among those options. Ultimately, though, he knew if that was his option of choice, he was choosing to end his military career. Keeble sat back in his seat, took a deep breath, and fixed his eyes on the horizon ahead. Screw it; just like jumping out of a plane, it was time to put his knees in the breeze.

"Hey, Private." Keeble stared straight ahead. "One day you're going to hear things about that group to your left. It's gonna be great things if I have anything to do with it." Who was he trying to convince more, the private or himself?

"Can't wait to hear them," the driver replied.

Keeble opened the door of the Hummer, stepped out, and secured his headgear. The Special Forces unit crest aligned perfectly with his left eye. Keeble's spit-shined jungle boots gleamed in the Georgia sun.

"Do you need me to wait for you?"

"Yeah. Why don't you stick around and enjoy the show?"

The driver left in search of a better parking space. Keeble crossed the road and stepped onto MacArthur Field. The field was named after General Douglas MacArthur, one of only five men to rise to the rank of five-star general in the U.S. army and a Medal of Honor awardee. Keeble regarded this ground he now stood on with honor and respect. The sheer audacity and disrespect shown to the field by the men in front of him was unacceptable. Worse than that was that it was very likely they had no idea of the level of disrespect they were showing. They stood there as if they were hanging on the block waiting for one of their homies instead of a highly decorated, highly motivated war hero. Keeble moved quickly on the grass, making no noise, as his training had taught him. When he was within ten meters of the group, he waited, curious as to how long it would take them to notice him. No one did, but he was surprised by one thing. For all the idle chatter and the lack of discipline, at least they all faced the same direction. A sign to Keeble that there was a level of discipline they didn't realize they already possessed.

"Anybody know anything about this Keeble dude?" Jones asked.

"H-H-Hell, nah. He kn-kn-know anything about m-m-me?"
Daisy stuttered.

"I hear he's a dick!" Keeble added, and his voice commanded
attention.

The group fell silent; several eyes opened wider and if thoughts
could be heard, "Oh sheeoot" would have been the statement.
The weathered, raspy voice they'd just heard didn't belong to any
of them. Without laying eyes on him, the men knew the voice
belonged to Keeble. Turner was the only one among them who
didn't have to put his body back into the position of attention; he
was already there.

"About-face!" Keeble ordered.

Turner, sharp and prepared, promptly obeyed the order.
The other men spun around at varying intervals. It was their
first opportunity to lay eyes on Master Sergeant Keeble. There
were a few chuckles, some because of the loss of balance, some
because of their embarrassment at being caught. Something not
missed by Keeble.

"About-face!" Keeble barked and the men turned back away
from him, again some of them off-balance. "Do you people understand what an about-face is?"

"Sir, yes, sir!" The response was in unison.

At least they could do something together and they all got it
wrong together.

"Who in the hell are you calling sir? I work for a living! When
you respond to me, you will say, 'Yes, Sergeant,' or 'No, Sergeant!'
Do I make myself clear?!"

"Yes, Sergeant!"

"When I give you an order of about-face, you all, not some
of you, *all* of you will move in unison. Do you understand!!?"

"Yes, Sergeant!"

"About-face!" Keeble barked again, now with their full

attention. This time, they all moved sharply, crisply, and as a military unit. *Not too bad*, Keeble thought. *They listen when you get after them a little bit. This group might be able to do something after all.* Keeble walked closer to the men to make a better assessment of the group.

"We now do everything together as one. There is one leader and one group." Keeble spoke as he walked in front of the row of men. A number of the men were taller than he was, especially Big Lev. He knew they were sizing him up as much as he was them. As he neared the last man in the row, he heard whispers and some snickers behind him. He stopped. The whispers came from the center of the row, which is where Winston now stood. Keeble never turned to look at him; instead he stepped backward until he was right in front of him, Keeble's left shoulder just below his chin.

"Care to tell me what's so funny?"

Winston was insulted. At six foot one, he was being dissed by this bald-headed blowhard. If the military wanted to train him for an important mission, they were going to have to give him something better than this fitness instructor.

"Sergeant?" Winston feigned innocence.

"Care to tell me what's so funny?"

"Army can't do no better than a grown-up version of Shaun T," Winston said to more snickering and laughter.

"That joke never gets old. That toothless whore you call a mama said the same thing last night."

Provoked by the comment, Winston instinctively reached out toward Keeble. Keeble had intended to evoke that type of response, actually hoped for it. Before Winston could get his hands on the old sarge, Keeble bent at the knees, shot an elbow into his sternum, taking his breath and causing him to bend forward where his chin met the crown of Keeble's green beret, which he happened to be thrusting toward Winston at the time. Keeble caught him as his body fell limply on him. The head butt to the chin forced his jawbone to jam into the base of his cranium, rendering him unconscious. This was a warning shot cast over the bow. Keeble figured ten seconds top and Winston would be twitching back to consciousness.

"Hey, you can't do that. You can't physically assault a soldier," Turner piped up.

"You're absolutely right. I can't. But I can protect myself."

"You provoked him," Jones said.

"Or did I merely respond to his provocation?"

"This is the army," Jones countered.

"Son, you're not in the army now. You're in my unit. All of you, handpicked for a highly dangerous mission. As I understand it, you are in this man's army on a volunteer basis because your other array of options involved penal institutions. What I am going to give you, all of you, is an understanding of a higher calling. Somebody get Mickey Mouse here up; explain to him that Shaun T, Mr. T, or motherfuckin' Ice-T is running the show. This is the beginning. If you're ready to go to hell and back, I'll guide you. I've been there a few times myself," Keeble concluded.

Keeble waved to the driver of the Humvee. It was time to head to the barracks that he would soon call home. "Journey begins tomorrow at zero-six-hundred."

7

ASMU 416 was the acronym the army and the CIA assigned to this twelve-man unit. The soldiers, all of their military belongings, and some personal items were being transferred by military cattle truck to B-6, their new barracks. The cattle trucks used by the military would get troops from point A to point B with the least comfort and most efficiency possible. It could comfortably seat eighteen adult men. In basic training, a platoon of thirty-four men and all their newly issued military gear stuffed in a duffle bag would be moved like cattle to their initial training station. With twelve men inside the truck, it was the army's version of a limo ride.

Still unsteady and a little shaken from his encounter with Keeble, Winston was not sitting among the men. He stood grasping one of the metal poles supporting the inside of the cattle car, pissed that he was caught off guard by Keeble. He looked out the window as the cobwebs cleared and his anger mounted. He wished he could opt out of this crap; the circumstances that forced him here were bullshit. It was his impression that some of the men taking part in ASMU 416 were doing it on a voluntary basis. Not him. The military was always quick to point out his exceptional performance whenever he got into a scuffle, but they were also quick to allude to his past criminal activity. His options after his last fight were to join Unit 416 or face the California pen. They used money to finally convince him to join Unit 416. After getting coldcocked and embarrassed today, the pen didn't seem like the worst option. He had two and a half more years of them being able to hang that old bullshit over him. As the cattle truck continued toward an area of the base he was unfamiliar with, he contemplated how to get away from it.

Darrell Jones, who was always ready with a quick word, decided to take a look at the other eleven men surrounding him in the cattle car. He was familiar with Winston, Smith, Turner, and Daisy. Fort Benning had been their home base as well as his. The other seven men he was sure he would get to know well very soon. All of the men were African-American with the exception of Jack Daisy. This was definitely a group of characters that Unit 416 had brought together. Jones looked over his transfer orders for the hundredth time. As he looked up, he noticed the guy across from him doing the same thing. His stenciled name tag read JACKSON. He nodded toward Jackson's transfer order. Jackson tipped it and nodded his head, acknowledging they all appeared to be in the same boat.

"Ass-moo!" Jones blurted out. "Any one of you cows know you were about to become asses?"

Jones and Jackson laughed and drew a few chuckles from some of the other guys. The sound of laughter momentarily drew Winston out of his head and into their world. Not buying into the humor though was Turner. He continued to sit quietly as the cattle car jostled him back and forth.

"Where you guys from? The same area?" Jones knew they

weren't from Benning. The unit insignias on their left shoulders were from different bases.

"Me, Wallace, and Hines are from Fort Campbell. Ford and Garrett are out of Fort Hood. Parker was at Fort Lee and Mitchell, we ain't sure about him. Mark him down from outer space." Jackson and the guys laughed; he had become the unofficial spokesperson for them. "Mitchell's from Fort Sill, but it might as well be outer space."

"I'm Jones and that's Smith, Winston, Daisy, and the lump on the log down there is Turner." Each man nodded acknowledgment when his name was called. Turner, though, turned his eyes to them for a few seconds; then his attention went back to wherever it had been before.

"I guess he's like Mitchell, huh?" Jackson asked.

"That cat's from another solar system. But we been here at Benning for a minute, some longer than others."

"Where are you guys from? I mean, like home," Jackson asked the Benning group.

"Terrell, Texas," Big Lev responded.

"B-B-Bronx, NY," Daisy added.

"Chi-town," Jones said.

They all glanced at Turner who was still sitting quietly. He could feel all the eyes on him.

"Little Rock, Arkansas," Turner responded to satisfy their interest but he never made eye contact with any of them.

Winston didn't bother to participate in this little how-do-you-do. It wasn't worth his time to be bothered with these fools. Jackson picked up on his attitude.

"Your boy always make friends so quick?" Jackson looked in Winston's direction with a smirk. "What about you, blood? Where are you from?" Jackson asked.

"Yo, nigger! What you say?!" Winston snapped. "Kelly Park

Hustler, fool. I ain't no bum-ass clood, nigger!" Winston said to Jackson. Blatant disrespect; these motherfuckers had no idea who they were messing with. He would deal with this asshole and then that motherfuckin' Keeble was gonna get got.

"Nigger? You should have done something to that nigger who dropped your ass," Jackson shot back at him, ready for a fight.

Winston let go of the railing and started to charge at Jackson. Quick to his feet, stepping between them and grabbing Winston, was Big Lev.

"This ain't the time, bruh," Lev said with a serious voice and a disarming smile. It was clearly understood that none of that would be happening today. "He's just ridin' ya a little bit. You'd do the same thing."

Winston yielded to the behemoth Lev, but did not take his eyes off of Jackson. Shit, he knew Lev was right and could feel himself a bit unsteady from his earlier altercation with Keeble. But Winston wasn't going to admit to any of it. The pumping of the air brakes could be heard as the cattle car began to slow to a stop. Lev, Jones, and Winston reached up to the metal poles to steady themselves as the truck jerked them.

Standing in front of the B-6 barracks at parade rest was Staff Sergeant Luiz Rodriguez. His military cover sat tight on his head, the bottom of which met his Ray-Ban glasses. The eyes were completely covered by the mirrored lenses. There was a pencil-thin mustache and a squared jaw. His fatigues were so well pressed, they could stand without him and the spit shine on his boots showed a reflection that rivaled the mirrored lenses. He was the poster image of the army come to life in the hot Georgia sun.

As the door to the cattle truck opened, Rodriguez snapped to attention vigorously. You could hear the pop as his hands smacked his thighs and the heels of his boots came together simultaneously.

Turner was already halfway out of the truck with his gear while the rest of company was still inside casually gathering their gear like they were at summer camp. Not sure what was coming next, they proceeded with caution. To this point, there had been very little briefing or preparation as to what their next steps would be.

"Fall in," Rodriguez said. But not with the authority of the old drill sergeant he was. He watched as the rest of the men continued taking their time to exit the truck. Apparently, he had not provided them the proper motivation. Fifteen seconds in and these assholes were already on his broke dick side.

"You sons a bitches are startin' off on the wrong goddamned FUCKING FOOT!!!!" Rodriguez's voice started off low and menacingly grew to a crescendo.

Now there was a fire lit under the new Unit 416 members. They practically ran over the top of one another, tossing their gear out in front of them. Rodriguez fought back his laughter at the sight of them trampling one another in an effort to get out of the truck.

"This is not Club fucking Med! When you are told to fall in, you do it expeditiously. When you are told to move, I don't give a damn if you make the wrong move. But you had better get your hind end to do it quickly. Is that understood?"

"Yes, sir!" they shouted as they gathered into a makeshift formation.

"Don't you call me sir, goddamn it! I work for a living! Drop and give me fifty. And you'd better call me Sergeant after each one of them." The men dropped quickly and began to sound off. One, Sergeant; two, Sergeant; three, Sergeant as they pushed. Rodriguez was pleasantly surprised; Keeble must have gotten into those asses already. He looked the group over, trying to determine who the first victim had been.

"On your feet!" he interrupted. "Nothing would make me happier than to have you push Fort Benning, Georgia, clear to Alabama, but we got shit to do. I am Sergeant Rodriguez and I will reside with you in B-6 for as long as you call this place home. Master Sergeant Keeble will train you and make sure you are prepared for your mission. Your bunks and lockers are already set up for you. You will find your name on the bed in the partitioned area assigned to you. You have shirts, shorts, shoes, and socks, all in your sizes, waiting for you. You have exactly six minutes to get your gear squared away, change your clothes, and meet me back out here. Chow is in one hour and there's six miles of roadwork that takes us to the mess hall. Any questions?"

Things were happening so fast, the crew barely had a chance to gather their breath, much less gather any questions. They looked at one another dumbfounded and their eyes settled on Jones. There was a consensus that if there was someone with something to ask, it would be him.

"If Keeble is training us, why are we running to a mess hall to eat?" Jones asked.

As Jones waited for a response to his question, he caught a glimpse of Winston. The look on his face advised him to keep his mouth shut. Winston knew the more yapping Jones did, the less time they had before chow and the harder the run would be.

"Respectfully, Sergeant, I would like to withdraw my question," Jones acquiesced.

"All right, men, fall out," Rodriguez ordered and thought to himself, *there's always one.* He watched as the men scurried into the barracks with their gear in search of their respective areas. Rodriguez hustled in behind them. Being late to his own formation wouldn't be a good look.

8

Keeble unloaded the military-issued olive-green duffle bag from the Hummer. He looked down at his name stenciled on the bag, MASTER SERGEANT MILES KEEBLE, before strapping it onto his back. Within the last twenty-four hours, he had gone from being on the verge of medical retirement to embarking on a training mission about which he was still unclear, still wondered what its true purpose was. He was a true military man and at the moment, details of the mission were on a need-to-know basis. He still had a career and that was all he needed to know.

The barracks where Keeble would be staying were among the oldest on the base. A-10 was centrally located in a loop of barracks but the nearest barracks to either its left or right was more than four hundred meters away. Behind it was a heavily wooded area with a drop of at least a hundred feet. In this secluded area, the darkened windows gave it the appearance that the barracks had been abandoned and neglected for years. Taking in the dilapidated surroundings, Keeble said to himself, "This just keeps getting better." He'd seen enough barracks in his day to know he was set up in old-school housing with big wide open bays; there was no telling how many soldiers would be jammed together in here. So this is how they set up the guy who would be training an elite fighting force for them.

His keys were marked for unit A-10. He double-checked them again, hoping that another number would magically appear and send him in a different direction. Reaching for the door, he was not surprised that it was unlocked. It might have been a bigger surprise if the door was locked. What did give him pause though was that the room was just twelve feet deep and ran the width of the front of the barracks. The heavy metal door that now stood in front of him twelve feet away did seem peculiar though. As he reached the door, Keeble found that this one too, was open.

Instead of finding an empty room with an open bay in front of him, he stepped into a different world. The room was dark; it almost felt like an old darkroom used for processing camera film. Keeble quickly adjusted his eyes and spotted a series of illuminated maps lining the back wall—maps from different parts of the world: Europe, Central Asia, Asia and the Middle East, but it was the map of Afghanistan that held his gaze a little longer than the rest. The hum of computers brought his mind back into the room. He could hear computers even though he couldn't see them. The old run-down barracks was a shell, housing a dimly lit mini command center.

"Glad you could join us." The voice coming from the left of the room was that of Colonel Jameson. As he spoke, lights came up on a conference table where he sat with two other gentlemen, one on each side of him. The three chairs they sat in faced one chair on the opposite side of the table. "I understand you had your first look at the troops."

"Yes, sir, I did," Keeble said as he turned toward the men. Without another word, it was understood that there was some work ahead of them. He dropped his duffle bag as he stepped toward the waiting chair at the conference table.

"Have a seat," Jameson invited. "We have a lot to discuss."

Keeble nodded; it was time to find out what he needed to know. On the conference table in front of him were twelve thick packets. He picked through a few of them. Daisy, Jack; Jones, Darrell; Winston, Mike. The last name made him chuckle; this was his new best friend. It was a complete history on the twelve soldiers that would be under his tutelage. Dates of birth, parents, siblings, children, crimes committed, favorite color. The information was endless.

"It's time to discuss the purpose of this mission." Jameson shot straight, eyes honed in on Keeble.

Keeble nodded. "That sounds good to me, sir. Now I know you and I have no doubt everyone here is keenly aware of who I am. How 'bout I meet everyone else?" His eyes locked onto Jameson. This wasn't a matter of intimidation, it was a matter of focus. Shit was about to get real for everyone in the room.

Jameson looked to his right and quickly introduced Harlow and Goldberg.

"We are infiltrating and disrupting an arms-dealing cartel in Central Asia. We want to put an end to them."

Arms dealing? CIA? What the fuck did I bite off? Keeble was taking in the enormity of the mission. "Isn't this group a little small for that?"

"Not when you are keeping the operation off the books," Harlow stated as a matter of fact and let the comment twist in the air until it fell silently on Keeble.

"The influx in the number of firearms in Central Asia is increasing at an alarming rate." Goldberg broke the silence. Behind them, a screen was uncovered and images popped up on the screen as he spoke. "Drugs and small arms are intricately interlinked in the region. They are trading the drugs for weapons to terrorists who are then using the weapons to attack our troops and citizens that are in those countries."

"So the CIA is doing what?" Keeble interrupted. "What are you doing to infiltrate the cartel?"

The two CIA agents paused before speaking. More images flashed on the screen.

"The CIA," Jameson picked up, "has been in this fight for several years with varying levels of penetration, but ultimately, they have failed to get deep enough into the cartel to destroy them. Six weeks ago, the CIA lost another case officer." As Jameson paused, images of the agent flickered across the screen. The agent stateside, with his wife and small child, images of him meeting with the cartel, and finally an image of his dead body with his decapitated head five feet away. "His cover didn't stand up. This operation has decided that they need real criminals. That's where we fit in. Every year, the U.S. military recruits roughly sixty thousand soldiers for all its branches. The army gets the lion's share of those recruits. As you know, not every record is spotless when they come to us. The men you met today have plenty of spots on their records. What they don't have, we are in the process of building up for them. We want to make sure that any checks done on them can stand up. These men have been hand-picked, identified as the ideal candidates for this objective. You are the only man who can prepare them mentally and physically for the task and there is little doubt on my part that you can relate to them."

"Yes, sir." The idea of this possible sacrifice sickened Keeble. There was no way he would be able to shape twelve soldiers into what the CIA wanted to get from them. He might as well lead lambs to slaughter. "Sir, I'm not sure I'm your—"

"They are killing Americans, soldier. And this is the only way

I can keep you in the active military. It's harsh, but those are the facts." Jameson stood, indicating this meeting had reached its conclusion. Harlow, Goldberg, and the screen rose with him. "Read the files. There's also a briefing package to help you get familiar with the new digs; you're going to be here awhile."

Keeble watched as the wall behind them separated, revealing an elevator door. As the door opened, the three men stepped in. *That shit ain't army issue for sure*, he thought. There was so much more to this picture than he had imagined.

The three men stepped out of the elevator in silence. The motion sensor picked them up and lit the two-hundred-yard corridor that led to their exit. For fifty yards, the only sound that could be heard was the clicking of their shoes as they struck the floor in unison.

"So this is your guy, the one you handpicked?" Harlow asked Jameson.

"Roger that. Marv gave me his name six years ago as a soldier worth keeping our eyes on. His background fits perfectly with these guys; he'll know what it takes to push them through," Jameson said.

"He's a good man. Things got a little shaky around him in Nerkh, Afghanistan. We kept a close eye on him; he never wavered in his commitment to the military or his mission," Goldberg added.

"He's a soldier, always going to be. He'll adapt and embrace this assignment too," Jameson confirmed.

"Hope so. This isn't fly-fishing in Moncks Corner, South Carolina," Harlow added with what seemed to be his first smile in years.

It was a smile shared by all three men. Harlow, the WASP; Goldberg, the Jewish one; and the African-American kid Jameson from the other side of the tracks could trace their bond back thirty years to a fly-fishing hole in Moncks Corner, South Carolina. Never in their wildest dreams could they have imagined their lives would still be intertwined, hatching a plan to break up an arms cartel in Central Asia.

Reaching the end of the corridor, the men shared a few more rare smiles before reentering the world that existed for them today. They shook hands knowing the pact between them was sacred and the mission in front of them would protect thousands of American lives.

9

Five miles into the run and Rodriguez hadn't lost a man. Even the big guy was doing pretty well. With one mile to go and a 20 percent incline, it was time to push them to see what they had. His job wasn't to break them; he wasn't even there to condition them. His job was to keep a watchful eye on them.

"I don't know what you been told," Rodriguez began to call cadence as they pushed up the incline of their last mile.

"I don't know what you been told," the men replied.

"But Eskimo pussy is mighty cold."

"But Eskimo pussy is mighty cold," the men followed.

"Sound off," Rodriguez led.

"One, two," they replied.

"Sound off."

"Three, four," they replied.

"Break it on down now."

"One, two, three, four, one, two . . . three, four."

It was a call-and-response from a squad leader to the company he was leading on a run. During a run, the cadence kept the runners on the pace. It forced the runners to breathe, helped them to endure the run; it also took their minds off of the running activity.

Two of Rodriguez's best attributes were being controversial and crude and often his cadence would reflect that. Hell, there were no women among this group and even if there were, he wouldn't give a damn. The men repeated lyrics to cadences they'd never used before and it brought smiles to their faces more than a time or two.

"I'll be damned," Winston said as he looked around. He was none the worse for wear from the run.

"D-D-Don't tell me?" Daisy stuttered.

"Son of a . . ." Hines just realized it as well.

The mess hall they'd just run six miles to get to was across a field directly in front of the B-6 barracks.

"Sergeant, are you serious?" Winston asked.

"Always assess your area. Immediately. If you don't know where you are, anybody can run you in circles." Rodriguez smirked.

The humor of the moment failed to find its mark with the men. They were so rushed to get changed and get back outside for the run, that none of them had taken the time to study their environment. Even Turner, who demonstrated the most discipline among this group, had allowed himself to be caught up in the rush.

"Remember, gentlemen, preparation can make the difference between life and death. Fall out and get you some chow."

Still sweating from the run, but hungry as all hell, the men rushed the mess hall. Some hit the head before getting in the chow line. Big Lev didn't have time to waste. He had plans of being the first one and the last one in line, and then he'd make room for seconds. Food for the men of Unit 416 was a nonissue.

For this special group, there would be no limit to what they ate or how much. This program was being funded by an off-the-books CIA slush fund. Rodriguez would soon learn that every-thing here, even the new Under Armour running gear, was being taken care of by the CIA and not by a military allotment.

"Take your time eating. This isn't basic training, but you are going to be together most of the time, so it is going to feel like it. You are free to do what you want on your off-duty time; there just won't be much of it. Bed check and lights out is twenty-three-hundred hours. That's mandatory. Master Sergeant Keeble will be ready for you at zero-six-thirty, but the question is, will you be ready for him?"

"Yes, Sergeant!" Turner fired off emphatically.

Rodriguez was looking for a unified roaring response from the men, a rallying cry or some cheers. All he got was Turner. Crickets chirping would have made more noise. Lev was in the chow line pointing at the next item he wanted put on his over-flowing plate. Winston stared blankly at him while several of the men were coming out of the latrine. Daisy had tissue stuck to his shoe.

Keeble has got his work cut out for him with this group, Rodri-guez thought. He wasn't sure what the nature of the training was for these men or their purpose for it. All he knew was that this temporary duty assignment was paying him very well for his ser-vices as a babysitter.

"Do you know Keeble?" Winston asked with a bit of an edge to his voice.

"Sure, I go way back with him. Don't think he knows I'm here, though. He'll be in for a shock," Rodriguez answered.

"He'll be in for a lot of shocks," Winston grumbled as he passed Rodriguez and found a seat at a table.

Rodriguez didn't have to wonder anymore. It was Winston

who'd gotten his ass whipped by Keeble. He always went after one of the toughest ones in the group. Keeble was never going to change. Rodriguez moved to the chow line to grab something to eat.

Big Lev finally had all he wanted on his plate and walked carefully, trying to keep anything from falling as he made his way to the table where Winston sat.

"You get enough?" Winston looked the plate up and down.

"Big man gotta eat," Lev said with a disarming smile, but his arms flexed as he picked up a leg quarter.

Big man, Winston thought. *If it came down to it, I'd fuck his shit up too.* The sight of Turner headed his way broke his train of thought. "Look at that bootlicker right there. I mean, really, nigger. 'Yes, Sergeant,'" he whispered to Lev.

"Humph." Lev grunted with a mouthful of chicken.

"Humph, what, dog?" Winston asked with an attitude.

Lev looked at him for a second, then said, "You gonna fight everybody today, bro?" It seemed like one of his new jobs was going to be keeping this fool from jumping on everybody that walked past him.

"Thinking about it," Winston responded flatly.

Big Lev chuckled to make sure Winston understood there was no beef between them.

"Fuckin' Rodriguez." Keeble now sat in the heart of the command center of the A-10 barracks, getting comfortable with his new home. He was a little more than a half mile away, but surveillance equipment put him in any and every room he wanted access to. In front of him were eight monitors. Files of the twelve men now in his charge were spread before him. He was scrolling through their profiles digitally and manually. He would click a link on their digital profile if he needed in-depth information on one of the soldiers. There was a monitor designated for the B-6 barracks, complete with audio if that became necessary. He was now enjoying the view of the ASMU mess hall monitor. And there was Luiz Rodriguez. The last time he had seen him was at Advanced Airborne School at Fort Bragg.

"How did they get your ass over here?" Keeble asked the monitor.

10

Lights out was more than thirty minutes ago, but that didn't cause the activity in the B-6 barracks to cease. Most of the men had turned in at lights out; Daisy didn't waste any time and hit the sheets before 2200 hrs. Jones was busy setting up two of his laptops in his space to make himself at home; Turner had spent the last forty-five minutes on his knees praying, while Winston and Big Lev were still running the gift of gab.

"That motherfucker is still on his knees," Winston whispered after he peeked over to Turner's area. "I hope he's praying to find out what this mission is about. They tell you anything?"

"All I know is that it's dangerous but . . ." Lev answered.

Winston paused before his next question. "So what's your story? Levern Smith, right? Texas A&M? You were wrecking shop as a freshman. How a big nigger like you end up in the army?"

"Fuck around with the daughter of the booster club president and have an orgy with her sorority sisters; drop a few mollies and see how long you last on campus. Then beat the shit out of a couple of assholes and the next thing you know, you're serving the army instead of jail time."

"You was fucking around with them white girls, huh?" Winston knew the answer to that question.

"Nobody would have thought twice about it if they weren't."

"It was this or the pen for me; judge gave me a choice. I should have taken the pen. I can't stand it in this ma'fuckin' army," Winston said.

"Aw, it ain't so bad. We get three squares and a bed, and the way I got to eat today, I don't give a damn if they send me to Timbuktu."

"You stupid, bro." Winston didn't mean it as an insult; it was just how he talked. "Three hots and a cot is the same deal you get in the pen."

"For thirty cents a day," Lev joked. "So, how they get you?"

They both heard movement. Thinking it might be Rodriguez, their conversation came to a halt until they realized it was Turner finally coming to an end of his prayers. Turner gathered up a shaving kit, walked toward them as he made his way to the latrine.

"How's Jesus doing?" Winston asked him as he came near.

Turner walked a couple of steps past them before he stopped. "Busy: he's been watching out for you," he said without looking back at Winston. He let that marinate for a few seconds before continuing on to the latrine.

Winston was dumbfounded, but Turner's comment brought a big smile to Lev's face.

"That brother's deep into his own thing," Winston said as he watched Turner go around the corner.

"You'd better get out of the kiddie pool before you mess with that brother."

"For sho'."

Then the sound of a crash startled them. This noise was in Jones's area near the latrine. As Lev and Winston went to see what was going on, they could hear Jones, who had launched into a profanity-laced tirade. When they got there, they could see the tirade was directed at Turner.

"What happened?" Winston asked.

"This simpleton trashed my equipment!" Jones pointed at Turner.

"Keep your voice down," Winston said. "You're supposed to be in bed."

"Who can sleep with you two running your mouths?" Jones made it clear he was aware that he wasn't the only one breaking rules tonight.

Turner mumbled an apology while starting to clean up the tangled mess he had gotten himself into. On his way to the bathroom, Turner had stumbled over some of the wiring Jones had run across the floor to power up his computers. The only light in the area was emitting from the screens of the computers. Anybody going to the bathroom would have tripped over them.

"What the hell!?" Rodriguez shouted. He pointed a flashlight as he came around the corner. If he was using the flashlight to keep from disturbing the other men, it was a wasted effort because his yelling woke the majority of them. "Lights out is lights out! You all are acting like you're having a block party!" He shined his light on them, then onto the mess in front of them.

Some of the men checked on the commotion while others didn't bother. Rodriguez wasted little time in confiscating the laptops. With the training that lay ahead of them, there wouldn't be much time for these kinds of distractions and they shouldn't have been brought there in the first place.

"Time to call it a night!" Rodriguez said firmly for all of them to hear.

Winston looked Rodriguez up and down before he moved. Lev and Turner did the same and left Jones fuming on his bunk as he watched Rodriguez leave with his computers. Rodriguez circled the barracks looking for any electronic equipment he could find. He grabbed what he could carry and took it to his quarters, then came back for the rest.

Yep, he thought, *Keeble will have his hands full with some of the locos.*

11

Dawn was still an hour away, but Keeble was wide awake. His last data entry occurred shortly before 0100. By his estimation, he'd slept almost four and a half hours. It was the most sleep he'd had in the last eighteen months that wasn't interrupted by a nightmare. Excitement for the first day of training was his alarm clock this morning. He pored over the men's profiles, getting to know as much as he could absorb before briefing himself on the training schedule. Today would begin with PT at 0630, chow at 0830 before weapons would be issued at 0930. They would report to the firing range at 1300 hours for the remainder of the day.

Any minute now, the B-6 barracks would spring to life, and Keeble couldn't wait to see what tricks his old buddy had up his sleeve. He pulled up the surveillance cameras for the barracks. In one monitor he had split screens of the partitioned areas the men slept in. On another monitor, he was able to pull up the separate area where Rodriguez slept. The cameras seemed to cover every angle imaginable in there. The cameras in Rodriguez's room weren't nearly as invasive. As expected, the men of the newly formed Unit 416 were sound asleep. Rodriguez, though, was as wide awake as he was. His lights were on, he was already fully dressed in his fatigues, and he was looking at his watch. Keeble guessed that Rodriguez also could not wait for 0530 to arrive. Keeble turned on the audio switch for the barracks; this would be worth listening to.

Keeble watched in silence as a few minutes passed, waiting until his watch struck 0530. His watch was in sync with Rodriguez's, because he began to move at that exact moment. Rodriguez reached down for something, but Keeble's view was blocked by the bed. When Rodriguez sat back up, he had a bullhorn in his hand. Keeble shook his head yes.

Rodriguez shot to his feet, ran to his door, and snatched it open. Watching this on the monitor, Keeble thought that the door might come off its hinges. Rodriguez turned on the lights in the open bay and blasted the bullhorn. He ran in and out of the partitions, yelling and screaming that it was time to wake up.

"What the hell are you doing still asleep? This is the army not the goddamned air force!" Rodriguez barked.

Keeble got a kick out of the shock on the men's faces. He was also shocked to see Turner standing at the ready; he'd gotten a head start on all of them. Some of them jumped out of bed; others moved more slowly. Big Lev was not one of the quick risers. He lost his balance and fell to the floor before making it to his feet. There was one bunk, though, that had not moved.

Unfazed by all the racket was Jack Daisy. He was curled up in a near fetal position. The sight of Daisy lying there drove Rodriguez ballistic. He blasted the bullhorn again and there was still no movement from Daisy. What in the hell was wrong with him? He knew good and damn well he couldn't have lost one of them before they started training. Rodriguez dropped the bullhorn and walked closer to him. That's when he noticed the earplugs in Daisy's ears. Now Rodriguez was really pissed; he should have spotted them last night. Rodriguez snatched the foot of his bunk and flipped it, sending Daisy over onto the floor.

"Time to w-w-w-wake up, Sarge?" Daisy asked, looking up and rubbing the sleep from his eyes.

"*Punta!* Yeah, it's time to wake up." Rodriguez shook his head. "PT is in an hour and you'd better have these barracks squared away before you show up." There was no enthusiastic "Yes, Sergeant!" after that comment.

They just don't get it, Keeble thought as he watched the monitor.

At 0630 Rodriguez and the men emerged from the barracks to a waiting Keeble. His blue Under Armour shirt matched those of the rest of the men, but instead of black running shorts, Keeble wore black sweatpants.

"Good morning, Sergeant Rodriguez. Good to see you again."

"Master Sergeant Keeble." He moved to the front of the formation so that he was standing face-to-face with Keeble. "Good to see you," he said in a low tone so the men could not hear them. "You look good, Miles." He knew full well what the man had been through eighteen months ago.

"Getting there. We'll catch up." Keeble spoke volumes in five quiet words.

"Looking forward to it." Rodriguez understood.

"Are these men ready to train?" Keeble snapped to attention.

"They are all yours, Sergeant." Rodriguez did an about-face and marched back into the barracks as his night shift had come to an end.

"People, we didn't get off to the best start yesterday." Keeble's eyes met Winston's as he said this. "I don't know about you, but I think this is going to be a brighter day." Keeble's attention moved about the men, but he could still feel Winston's eyes boring holes in him. "I am here because the army knows there is something special inside of me. You are here because the army believes there is something potentially special in you. It is my responsibility to bring it out of you. Every day you spend with me will take you further away from potential and closer to that reality. Let's get it started."

The men listened with apprehension, not sure how to take Keeble. Winston sucked his teeth silently. *Fuck that motherfucker,* he thought to himself, because he wasn't about to let that shit slip out of his mouth. There would be plenty of time to show Keeble that he wasn't one to be messed with.

Keeble led his men on a two-mile run. The seven-minute-per-mile pace would be a good one to get their heart rates up. Their personnel files told him that they had all maxed out on their PT Tests; they were all capable of at least six minutes per mile.

The run concluded at a half-mile obstacle course. Years had passed since the last time Keeble ran it. It was one of the toughest ones at Benning then; now it looked to be more daunting than ever. Its nickname was Death Wish; when most people ran it for the first time, they wished they'd died. It had rope crawls over water pits, monkey bars, low crawl pits, a three-foot-high hurdle gauntlet, and a hell of a climbing monstrosity. Keeble knew that wasn't there before. It had a twenty-five-foot rope climb. Once over the top, there was a thirty-foot horizontal ladder leading to a twenty-foot vertical climb. At the apex of that climb, you had to shinny over the top onto rope netting where you could finally climb down forty-five feet to free yourself of the monstrosity. It fascinated Keeble.

"How about it, Sarge?" Jackson asked.

"Huh?" Keeble was caught up in the memory of once setting a course record here.

"Do we get a crack at it?" Mitchell sounded anxious.

"Well, we didn't come here just to look at it."

"You ever run this before?" Winston asked Keeble, his tone making it more of a personal challenge. He looked Keeble up and down, and then glanced toward the course. He was practically begging Keeble to take his challenge.

"It's changed, but I've done it a time or two. However, today's not my day. Let's see what you all can do with it."

"You ain't said nothing but a thing. What are we waiting for, dogs?!" Winston shouted to the guys as he took off. He would show Keeble how he'd gotten the obstacle course record in boot camp.

The men fell in behind Winston and attacked the Death Wish obstacle course. All of the men showed lots of athleticism and moved with a great deal of fluidity. Even little Jack Daisy was right in the middle of the pack. But it was Winston and Jackson who tested each other as they led the pack. Keeble shook his head knowing they couldn't keep this pace. Once they reached the halfway point, that pace would drop in half. He could see Big Lev already beginning to struggle. The course was designed with a leaner frame of man in mind and that was a lot of body for him to be hauling through it.

As predicted, halfway through the obstacle course Jackson was resting, stopping, and gasping for air. Men in the best shape needed to pace themselves. Winston, though, was still going at it strong, determined to show Keeble and the rest of Unit 416 who was the man. As he approached the monstrosity, he finally allowed himself a break. Hands on his waist, he took three long, deep breaths before grabbing the rope. He pulled himself up using only his arms. He bear-crawled the horizontal ladder and shot up and over the vertical ladder. As he climbed down the netting on the other side, he let go with about fifteen feet to drop, landing on his feet in the pit below. He attacked the hurdle gauntlet to finish the course.

Holy shit, Keeble thought, *that wasn't bad for a first time.* Winston was bent over catching his breath. He stood up as Keeble walked toward him. He had proven his point and wanted to look Keeble in the eye as he crowed. As Keeble walked by, he never looked in his direction. Instead, he was focusing on the other men as they were coming in.

Mitchell, the nut job from outer space, saw what Winston did coming off of the monstrosity and decided to free himself twenty feet above the pit but twisted his right ankle on his landing. When Big Lev finally cleared the monstrosity, he was dog-ass tired. But he had a lot of dog in him and gathered himself for the last stretch. Some of the guys gathered around to cheer him on. Lev had cleared a couple of the hurdles in the gauntlet when he realized he was running on empty. Frustrated and fatigued, he gathered all the strength he could muster and fired out at the next hurdle as if it were a tackling dummy, letting out a primal yell as he struck it with his massive chest and shoulders. The sound of his body against the hurdle echoed, but the impact was so hard, it dislodged the log at the top of the makeshift hurdle.

Keeble and all of the Unit 416 men stood in stunned silence as Lev dropped to his knees to gather his breath. He didn't want to move, not because he was injured, but he just knew he was in big trouble again.

"What the fuck?" Wallace was amazed by what he'd just seen.

Keeble was as blown away as any of the men, but he never let that show on his face. *That was impressive*, he thought. At the moment, he was thrilled that he had dropped Winston yesterday and not this freak of a human being. "Gentlemen, I think we're done here for the day. Fall in."

Keeble marched the men back to the barracks. The obstacle

course had taken its toll on a couple of the men and there was no way he was going to make Mitchell run on his twisted ankle. There was too much work ahead of them and he was not willing to sacrifice anyone yet.

12

Weapons were picked up in the armory barracks after breakfast. Jameson had each man's M16A2 rifle shipped from his respective unit to B-6. In addition to that, he had an added treat for his Unit 416 trainees. There were twelve brand new Special Forces Compact Automatic Rifles (SCARs). This weapon would soon become their new best friends. At 7.95 pounds fully loaded with a thirty-round clip, the SCAR weighed almost a pound less than the M16A2 rifle. The weight difference of one pound held a huge tactical combat advantage.

Keeble inspected the weapons to make sure they were unloaded. All ammunition would be issued at the firing range; no one was permitted to have a loaded weapon or ammo en route to a training exercise. Satisfied with the inspection, Keeble ordered the men to strap their M16s over their left shoulders and the newly issued SCARs over their right shoulders. Keeble was the only one without his weapons. They fell into formation in two six-man columns, similar to the way their bunks were set up in the barracks. Keeble's attention was drawn to Jack Daisy; his uniform seemed to be a little off. It looked like his boots hadn't been shined in months. He kept looking from his right shoulder to his left; and there was a bit of a goofy grin on his face.

"Forward, march!" Keeble ordered. After a couple of strides of not being in stride, Keeble started a cadence for them to get them in step and they proceeded on the four-mile hike to the firing range. No matter what the cadence was, he could hear Daisy stuttering his way through them. And there was that grin that never left his face; he sure was happy about something.

Lunch at the firing range was an MRE, a self-contained individual field ration. The meal was designed for nourishment, not for taste. But after eating enough of them, the men eventually developed a taste for them. Keeble had eaten so many things in jungles, wetlands, swamps, and deserts that MREs had become a four-course gourmet meal.

Once on the firing range, Jack Daisy was where he wanted and loved to be. This was his home and that grin didn't seem to be quite as goofy when he was laying down fire. All the men were excellent marksmen, as evidenced by their files. Seeing them on the range told the real story. They fired their own M16s at stationary pop-up targets. Each man had his own firing lane; in a prone firing position they shot at pop-ups ranging from ten to three hundred meters. They had one shot at each target. The targets would pop up randomly at varying distances and remain standing for three seconds. If they weren't shot down, they would disappear and that target was recorded as a miss. The men had forty targets and two minutes to complete the drill.

Keeble took his position in an eight-foot-high chair, twenty meters behind the men. He watched through binoculars as the men took down targets as they popped up in their firing lanes. It would take a second or two for the men to recognize the target, aim, and shoot. Not lane three, where Jack Daisy was; Daisy had instantaneous recognition of the targets. He was picking off targets before most of the men even knew they were there. It was as if he knew what was coming next. Keeble lowered his binoculars and looked toward the firing range captain's tower. He held up three fingers and nodded his head. He had to give Jameson credit for the research on these men. He'd pegged Daisy as the one to keep an eye on. The captain looked at Keeble, then downrange for a few seconds and back to Keeble. He shrugged his shoulders and shook his head as if to say, "I see it too, the fuck?"

As they moved from different shooting ranges and scenarios, Keeble was convinced they were all very, very good. But the cream always rises to the top, and in this situation, the cream kept coming up Daisy. Daisy was truly exceptional with his M16. Most soldiers do better in a particular position, scenario, or area. Not Daisy. Whether he was standing, moving, sitting down, or in a prone position, Daisy was the premier marksman among this group with an M16.

After running the men through the different ranges and assessing their skills, Keeble gathered the men together for a break. "All right, men, smoke 'em if you got 'em; take this fifteen before I take 'em back and we're going to work with the SCARs when we get back at it."

"Yes, Sergeant!" Turner and Daisy said in unison, but most of the men were already clearing their M16s of any rounds from the chamber so they could take their break.

Winston stared blankly at Turner and Daisy. Lev nudged him to break his train of thought. Lev could see Winston's mind working, likely calling them the bootlicker and the goofy white guy.

"Fucking ebony and ivory over there," Winston said to the big man as they started walking off the range.

As the men broke out for their well-deserved break, they

stacked their weapons into a makeshift gun rack, using one weapon as the centerpiece and stacking three weapons around it. It wasn't much, but it was one of those little things that let Keeble know there was something in these guys.

Keeble and the shooting range captain weren't the only ones impressed with the shooting skills of Jack Daisy. A couple of the fellas gave him a head nod or a thumbs-up as they passed by him. He shrugged his shoulders as if to say it was just a good day on the range.

Keeble knew better; there was no way he could chalk this up to "just a good day on the range." His file proved he never had a bad day on the range, but watching him firsthand, it was like watching a weapons veteran with ten years of experience.

"You taking a break, Daisy?" Keeble asked as he approached Daisy.

"N-N-No, Sergeant. I, I, I mean y-yes, Sergeant," Daisy stuttered.

"Which one is it?" Keeble asked.

"I w-w-want to use the SCAR."

"I'll see to it that you do. You like that M16 don't you?" Keeble watched the smile broaden as Daisy nodded. "Once you start using the SCAR, you'll fall in love so fast, you'll think you're cheating on the M16."

"T-T-That's m-my g-g-girl."

"The SCAR will be your woman or your bitch, whichever you prefer, as your number one." Keeble let Daisy ponder that for a second. "Where'd you learn to shoot like that?"

"The army," Daisy replied.

"Don't bullshit me, son." Keeble thought he answered too fast and without a stutter. "You don't get that good in a year and a half unless you're shooting every day. And you haven't been shooting every day." Keeble paused for a second. "Shooting like that is special. You can learn to hit targets, but spotting them as fast as you can, then settling yourself to fire, that's a gift. And it takes time to hone that gift. It takes years."

"M-m-my daddy and m-my uncle." Daisy withdrew into his thoughts.

"They were vets, right? Vietnam?" Keeble said. He could see Daisy's thoughts questioning how he knew. "I read your file. You shot with them a lot?"

"All the time." Daisy's voice was clear of the stuttering. "My daddy taught me how to shoot when I was four. Shot my first automatic weapon at six. He taught me to shoot an M60 for my ninth birthday."

"Hell of a present," Keeble said.

"Yeah, well, the next day he killed my mama and committed suicide. T-T-That w-was a h-h-hell of a a a present. F-F-From th-then on I got good with my uncle." The stutter returned.

Keeble had no words to offer. Instead he gave Daisy a minute to process whatever he needed to work through. "You good?"

"Yeah, Sarge." Daisy was ready to move to the next subject. "So, are you any good with that SCAR?"

"Follow me and tell me what you think." Keeble went to the rack where his soldiers had rested their newly assigned SCARs and let Daisy grab one for him. He whistled to the range captain's tower. "Set range two and three on two-second intervals."

"Roger that," the range captain shouted back.

"Stay at least fifteen feet behind me at all times," Keeble said as he locked and loaded the SCAR and inserted his earplugs. "Ranges clear!"

"All clear!" the range captain replied.

Keeble took a standing position between the ranges and waited for the targets on ranges two and three to begin popping up. The targets came up simultaneously on each range. He started with range two, picked off the pop-up at two hundred meters, switched to lane three and nailed that target. When the next target popped up at sixty meters, he nailed it before zeroing in on lane two's sixty-meter target. Hearing weapons firing on the range, the men came back to see what was going on. Most were surprised to see Keeble alone firing at the ranges and not missing a beat. Twenty targets had come up on each lane and Keeble hadn't missed one. Keeble dropped the spent magazine, inserted a fresh clip, and dropped the next twenty targets on each lane.

Daisy could not believe what he had just witnessed, eighty targets in less than a minute and a half. Keeble cleared the weapon and dropped it to his side. As he turned to face Daisy, he saw the rest of his captive audience. The other men of Unit 416 were standing there, mouths open and eyes wide. As Keeble scanned their expressions, his eyes paused ever so slightly as he caught a glimpse of Winston. Keeble would have paid a thousand dollars to hear what was on his mind at that moment. Keeble then walked closer to Daisy.

"I'm tellin' you, you gonna fall in love with this thing right here," he said to Daisy. "You men grab one of the SCARs. Once we get the weapon zeroed in for you, it is yours, just like the 16," Keeble called to the others.

Still dumfounded by what they'd witnessed, the men moved slowly toward the rack of SCARs and grabbed the next available one. Daisy turned to head for the rack when Keeble stopped him.

"There's only eleven left up there." Keeble handed Daisy the one he'd just used.

"T-T-That was amazing."

Keeble just shrugged his shoulders. "It was just a good day on the range." To which Daisy laughed. "It's a special gift and you got it. Like we used to say in the hood, game recognize game."

The men spent the rest of their training afternoon learning everything there was to know about their new weapons. Sights, ammo, breaking them down, proper cleaning, and putting them together again. And all the while, skinny Jack Daisy from the Bronx was in hog heaven.

13

After the long day on the range, the men marched back to the barracks and looked forward to some down time before chow. But the reward for the evening was PT. The M16s were returned to the weapons' room but the SCARs stayed with them. The two-mile run in their fatigues and military boots would have been enough with the first day of training they'd had, but to make the run with the SCARs above their heads, the men were put through it. Mitchell was still dealing with his badly turned ankle and struggling mightily through the run. The thought of quitting entered his mind more than a couple of times, but he gutted it out.

Dinner was served in the mess hall at 1900 hours and eight minutes later there wasn't a spot of food to be seen on their plates. It was like being back in basic training. Food and bringing this day to a close were the only things that would satisfy them at that point. Once dinner was finished, the men had a few hours to themselves to do what they wanted. Tonight was a night they headed for the barracks.

Rodriguez met Keeble at the empty mess hall at 1930 for what was their scheduled daily briefing. This would be the first of many to come in the days ahead. Keeble briefed him on the day and advised him that he probably wouldn't have much of a ruckus out of them tonight.

"You weren't supposed to know I was here," Rodriguez said.

"They didn't tell me, but I found out last night; you won't believe the equipment that's up at A-10. I can see damn near everything in their barracks," Keeble bragged.

"No shit?" Rodriguez chirped.

"Blows your fucking mind. It's a one-man command center with equipment I hope I figure out how to use before I finish training these guys."

"You think they'll stick?"

"That's the hope, but realistically, they know they will lose some along the way," Keeble said, planting a seed for the next question to be asked.

"They?" Rodriguez pushed for an answer.

Keeble looked at him, but didn't say a word for a few seconds. That would be the extent of that conversation for the moment. Finally, "Tonight's a good night to have your jump boots on when it's dark."

It took a second for that to click with Rodriguez. Jump Boots was code for a dive known as JB's where lots of military hung out; they would connect after lights out. It was a favorite old hangout where they could go to knock back a couple of cold ones, catch up on some old times, and get filled in on some of the new ones.

"This is some bullshit," Mitchell said as he elevated his swollen ankle, trying to find some relief. It was after 2200 hours and most of the men were already in the sack.

"I don't know how you made it through the run with that ankle," Ford said as he examined and moved it. "Does that hur—"

"Motherfucker!" Mitchell reacted to the pain. "Leave that alone."

"I can't tell what's going on without testing it," Ford reasoned.

"You ain't no damn medic; you keep touching it and he's gonna break it off in your ass," Garrett teased his buddy from Fort Hood.

Ford started to reach out for the ankle again but was stopped by Turner. He'd been to the mess hall and returned with a bag of ice that he placed on Mitchell's foot. If he wasn't able to get that swelling down by the morning, there was no way he'd be able to get that foot back into a pair of boots.

"Keep that on for a half hour," Turner advised before heading to his bunk.

"Appreciate it," Mitchell said to Turner but it was too late. Turner was already gone; Garrett and Ford moved on to their bunks as well.

Winston and Lev were sitting together again, huddled in conversation. Winston was one to keep his distance from people until he'd been around them for a while. But something about Lev kept Winston talking to him and the two were quickly becoming friends.

"I know you ain't serious?" Lev couldn't believe what he'd just heard.

"For real, man. As soon as he gives the lights out, fifteen minutes and let's burn out of this motherfucker. I need some beer and I ain't the only one that could use one. I got a hookup; trust me," Winston said with a wink.

"Half these guys are already shut down for the night and they ain't tryin' to find no trouble, not yet anyways." Lev reached for the big picture.

"I'm tryin' to test a couple hearts in here, to see who's real. I mean if a nigger is about that life, they'll let us know. Real niggers ain't gonna give a fuck about them and they rules." Winston wasn't just challenging the other men; he was issuing a challenge to Lev as well.

Lev met eyes with Winston; he understood the only way he was going to prove himself to this man was to step out with him. The only question in his mind was how many others would be joining them. As he let that thought fade, another question popped into his head. It was time for real talk. "What you be lookin' at that man like that for?" Big Lev asked Winston.

"What you talking 'bout?" Winston looked around to see who Lev was talking about.

"I saw how you was checking Keeble out. At the range, PT, and at chow."

"I don't trust that nigger; that fool done tried me. I'd a done burnt that fool by now if we was in Compton." Winston paused as he saw Jackson passing by. "Jackson's ass too, now that I think about it."

"We done finished that with Jackson. You, me, him; we all in the same boat. But, shit, if that fool Keeble was in Compton, he'd a seen you a mile coming," Lev said.

"You right. He was hell on that range today. I ain't never in my life seen a nigger use a burner like that before." Winston almost smiled, but true to his thug life, he swallowed it before it got too far away from him.

"Oh shit, that thing on your face has corners that turn up, huh?" Lev caught it.

"Aw, fuck you, man."

"That obstacle course, though, you tore that shit up. Did you play ball somewhere?" Lev wondered.

"Not unless you counting high school. I couldn't stay on the field 'cause I was always on them streets. Far as the obstacle course, I was showin' Keeble what's up. Plus I knew your big ass was back there and I needed to get the hell out of your way."

"Shit, I was tired. The quickest way for me to get off the practice field at A&M during two-a-days was to tear some shit up." Lev let out a big laugh, which almost turned those corners up on Winston's face again.

"Lights out!" Rodriguez commanded as he emerged from his quarters at 2300 hrs. He was shutting down all activity. As he entered the bay area to do his bed check, the lights were already out. Bunk after bunk, the men appeared to be sound asleep. *That was a hell of a first day*, he thought.

Rodriguez made a quick change into some jeans and a T-shirt before slipping out of the side door of his barracks and approaching the door to the A-10. Keeble was coming out of the door with a small case in his hand.

"Your car's on the other side; let's head that way," Keeble said.

"How did you know that?" Rodriguez was confused; he was sure he wasn't seen moving it.

"Hell, I watched you do it."

Rodriguez looked past Keeble to the door of barracks A-10. "*Que pasa?*"

"Told you; I can see everything."

"*Sí?*"

"Yes."

"And who's going to monitor the men while we're out?"

"I got that covered." Keeble pulled an iPad from the case he carried. Within seconds, he pulled up the split screen monitor of the barracks on the iPad. "If those guys are what I think they are, they'll be dying to do something just to make a fuck-you statement. It also wouldn't surprise me if they couldn't move a muscle, but if they do, we'll know."

"Holy shit!" Rodriguez said.

"Tip of the iceberg, my friend; tip of the iceberg," Keeble added.

"I want to see that command center."

"In due time. Right now, I need a cold one or six or seven." Keeble wasn't yet ready to show Rodriguez something he didn't fully understand.

14

Winston was the lookout man while Lev was busy trying to rouse the others. Jones, Daisy, and Wallace jumped at the idea of getting their hands on some cold beer. Turner thought about it long and hard before deciding to join in. The rest of the men were too beat to get out of their bunks. As they snuck out of the barracks, Winston could have sworn he caught a glimpse of Jackson watching them.

What a puss, Winston thought to himself. He was glad Jackson wasn't hanging with them. He wanted to tear him a new one and it would be hard to explain how Jackson got his ass whooped in the morning formation. One after the other, the six of them made their way out of the door headed for the end of the road.

"How'd you know Rodriguez would leave?" Lev asked Winston.

"I was watching Keeble; seemed like he was up to something when he talked to Rodriguez. Ole boy was speaking in code. Wasn't sure what he was saying, but Rod-man seemed to be slow on the pickup."

"So now what? We taking a long walk to a bar?" Daisy asked, looking from side to side as they reached the end of the road and all eyes fell on Winston.

Winston ignored Daisy and instead pointed off into the distance. Seconds later, there were headlights approaching from that direction. Winston held his pose until the twelve-passenger van stopped in front of them. As the men piled into seats in the back, Winston jumped into the passenger seat and gave a pound to the driver.

Within minutes, they were in a nearby hangout sucking down beers as fast as the bartender could get them up.

"That's not a problem?" Rodriguez was looking over at Keeble's iPad. "They left the barracks."

"Think about it; so did we," Keeble said with a grin as he watched them leave. "They'll be back; I'll bet you a six-pack." He slid the pad under his arm as they approached JB's.

"As I fucking live and breathe, the first round's on me. Got me a real live hero here!" a short, heavily tanned woman with a gravelly voice said as Keeble and Rodriguez entered the bar.

"Marge!! You still here?!" Keeble yelled back at her.

"Well, where the hell am I going?!" Marge yelled.

"Hot Rod, you ain't startin' no fight in here tonight, are ya?"

"Only person I ever fought in here was you," Rodriguez said with a laugh.

"Hold this, sugar," Marge said as she dropped her tray in the nearest patron's lap before rushing over and bear-hugging the two of them. "I'd say welcome back to JB's, but I'll just say, welcome home." She looked Keeble in the eyes and took him in before she spoke. "You good?" The question from Marge was much deeper than the words and it wasn't lost on either Keeble or Rodriguez.

Keeble met her eyes. "I'm good." But he knew she was searching and Rodriguez was waiting too.

"Glad you made it home." Marge knew the last battle was still raging inside of him. "Grab you some seats; Marge is takin' care of you tonight."

"I've heard that before," Rodriguez said with a wink.

"Your wife know you talk like that?" Marge playfully snapped a towel at him and shooed him on his way.

Keeble and Rodriguez settled into a table and waited for the first round to arrive. As Marge waited for their first rounds to come up, she pulled out her cell phone, scrolled through it until she spotted the number she was looking for, and hit the send button.

Several rounds of beer passed before the men and they were feeling good. Isolated from the rest of the patrons, they began to loosen up to one another.

"So I'm sitting there in front of this fat motherfucker, right? He's peering over the rims of his horn-rimmed glasses, with this look on his face like he thought he was going to get a rise out of me," Winston said.

"That's how they do," Daisy said, shaking his head.

Winston looked at Daisy; there would be no more unwelcomed interruptions from him. "He couldn't wait to send me up, but then the mama of the kid I saved went to bat for me, you know, if I didn't save her kid, the kid wouldn't be here and that kind of shit." He paused for a second as he thought about what she had done for him, but he didn't want to show how moved he was. "I think I fucked her," he said with a chuckle. "I don't know. Anyway old hard ass bought it. He asked me straight up to make a choice, the pen or this bitch here? So I chose this bitch. You know, fuck it, it was a way out of Compton without being in a box. What about you, little man?" Winston turned up his beer and took a long swig.

"It wasn't a judge that got me," Jones said as he looked pointedly at Winston. "There wasn't a judge in Chicago capable of maintaining dominion over me."

"C-c-c-ome a-a-again?" Daisy struggled to get out.

"I worked some magic to get released from jail; I was all set to find my next hustle until I had a run-in with the Chinese Mafia. Fifty yards from the station, a Cadillac SUV skidded in front of me. People nearby scattered, but I foolishly stood my ground. Running wasn't going to benefit me. I was into them pretty heavy for money and even if I attempted to evade them, it would only be a matter of time before they pinned me down, especially in Chicago. After being sufficiently accosted by a couple of henchmen, I crawled out of the alley they left me in, found the nearest recruiting station, and was on the first thing smoking out of Chi." Jones took a sip of his beer.

"S-s-so t-they ran you o-o-out of there?" Daisy took in Jones's story. "I-I-I ain't n-n-never run from n-n-nobody," he added with a laugh.

"No doubt you wouldn't have time to if you decided to engage them in conversation first," Jones quickly responded.

Daisy wasn't completely sure what Jones had said to him, but he was sure he would be insulted in the next five minutes when he figured it out. He'd told the guys he was in the army because his next stop was homelessness. His uncle had bailed him out for the umpteenth time and his aunt couldn't take the stress anymore. Will and Ethel had raised him from the time he was nine after his parents had died in a murder/suicide and he was the one that found them; soon after that, the stuttering started.

His uncle had a soft spot for him and took him in. He and Jack's dad were decorated Vietnam War veterans, only Jack's dad didn't adjust well back in the real world. Jack's mother was wife number four and twenty-three years younger than Jack's dad. After the murder/suicide occurred, Will felt obligated to take care of his brother's boy until the mounting arrests and hanging on the street corners became a daily occurrence. The last arrest already had a warning attached to it; it was either shape up or ship out and his uncle didn't hesitate to pull the trigger on shipping him out. Jack tried to convince them that he could change, even threw his best slightly goofy grin on his aunt; it used to always break her, but that last time she wouldn't even look at him. If she had, she would have given in. As his uncle gave him some recruiting information, he was getting out the words "Army, h-h-here I c-c-come."

"I'm noticin' a common theme here, fellas," Lev said. "I was 'bout to get sent up myself if it wasn't for old man Jenkins."

"Old man Jenkins, who is that?" Jones interrupted.

"He's a lawyer who had a farm that my granddaddy used to work on back home. Most people in Terrell are surprised when they find out he's alive, much less practicing law. He gettin' on 'bout eighty now. Boy, I must'a drank a tanker full of lemonade out on his farm." Lev shook his head as he reminisced. "I beat the shit outta this dude that was whippin' up on his wife and I ended up in jail. Old man Jenkins worked it out so I could keep my ass outta jail. Gettin' me in the army was the best way to get the hell out of Terrell. He gave me an army recruiting brochure and that put me on the way here."

"I wasn't looking at any troubles, at least not with the law," Wallace said. "I was just ready to get away from Atlanta and my family."

"Nigger, you hiding in the army from family?" Winston couldn't believe what he was hearing. He thought Jackson was a bitch ass, but this was taking the cake.

"My pops is a preacher, a big church and a large following. It's a different kind of pressure." Wallace said there was a lot more to be told, but now wasn't the time and he didn't know enough about these guys to share any additional details at the moment. Instead, he took a long draw of his beer signifying that he was done talking.

The one person they hadn't heard from yet was Turner. He listened intently to each of them. Processing and analyzing them. He could feel the others turning their attention toward him.

"I hadn't been out of the pen for long and was starting to fall back into my old life. Banging in Little Rock was a way of life. I couldn't find legit work and my homies were the only ones showing me love. But the only way they would completely let me back in was if I burned a dude that got one of my homies. And I was ready to do it, you know. I tailed the dude, had the choppa in my hand ready to smoke this fool and I thought about my moms and the promise I'd made to her. I wasn't tryin' to see no more of them blues, man. Kill somebody you don't know on the outside and you getting some time or worse. They tell you to kill somebody you don't know while you in this piece and you cashing a check." Turner watched as they began nodding their heads. "I worked on Black Hawks and was camped out in one pretending I was flying it when a colonel rolled up on me and told me I was getting transferred."

"Dark-skinned black dude?" Winston asked.

"Yeah, that's him."

"Ma'fucker rolled up on me when I was in the brig, 'bout to get booted out, and hit me with them papers," Winston added.

"Got m-m-me off th-th-the range," Daisy recalled.

"I got the same paperwork," Wallace said, but offered no other details.

"I was in a pit fightin' three dudes in my unit. Everybody else was standing around to see how this thing was gonna turn out."

"The fuck you was doin' in a pit, fightin'?" Winston was calling bullshit on this story.

"My commanding officer wanted to see how I would make out." Lev knew he was being called out; he let it ride. "After I finished tearin' them a new asshole, I climbed out of the pit and the next thing I know, a colonel is handing me some transfer papers."

Winston looked Jones up and down, wondering what hell he must have unleashed to end up with them. "What about you, little man?"

Jones took exception to the snide remark, but having heard them all his life, he just kept it moving. "I was arrested for accessing highly classified military information with my computers and a gaming system. Apparently they were searching for a more effective use of my unique abilities." Satisfied that it would take them a few seconds to catch up with his statement, he took another sip of his beer.

"It's probably a good time for us to head back to the barracks." Turner was checking the clock on the wall.

Winston wanted to push the envelope further, stay a little longer. He met eyes with Turner's. If it was just him and maybe one or two other guys, he would have demanded they stay with him. But for five of them to make the run they did with him, he was satisfied with their hearts. He signaled his friend who drove the van, letting him know that it was time to get them out of there.

Four Heinekens later and nursing number five, Keeble filled Rodriguez in on the men who were under their charge. All Rodriguez knew about this temporary duty assignment was that there were twelve men who were handpicked for a special military operation and he was receiving a three-thousand-dollar supplement for babysitting them, a detail he didn't share with Keeble. Keeble did let Rodriguez know that an entity outside of the military was funding the operation and the stakes were very high. An image of a van came into view on the iPad and caused Keeble to pause. He pointed it out to Rodriguez and they watched as the six men stumbled out of the van and back to their barracks.

"Told you they'd be back; just needed to blow the air out." Keeble would never let Rodriguez know he was relieved they'd returned.

"It's getting pretty late. Probably need to get back so you can catch some z's."

Keeble looked down and took a slow swig of his beer before placing the bottle on the table. "I don't need much sleep these days. My mind doesn't let me."

"Afghanistan?" He could see Keeble drifting into his thoughts.

"Yeah, it . . ."

Before Keeble could get the story going, his attention was drawn to the door of the bar as it was opening. As Keeble's eyes widened, it caught Rodriguez's attention and he turned to have a look. She stood five foot ten, thanks to the three-inch heels. She was a natural beauty who never required makeup and she had a body that could have inspired the Commodores' song.

"Well, look at what the cat drug in," Marge said, as she quickly grabbed the woman by the arm and ushered her to the table where Keeble sat with Rodriguez. "This is Luiz Rodriguez and Miles Keeble. And this is—"

"Rita Perez," Miles interrupted. No introduction was necessary.

"Kee, looks like you have some more catching up to do and I'm on duty. Want me to wait, or what?"

Rita looked at Keeble and smiled. Her teeth were as perfect as he remembered. "No, bro. I'm not going to be too long, but I think I might be able to catch a ride back."

Keeble gave the iPad to Rodriguez to keep with him. As long as he didn't touch any settings, he'd be able to monitor the troops on his way back to the base. Rita Perez walked slowly to the abandoned seat, allowing Keeble the opportunity to enjoy her short stroll.

Keeble spent an hour with the one that got away before having her drop him off at the barracks. Not wanting to disturb any of the men in the barracks, he had Rita kill the engine and the lights when they were within two hundred meters and they coasted to a stop.

Keeble got out of the car, watching as the car drove away slowly in the darkness. After a few seconds, the headlights came on and the car picked up speed. Rodriguez picked up Keeble on the computer as he came toward B-6. Rodriguez chuckled as he watched Keeble approaching his side door. He watched on the monitor as Keeble raised his hand to knock, but before he could tap on the door, Rodriguez snatched it open.

"I thought you'd spend more time than that with her, make a night of it. Didn't think I would see you until PT," Rodriguez said, hoping to get a rise out of Keeble.

"I see you figured out how to use the surveillance on the pad," Keeble responded flatly.

"Too soon for anything like that; we'll see where it goes though. Whatever it is, we'll just take it slow."

Keeble was cautious, but he didn't hide the fact that he liked her. "I'm gonna turn in; catch a little shut-eye if I can. Let me have the new toy." Keeble stuck out his hand as Rodriguez reluctantly handed over the goods.

"I still want to see what you got up there at A-10."

"Rod, we're going into day two. We've got a long way to go; there's time."

Keeble retired to his barracks to get what sleep he could, which he anticipated to be next to none. The thoughts of his men in Afghanistan usually kept him company, but tonight, they were a little clouded with thoughts of Rita. Welcomed, pleasant thoughts for a change. He settled into his command center to observe the monitors. One of these nights, he thought, he'd get to see what his new bed felt like.

15

Reno Wilson loved what he was doing. Every day that he woke up, he knew he was serving his country and making the world a safer place for his young family. He'd been in Afghanistan for three years getting closer and closer to Anemah Maasiq; today was the day he would meet the man face-to-face. He had a driver and one other passenger in their vehicle as they led a Tashkent Cartel convoy through Uzbekistan. They were headed to the Afghan border for a meeting to exchange weapons for opium. His work was beginning to pay off. He'd been building trust with the cartel in an effort to infiltrate Maasiq's organization and tear it down from the inside.

"Is everybody still cool back there?" Wilson spoke into a headset while keeping his eyes on the road in front of him.

"Looking good," a heavily accented voice came back through his headset.

"We're going to pull over in a few seconds; we're half a mile from the border." Wilson checked his watch. It was only twenty after one, ten minutes before their scheduled exchange on this lightly traveled route.

"I follow you," the voice said.

Wilson pulled over and the convoy followed suit. Every passing second seemed like a minute as he could feel the anxiety building up inside of him. He felt like it would be ten of the longest minutes of his life. He kept his eyes to the southern border waiting for a sign of the approaching convoy. Less than five minutes later, he finally saw the convoy approaching.

"I have the contact in sight. We're going to get closer to the border." Wilson pulled his car back onto the road and approached the border while his convoy followed suit.

He stopped his vehicle about twenty meters from the border. The convoy from the south pulled up and stopped right at the border. Wilson took a deep breath before getting out of his vehicle. He walked to the border and greeted three of the men speaking in the Dari language as they stepped out of the vehicle. The men greeted him warmly and that relieved some of his tension. That's when Maasiq climbed out of the backseat of his car. He wore white with a green vest, had a matching green pakol on his head, and stood six foot three. Wilson noticed his eyes; they were ice cold and seemed to be empty of a soul. They exchanged a few words in Maasiq's native language before he instructed Wilson to proceed. Wilson looked back and waved his convoy to come forward before turning his attention back to Maasiq; they all knew what they were here for. The lack of movement from the convoy caused Wilson to pause.

Wilson excused himself from Maasiq, assuring him that there was no problem. As he turned around again, he waved to his convoy once more in an effort to get them to join him. As he walked toward them, he could feel his stomach sinking. His pace began to slow before he finally came to a stop. He could feel the weapons being drawn on his back by Maasiq's men. He turned his head slightly to the right before turning his attention back to the men in his car. He saw them slowly raising their hands in a futile effort to surrender. Wilson then looked to the Tashkent Cartel; they made no effort to offer any assistance to him.

Wilson spoke in Dari and asked for his life to be spared, but refused to turn and beg these pigs for his life. The only response he received was the sound of gunfire as it rang out. He saw bullets as they ripped into the vehicle he'd once sat in and felt the pain as the hot ammo pierced his skin and shredded through his body, separating the soul from his life.

As his lifeless body fell to the ground, Maasiq's men continued to empty round after round into his carcass and the men who'd shared the car with him. Once Maasiq's men stopped the onslaught, the men from the Tashkent Cartel finally emerged from their vehicles. They walked by Wilson's vehicle, making sure there were no signs of life inside and gave a few kicks to Wilson's body as they stepped over the blood-soaked victim.

There was a friendly greeting between all of the other men and laughter as they pointed at the bodies of the slaughtered men. The men from the Tashkent Cartel got into the cars of Maasiq's men, and Maasiq hurried his men to the Tashkent vehicles. Within seconds, the convoys were moving again. The only vehicle left at the border was the bullet-riddled one belonging to Wilson while his bloody body lay in the road in broad daylight at 1:30 in the afternoon.

16

Cell phones ringing at 4:30 a.m. were no longer a shock. Harlow answered the phone and listened. There was a time when he would have said hello; now he simply said, "Harlow." After that the information would begin to flow. Calls at this time of the morning weren't filled with good news and cheer. This morning's call would be another one that fit that bill.

"Goddamnit!" he said as he hung up the phone, realizing that now wasn't the time to let his emotions get the best of him.

He wasted no time in getting Goldberg on the line. "Marv, we need to get Lawrence to Alexandria this morning; we have a situation. How fast can we make that happen?"

"I can place a call to him to see what we can make happen," Goldberg responded on his end of the phone.

"We're having breakfast at Le Refuge at oh-seven-hundred. Let him know I'll send a private jet for him if necessary." Harlow's voice was tense and he spoke quickly.

"What happened?" Goldberg asked. He had known Harlow

too long not to pick up on his tendencies and Le Refuge was never open for breakfast.

"Problems at the northern border of Afghanistan. I'll give you more details later." With that, the conversation was over. He didn't give a damn if they had to move hell or high water; they were meeting at 7 a.m. and Jameson would be there.

Before he could jump in the shower, he received an urgent alert on his phone. It was an activity report on Keeble. Harlow quickly moved to the office in his now half-empty Georgetown condo. It was a reminder that the fourth wife with the great tits was part of his past. He cursed her as he fired up his laptop. He cursed more when he saw the images of Keeble with Rodriguez at JB's in the wee hours of the morning. Then he saw the images of Keeble with Rita and he cursed again, but there was some admiration.

"She could be number five," Harlow said as he printed out the file. Complications were not what this mission needed.

At 0540 Jameson was already in the air, on board the C-130 that had been held for him at Pope Air Force Base and headed for Dulles Airport. At max speed the plane would be there in less than an hour. He exchanged his BDUs for a suit during the flight. He wanted to blend in and his unit insignia would stick out like a sore thumb.

As Jameson emerged from the plane, a waiting car met him on the tarmac and whisked him off to Le Refuge in Alexandria. A maître d' met Jameson at the door and showed him to the back of the empty elegant French restaurant where his table awaited. It would be a few minutes before the gentlemen who'd invited him to breakfast arrived. It was Jameson's habit to always be early.

"I will show the other guests in when they arrive, monsieur."

"Merci," Jameson replied, and that pretty much wiped out the extent of his French vocabulary.

Looking over the menu, Jameson realized that all of the items were printed in French. He did recognize the French words for bacon and eggs, only because bacon is the same in French and English.

"You'll never figure that out," Harlow said, entering the private room with Goldberg in tow.

"So, tell me what was so important that we had to meet today." Jameson had little time to waste and because these were his friends, he got straight to the point.

Harlow smiled, acknowledging his friend, but aware that the maître d' was still hovering behind them. "You want something that flies, walks, or swims? I know you can't read French."

They quickly settled on an order, gave it to the maître d', and ushered him on his way.

"So, the meeting?" Jameson asked once the room was clear.

"We lost another person this morning. It was just after four a.m. here, one thirty in the afternoon there," Harlow began. "The operations officer," Harlow paused for a brief second, "was set up in Uzbekistan, the deepest run we've been able to make so far into one of their arms cartels." He fired up his laptop and pulled up a grainy image. "We've got a fucking terrible satellite feed and we're not close enough to hear shit. He was brokering a deal between the Tashkent Cartel and Afghan drug lord Anemah Maasiq."

The feed was a wide grainy aerial shot near the Afghanistan border. Jameson watched the footage as the whole operation went south on them. Worst of all was seeing the operations officer being gunned down in cold blood.

"All that in broad daylight. Someone is leaking our agents. Once we start to get close, we have an incident like this," Harlow said as he stopped the feed. "That's what we're up against. Do you know where Keeble was early this morning; do you know what he was doing?"

"I haven't talked to hi . . . wait a minute. You're tracking him?"

"We're tracking you too. Hell, we track everybody, and you know that. Don't take it personally. We have to stay on top of things. We're tracking Keeble's every move with and without these men and you should be too," Harlow said.

"This is the second day in; we're on track," Jameson reassured him.

"Erick's unhinged because that was one of his nephews lying out there. Erick brought him into the agency; recruited him out of college." Goldberg used Harlow's first name to reel him back.

"Keeble has to remain on point, focused." Harlow pulled out some photos and handed them to Jameson. He needed to move on to the next topic. Now was not the time for him to discuss his sister's son lying in a pool of his own blood at the Afghan border in broad daylight. "This is from last night, a bar called JB's."

Jameson scanned the photos of Rodriguez and Keeble. "These guys go back a long way; they were blowing off steam."

"Keep looking," Harlow said.

He flipped a few more pictures, and then he saw her image. "She is fucking beautiful." Jameson couldn't help himself.

"Rita Perez," Harlow said. "Works for Georgia Power Company. Six years ago, she almost became Mrs. Keeble. Keeble spent some time with her last night, not long, but long enough to make us curious. We don't need anything clouding his judgment. We can't trust him if he is out all night. How can he lead this group of men? These men need to get trained up in a hurry. We have to rein him in, and let me tell you what is more troubling than that. Six of those bastards took off from their barracks last night," Harlow said as he produced another set of photos. "These damn criminals have no sense of discipline or commitment! What the fuck were they doing out of the barracks? We need to scrap this whole fucking thing right now!" Harlow was becoming more incensed with each word he spoke.

"There is no need to panic. I'm sorry about your agent. Keeble is our guy; he'll get them trained up right. She's a beautiful woman and he's a man; it is what it is. Keeble is a mission-driven soldier and his number one commitment is to the army. He'll do what he has to stay in; he already has. But if he wavers, trust me, I will convince him to stay the course; that's on me. And as far as the recruits are concerned, they're not in basic training so technically they are free to do whatever they want with their own time as long as they are ready for their next day of training." Jameson let the statement hang in the air. Part of it was bullshit, he was furious that these men were out of the barracks last night, but he maintained a poker face in front of Harlow and Goldberg.

"We won't be staying the course," Goldberg finally said.

"Come again?" Jameson needed clarification.

"Our timetable has been stepped up. We are escalating training immediately. Tomorrow we are isolating these men to the Darby phase of training. You tell Keeble that the mission is the same, but our timetable has changed. We are going to get these men on the ground in Uzbekistan in the next thirty-five days," Goldberg stated.

"Thirty-five days?" Jameson didn't like the odds of their being successful in that amount of time.

"Those thirty-plus days will tell us which men among this group will give us the best possibility for success in Uzbekistan. Stepping up the training will help us separate the cream from the rest of the crop." Goldberg had summed it up.

17

PT on day two picked up where day one left off. The run was six miles and the pace was pushed to six minutes a mile. The men were to be tested and monitored every day. Keeble would challenge them, push them to the edge of their limits, and bring them back. If the edge was too much for them, then he would push them over it and move on.

Mitchell struggled with the run. He started out fine, but three miles in, he could feel the swelling in his ankle. He told himself that this was nothing but mind over matter. All of the men around him were grinding to sustain the pace. It was during the fourth mile that Mitchell began to compensate for his ailing ankle. Every time he would start to fall behind, Turner would drop back with him until they were the last two men in the formation.

Turner watched the rest of the formation move farther and farther away from them and sensed that Mitchell was ready to give in. Being beside him wasn't enough to keep Mitchell going, so he began to speak to him.

"In all these things, we are more than conquerors." Turner

stared at him with fierce determination. Mitchell didn't respond; he wouldn't even look at him as he tried to fight through the pain. "In all these things, we are more than conquerors!" Turner's voice rang out, commanding Mitchell's attention.

Mitchell looked into Turner's eyes. Turner's eyes burned with a fire that sparked something inside of him and he said, "In all things, we are more than conquerors."

As they repeated the words back and forth to one another, they picked up their pace. Mitchell ignored the pain and repeated the line. If he needed an extra push, he would look into those fiery eyes of Turner's that had the ability to lift him when he didn't have it in himself. They were able to catch up to the group and finish the run with them.

Once they broke formation for chow, Mitchell's train of thought and flow of positive energy stopped and his ankle flooded him with pain. He looked down to see that it was once again swollen to twice its normal size. He hobbled gingerly to the mess hall on it.

Keeble settled at a table by himself to read a newspaper. A passerby would think there was no attention being paid to the men, but Keeble was taking all the men in. They tended to segregate themselves with people from the same base. The one exception was Mitchell and Turner. They were engrossed in a two-man conversation that centered on Mitchell's ankle. He kept pointing to it as if he were giving a play-by-play of the injury. A sprained ankle. Keeble wondered what Mitchell would think if he showed him the damage that was done to his.

"All right, ladies. Teatime's over. You have thirty minutes to shit, shower, and shave before your asses need to be in formation at oh-nine-hundred," Keeble announced.

The men grumbled, but they wasted little time in clearing the mess hall. There were six shower stalls in their barracks and they knew it was every man for himself. Jackson, Hines, Wallace, and Parker were among the first ones in the shower but took the longest time to clear the way for some of the other soldiers. Jones and Daisy got in and out, which made room for Garrett and Ford. Turner and a hobbling Mitchell got in once Wallace and Parker cleared out. Jackson enjoyed the impatient looks on the faces of Lev and Winston.

When they fell into formation, Winston, Lev, and Daisy were among the last men to join them. Daisy may have been one of the first to get a shower, but the appearance of his uniform made it seem as if he had barely had a chance to get in there. Daisy's jacket was askew. Keeble could see that it was buttoned incorrectly and he had tissues hanging out of his pocket.

"Goddamnit, Daisy, attention to detail. Somebody straighten him out," Keeble ordered and Lev stepped in when no one else did.

Training for the morning was hand-to-hand combat done in front of the B-6 barracks. Keeble got right to work demonstrating techniques and then asked the men to employ them. Jackson surprised Keeble with his already developed level of skill and the other men picked up on the techniques pretty quickly. Winston, though, was a little slower on the pickup; it wasn't the style of fighting he preferred.

A little more than an hour had passed and Winston still felt like it was a waste of his time. Keeble felt it was time to raise the intensity. The men were divided into two groups that would face off against each other. The objective was to subdue your man. Once you lost two matches, you were out of the competition.

Mitchell, with his bum ankle, was eliminated first. One of the surprises was little Jack Daisy. And when he won a match, he would send them away with a little rap tune. Keeble couldn't tell what irritated Daisy's victim more, losing to him or having to take the loss with Daisy rapping about them. Keeble's other surprise was Winston's use of the techniques.

The competition came down to four men. There were two undefeated men: Jackson and Lev, and Winston and Daisy had one loss each. Big Lev couldn't be taken down because of his size and brute power. Winston's one loss came in a matchup with Lev, whom he was facing again, but he really wanted to get to Jackson, who'd just eliminated Daisy.

Lev exchanged a look with Winston before their matchup started. He knew exactly what was on Winston's mind. Winston wanted revenge for the little stunt the asshole Jackson had pulled in the shower, purposely keeping them waiting. When they locked up, Lev made sure it was understood that he could win this anytime he wanted to, before allowing himself to be subdued by Winston.

Jackson licked his chops at the possibility of getting his hands on Winston. He would have preferred the big man, so he could show everybody here who the alpha male of this group was. He was disgusted by the way Lev laid down and gave himself up.

"Why don't you spread your legs the next time you lay down like a bitch?" Jackson said to Lev as he walked by. He didn't whisper it; he wanted everyone to hear him.

Lev, to his credit, didn't snatch him up by his throat. He stopped walking, turned back to him, and stared at him before looking past him to Winston. He nodded his head and smiled, letting Winston know this was his best chance at getting his hands on Jackson. Then he looked back at Jackson. He never said a word as he took his place among the men and waited for those two to get after it. If he was able to get past Winston, Jackson would still have to see him.

Jackson was as aggressive as Winston when the match started, but it was Jackson's plan to get him going so he could counter

Winston and use his aggressiveness against him. They were locked in front of each other with their arms extended. Winston used his right forearm to chop Jackson's elbow and reached in with his right hand to grab Jackson by the throat. Jackson turned into Winston so Winston was behind him. Jackson snatched Winston's fingers from his throat, twisting and bending them outward with his left hand before shooting his right elbow to Winston's face, lifting it up and following that up with another elbow to his neck. *Now I got this motherfucker,* he thought. As Winston bent from the elbow, Jackson put his right arm around Winston's head so that it was trapped against Jackson's waist and he began to choke Winston out.

Keeble was about to call a halt to the battle when Winston fired off a left-handed uppercut to Jackson's gunnysack. Jackson's eyes opened wide as he felt the impact. Then he felt his testicles rise up through his stomach and into his chest before lodging themselves in his throat. The suffocating pain caused him to drop and curl up in a fetal position. He wanted to scream out in pain, but he couldn't gather enough oxygen to do that. Winston crawled on top of him and damn near dislocated his shoulder as he put Jackson into an armbar and drove his head into the ground as he waited for Jackson to submit.

"I think you won; won't you let him up now?" Lev said with a broad grin on his face.

Keeble looked at the crumpled heap that was Jackson and declared the competition to be over. Maybe it wouldn't have been a bad idea to go over some rules before they got this far in the competition. He dismissed the men for lunch.

"What about Jackson?" Parker asked.

"He'll be all right; we're right by the mess hall. He can drag himself in there once he gets it together. Dismissed," Keeble said as he headed for his barracks. It was another little test to see if anyone would stay with him, just like seeing if they could work together to make sure everyone had equal time in the shower. As he looked back, he could see no one stayed with Jackson, but Winston, to his credit, lagged back a little bit.

Keeble entered his barracks to the odd sense that someone else was already there. As he entered the command center, he saw Colonel Jameson sitting there. He'd flown to Benning after leaving Harlow and Goldberg in Alexandria. As Keeble looked around the command center, he noticed that some of the monitors and equipment had been removed.

"To what do I owe the honor, Colonel?" Keeble said as he saluted Jameson.

"Afternoon, Sergeant." Jameson gestured for Keeble to take a seat, but Keeble did not. "The rest of today's training follows the same schedule, but you and your men are moving out tomorrow morning at oh-six-hundred."

"What the fuck? Sir?" Keeble was not often surprised, but two days in and the mission was being aborted?

"I'll let that pass, Sergeant." Jameson's eyes could have drilled holes into Keeble. "The CIA needs this operation to move to the Ranger training immediately. You have thirty-five days to prepare them for their next phase of training. Our timetable to get these men to Uzbekistan has increased exponentially and their training will reflect that. Do you understand, Sergeant?"

"Yes, sir." Keeble didn't understand all of the variables at play but he'd been in the military long enough to know that things can change at the drop of a dime and they would explain themselves later. "Sir, based on the schedule, we won't be back here until zero-two-hundred if everything goes right."

"I don't give a damn if they don't get back here until oh-five-hundred. Come oh-six-hundred, these men will be entering a modified Ranger program tomorrow. I can't think of a better way to start applying the pressure to them," Jameson added.

"Thirty-five days, sir?" Keeble said, knowing that was all he had to build a cohesive unit out of this group. "I don't know if they're all ready to get across that line."

"That was never the plan. We don't expect all of them to get across the line. It is your job to separate out the ones that aren't able to cut it." Jameson let that comment hang in the air and settle in on Keeble. "It is on you to find out which of these men have the ability to do whatever it takes, at all costs, to succeed. You are the man for this job because that is every bit of who you are and what you have been your entire military career!" Jameson finished his statement and rose to his feet. He again met eyes with Keeble. "Let's get these men ready, Sergeant. You get it done."

What Jameson left unsaid was that at the end of the month of training, there would be no next block of training. When this block was finished, the survivors of this unit would be finding their asses on the ground in Uzbekistan.

18

At 0530, Rodriguez was rumbling through the barracks waking the soldiers up. The previous day's training had concluded just four hours earlier on a rain-soaked land navigation course. He made a beeline for Daisy's bunk to flip it first. The last two days of training had taught Rodriguez that Daisy needed a little extra attention. But this morning with limited sleep, he shot straight up out of the bed as the lights were turned on, still with the trademark grin on his face. All the men wasted little time hitting the floor this morning, even Mitchell. His eyes couldn't hide the pain he was in, but he was up and ready to go.

Turner was a natural on the course, outdistancing the rest of the men and completing the almost pitch-black, treacherous course in near record time. Turner kept an eye on Mitchell; he knew Mitchell was hobbled by his damaged ankle and the course was a problem for him. Once Turner completed the course, he doubled back to help Mitchell out. It was a violation of the stipulations set out for them to complete the course. It was every man for himself, but if any one of them failed to complete the course, they would all fail the task. Turner could care less about the rules; no one was going to fail the course if he had anything to do with it.

Keeble quietly observed Turner as he doubled back and did not stop him from assisting Mitchell even though it was a clear breach of the conditions for the test. Mitchell and Turner nearly came to blows as Mitchell initially refused Turner's help. Mitchell finally gave in when Turner threatened to jack up his other ankle and carry him to the finish.

When the course instructor tracked the two of them down, he warned Turner that he was jeopardizing all of the men by helping Mitchell. Turner argued that they would all fail if Mitchell didn't complete the course anyway.

"ASMU 416 is our objective," Turner said as he guided Mitchell past him.

The instructor was so mad he could spit fire. When the instructor called Turner a boy, it prompted Keeble to come forward from his observation point. Keeble stopped the instructor from following the two men. He took exception to two of his men being addressed as "boy," and without a word, he let the instructor know that one more step after his men would be a very painful one. The instructor understood that no matter what his directive was before they started the course, the rules for the day had changed.

As Mitchell completed the course with the help of Turner, they could hear the other men rallying for them as they approached the finish line. There were two minutes to spare when they crossed the line. Rodriguez and Keeble picked up on the bonding as the other guys cheered them on. The moment was ruined when Jackson tried to capture it by yelling out, "That's ASS-MOO for you, baby!" It was quiet so fast you could hear crickets chirping. Winston said, "Really, nigger, that was corny," which earned him the opportunity to drop for fifty. Keeble told them all that Ranger training was beginning immediately. They would be heading to Camp Darby at 0600.

As they left the course, Keeble informed Rodriguez that the training schedule had changed and the men would be leaving for Darby in just a few hours, but Mitchell would not be able to continue with the program. Rodriguez spent the few hours in between readying the men's equipment for departure to Camp Darby. He also had to prep Mitchell's equipment for his departure back to his unit.

As the men got themselves together, Rodriguez pulled Mitchell to the side and told him to bring his personal gear with him. Turner watched the two men as they talked. When Mitchell's head dropped, Turner knew that some bad news had been delivered. Rodriguez grabbed his equipment, taking it to a waiting car. Mitchell stopped to talk to Turner on his way out of the barracks. He thanked Turner for his help and confirmed that he would not be joining the rest of the men as they moved on to Camp Darby.

They fell into formation by 0600, dressed in PT clothes, and they carried their gear with them. The Unit 416 men were in need of more rest. Little did they know that last night would be the most rest they would receive over the next several weeks.

The mess hall had come to them this morning; there was a chow line set up for them to pass through once they were released from formation and before they mounted up in the Hummers for Camp Darby.

"Pick your gear up after you get something to eat and I would caution you not to try to overload on food. Training starts once we hit the ground at Darby. I am with you and I will keep pushing you, but you will be in the hands of the Ranger instructors. Unit 416 men do not back down and they do not quit! Fall out!" Keeble was on the path to motivation whether they were ready for it or not.

Rodriguez monitored the men as they moved through the chow line, paying attention to the amount of food they loaded up on. But he silently tripped at the sight of Lev and Turner, who were also keeping an eye on what the men were grabbing to eat. A couple of the men were listening to Keeble and watching each other's backs. The only one this morning who seemed to operate from his own agenda was Jackson; he was hungry and got a double helping of eggs and bacon. Rodriguez shot a quick glance at Keeble who simply nodded his head.

They scarfed down a quick breakfast and picked up the ninety pounds of gear that included their weapons, ammunition, and training equipment. Now an eleven-man crew, they split, with six men riding in one Hummer and five in the other. Ford, Garrett, Hines, Jackson, and Wallace got the better of the deal, gathering in Rodriguez's Hummer with some additional space. But the joy they were experiencing with a little extra room to Darby would be short lived.

The drive to Darby was not a long one, but it took them into a different world where their training would be conducted by the 4th Ranger Training Battalion. As soon as the men left the Hummers the instructors were on them and the Ranger training phase began.

The instructors were barking instructions. Garrett and Hines looked back at Keeble like they were cows being led to a slaughterhouse. Rodriguez was already pulling away. If they were looking for a sympathetic ear from Keeble, they were looking in the wrong direction. He was barking at them just as loudly and viciously as the instructors as he hustled his men out of the Hummer.

There were twelve Ranger instructors, one to watch over each man. With one less man as part of their group, now there was an extra pair of eyes to watch their every move. And true to Keeble's word, the training began immediately with testing their physical fitness. The men had two minutes to complete seventy push-ups; next they had two minutes to do seventy sit-ups, followed by twenty-one pull-ups before heading out for a five-mile run that was to be completed in forty minutes or less all while the instructors, clipboard in hand, graded their form and charted their progress. This was a Rangers basic readiness test on steroids.

Keeble watched with satisfaction as the ASMUG unit fought their way through the grueling demands of the readiness test. Jackson was the only one who almost ran out of time during the run. On his third mile of the run, the double helping of bacon and eggs came back to visit him and had him doubled over. Once he'd left them on the course, he managed to make the forty-minute time limit for the run.

They were given a few minutes to get changed before moving to the combat water survival assessment. There were no showers or any of the cozy trappings of B-6. Where they stood is where they changed.

"This is where your mind changes, where we find out how mentally tough you are, establish your tactical fundamentals, and prepare for your squad combat operations. The world outside doesn't exist anymore. Don't count the days and don't check the time. You are here; we are here until it is over." Keeble locked eyes with Winston. He was looking for a spark in them; Keeble wanted to see if he was it.

As the sun was climbing in the morning sky, Unit 416 found themselves walking across a suspended narrow bridge thirty-five feet in the air over a pond before they encountered a rope crawl, all while carrying about sixty pounds of their equipment and weapons. This was to be performed calmly without showing any fear of heights and once they reached the end of the rope crawl, they had to drop themselves into the pond and jettison their weapon and equipment while submerged in the water. Then came the climb up a seventy-foot tower before hopping onto a pulley that would plunge them back into the pond. This was done without a safety harness and if it wasn't done correctly, that man would ship out right then. The Ranger instructors knew that somewhere along the way, they were going to lose one of them. Keeble knew it too; he loaded up his equipment and jumped in with them, partly for old time's sake and partly to get a bird's-eye view of the next one to drop from the group.

After the course was completed for the fifth time, not a man was lost but they were nearing exhaustion. The course would normally be taken no more than three times in a day. Today's instruction and the instruction for days to come would consist of planning and executing daily patrols, performing reconnaissance, ambushes, raids, and learning how to perform stealth movements to a new patrol base to plan further missions.

Among the men, there was very little conversation during the training. Everything was moving at warp speed. They barely had time to catch their breath, let alone talk to one another. Winston kept his eye on everybody and they kept an eye on him. Sometimes it was a wink or a nod to Big Lev to let him know he was good and the big man was too. Jones and Turner felt that energy too. Daisy still had his grin, so he was all good with the rest of the men. Ford was beginning to slow, and the thirty minutes of downtime for an MRE couldn't have come at a better time for him.

"These sons a bitches is trying to kill us, ain't they?" Ford asked the guys.

"Keep your voice down," Hines cautioned. "They'll be back on us you keep talking like that."

"Goddamn, you niggers need to stop bitchin'. This ain't shit," Winston said. "We're just getting started."

"You right, bro," Lev concurred. "It's all about your mind," he said to the rest of the group.

"Did they tell you guys it was going to be like this?" Ford asked, looking at everybody.

"It don't matter what they told nobody. They told you the same thing that they told everybody else. We are being prepared for a high-risk mission. They ain't bringin' us no cupcakes and gumdrops to get ready for that."

"Brothers, I don't know what they have waiting for us for the rest of the day. But it would be in our best interest to consume our provisions and conserve our energies for what remains of our training day," Jones said.

The men turned their attention to Jones. It took some of them a few seconds to figure out what he was saying to them.

"Come again?" Jackson inquired.

"He said eat and shut up." Turner gave the condensed version.

"I h-h-have chicken à la k-king." Daisy grinned.

They began to dig into their MREs and limited their conversation.

"What's up with you, black?" Lev asked Winston.

"You had a point. Which one of those dudes that I used to be is gonna get the furthest here?"

"That's good stuff to hear."

Winston lifted his fist up and held it out for Lev. Lev lifted his fist and they gave each other a pound.

Lunch was followed by more instruction from the Rangers in their makeshift field classroom before they started to implement newly learned raid techniques. Their day would conclude with them on another land navigation course. They would spend close to seven hours on the course, two hours with light and five hours after nightfall on the treacherous grounds of Darby.

Hearing that they would spend another night trekking through unfamiliar ground did little to inspire Ford. The testing and educating was designed to stress the men both physically and mentally. Ford was the first one to begin feeling the effects before he decided to replay Winston's words, "This wasn't shit."

"You good?" Big Lev asked Ford.

"Yeah." Ford wasn't sure if it was a lie or not, but it helped him focus on the next task.

"Hell, yeah, you're good. You ain't ready to leave this, are you?" Winston challenged him.

"Hell no!" Ford answered with a determined resolve.

At 1700, the men were turned loose on the course with nothing more than a flashlight and a map. Each map was different from the next and contained a route order to the predetermined locations. This was a way of ensuring that no man was following another, and unlike last night, there would be no exceptions to the rule. The quicker they navigated the course during the night, the sooner their first day at Camp Darby would come to an end.

Rodriguez returned to Darby at 1800 as he'd been instructed. He, Keeble, and a couple of the Ranger instructors moved the men's equipment to the final marker destination. There would be no barracks for them tonight or for what would come to seem like an eternity. A pup tent and a sleeping bag would be their Ritz-Carlton while at Darby.

"We lose anybody yet?" Rodriguez asked.

"Not yet, but Ford was getting shaky. That's not bad though; any Ranger class that comes through here loses twenty percent of their class the first day, sixty percent in the first three days."

"Well, they still have a good day and a half to go," Rodriguez cautioned.

"We may lose a couple, but the instructors put twice as much on them as they would have put on a Ranger candidate. I tell you, these boys are pretty special. I can feel it. I've been watching them all day. For the most part, they ain't bitching and crying. They're grinding, pushing each other. They're still trying to find a leader among them, got a couple of them stepping up, even Winston," Keeble said as they began the work of setting up their base camp for the night.

Turner was the first to make it to the final destination and complete his first day at Camp Darby. Once he was checked in by one of the instructors, he found his pup tent, dropped his equipment, and was asleep before his body was prone. It was just after 2300. He was followed by Winston a half hour later, and ten minutes after that was Daisy, tired as hell and barely hanging on to his grin. One by one, they trickled in just before midnight. Ford was the last one in at almost 0100 and he did not look good. Wake-up call would occur in two and a half hours.

Ford dragged his weary body past Keeble. He felt Keeble's eyes on him. Land navigation was never a problem for him, but the two courses in two nights were taking a toll on him as much as the lack of sleep. It would be a very short night and one hell of a long day for Ford. He got out of his gear as fast as he could and waited for sleep to fall over him; it couldn't come fast enough.

Keeble waited for Ford to turn in before he did the same. He wasn't positive, but amid the snoring of the dead-tired men, he thought he could hear the sound of sniveling before it turned into a snore. Darby and her twenty-one hour days was close to claiming one of his men.

19

They were awakened by sirens at 0330. Day two began with them getting all of the equipment packed up. Ford struggled mightily to wake up and finally got it together. The two and a half hours weren't nearly enough z's to get him on balance for the day, but he wasn't willing to give up.

"It's in you, son, it's down in there. Let's go get it." Keeble was wide awake and ready to keep him and all of his men motivated. Two and a half hours of rest to a man that barely slept anymore was like getting a full eight hours of rest.

Breakfast was another fast pass through the chow line with the food going down just as fast as it came to them. None of them cared about the taste of food. At this point, it was all about consumption. The first day of training had taught them that the opportunity to eat was going to be rare.

Day two started with a three-mile run in uniform to Malvesti Field where an obstacle course was waiting for them. This course had a station known by many as the "worm pit," a shallow, muddy, twenty-five-meter area covered by knee-high barbed wire. They would negotiate this course several times, sometimes on their back and other times on their bellies.

They spent an hour on the obstacle course before moving to an outdoor classroom at the end of the field. They were issued communications equipment, which brought a huge smile to Jones's face. He was anxious to tinker with the hardware and manipulate its operating system. The kid was now in his candy store. There were multiple education stations set up that they rotated to in groups of three. The instruction was fast paced. They were introduced to troop leading procedures, use of field communications equipment, principles of patrolling, field craft, and basic battle drills focused toward squad ambush and reconnaissance missions. All of the men would have multiple opportunities to lead these drills. Hours of instruction were followed by twice as many hours of physical implementation of the techniques they'd learned before getting their next meal break. Jones barely grabbed some chow; his focus was on experimenting with the infrastructure of his communications equipment.

"You good, Ford?" Lev checked on him. Ford's day had started out shaky and little of it had changed for the better.

"I'm good," Ford lied.

Lev, Ford, and Jackson had been part of the same training group. Winston told them to keep an eye on each other and to keep pushing no matter what. Jackson had long forgotten about anyone else in his group; he was just trying to get himself through the day. So keeping Ford motivated had fallen on the broad shoulders of Lev.

Lev turned to Ford, and stared him in his eyes. "I got you, brother. Make sure you get plenty to eat; keep your strength up," he said.

"Fuck that. I need some sleep." Ford tried to get up a grin but was too weak for that.

"Forget about sleep. It doesn't exist anymore," Keeble said as he walked by to the chow line.

Lev looked at Ford and Jackson. "Hey, do what you can do when you can do it." He steadied Ford and they followed Keeble to the chow line.

After lunch, they were back at the education stations for more instruction. This time they covered airborne and air assault operations, demolitions, environmental training, and the fundamentals of combat operations. These three hours of instruction were followed by four hours of implementation. These lessons would be drilled into them, into the fiber of their being, over and over again. This was designed to instill in the ones who made it through the training the confidence, and the tactical and technical proficiency needed before moving on to their next training region and the next until there was no doubt about the preparation for the mission the survivors of this group would undertake.

Day two would conclude with a twelve-mile tactical rucksack march in full combat gear at night. They had a three-hour time limit in which to complete the march. At 2000 the march started.

Keeble couldn't have been prouder of his men and what they had endured during the last thirty-six hours. Although the day had been a struggle for Ford, he was still in it and not a single one of his men had bailed on the team.

"Big Lev, I want you and Daisy to lead the march. Push a twelve-minute mile for the first hour and then settle back to a fifteen-minute pace to finish out," Winston said.

"Roger that, boss," Big Lev finished while Daisy was still stuttering out the word *roger*.

"I'll bring up the rear; keep an eye on Ford." They nodded in agreement as they departed on the march.

Daisy, for his part, started a rap to help Lev set the pace. Lev rolled his eyes at the thought of listening to him spit stuttering rap lyrics for the next twelve miles. The humorous lyrics absent of any stuttering both entertained and amazed Lev. How could a man who spoke with such difficulty rap so effortlessly?

Keeble nodded as he observed Winston taking leadership of this group. Winston took a look at Keeble and met his eyes with a cold stare, still wanting to get at him but he had more pressing matters at the moment. Winston turned, geared up, picked up his left and right, and fell into the rear of the group. Keeble waited a few minutes before falling in behind them with the hint of a smile on his face.

The good feeling would be short lived, though. Ford would become a casualty on day two. Ford blacked out six miles into the march. He never slowed or wavered; instead, he crashed and burned and never knew what happened. Keeble stayed with him until a medevac removed him from the trail. His body couldn't finish what his mind had started. Although Ford had fallen, Keeble was satisfied with his effort. However, he was done with Unit 416.

The remaining men completed the ruck march prior to 2300 and no one else was lost. By the end of day two, Unit 416 was down to a group of ten men. Keeble knew the attrition rate for the first few days of this type of training, so to lose one man instead of six or seven out of the eleven was a huge victory for the group.

That number would grow over the next several days, but tonight, the ten men who successfully completed the march would feel good about their accomplishments of the past two days. Daisy started to give the men a celebratory rap, but it was cut short by the sound of music playing. Jones had altered his mobile military communications system to pick up music from a station that was playing sixties Motown. The sound brought smiles to a group of weary men as they drifted off to some much-needed rest. An immediate halt would normally be put to this type of activity for men who were in training. But this wasn't a normal group of trainees and although he wouldn't say it, Keeble was astonished by what Jones had done with the equipment.

20

"Somebody want to explain to me what the fuck we are doing here?" Lev asked, hoping someone could provide him with a decent answer.

"Don't ask me, big man. I don't know what sense it makes to jump out of a perfectly good airplane," Winston said while shaking his head.

The ten men were sitting on a tarmac, wearing full combat tactical airborne gear, preparing to walk up the tailgate of a C-130 Hercules airplane. In the midst of all the other training they were receiving, they were also given a crash course in airborne training. Most of the men were taking it as the next thing to come. A couple of them had never flown on an airplane, much less thought about jumping out of one. Lev was apprehensive at the thought of taking his big body out of that iron bird.

Turner sat quietly, said a prayer, and tried to contain his enthusiasm. He couldn't wait to get up in the air in something, anything, even if it meant he would have to jump out of it. If he'd had his druthers, he would be the man flying the aircraft instead of taking a ride.

"C-130 rolling down the strip, airborne daddy gonna take a little trip." Keeble was singing an airborne cadence as he walked among his men checking their equipment. "Stand up, hook up, shuffle to the door. Jump right out and I count to four. If my main don't open wide, I've got another one by my side. If that one should fail me too, look out below because I'm coming through."

"Still don't trust that fucker," Winston mumbled to Lev. He looked around at the men to see who was taking to this bull.

Jones, always one to question the practical sense of anything he encountered, had a question for Keeble. Keeble was sliding into his jump master harness. It had been a while since his last military jump and he was anxious to get his knees in the breeze but today, he would just serve as a jump master on their first jump.

"Sergeant Keeble, I'm sure that you can understand that on an occasion such as this, there may exist some tension among my compatriots. The cadence you just chanted draws attention to the potential mishaps when one exits an aircraft. It doesn't necessarily invoke thoughts of the type of outcome that we are seeking today."

"Okay." Keeble lost concentration on what Jones was saying after "potential mishaps." "Why don't you play that song that we talked about?" He knew Jones was still manipulating his communications equipment.

More than happy to show off what he had done with the equipment, he switched on a handheld controller and the music from "Fly Like an Eagle" began to play. What the other men and Keeble weren't aware of was that he had hacked into their communications equipment and linked the music into their headsets.

"How did you find time to . . . ?" Keeble's voice trailed off as he watched Jones smile and shrug his shoulders. According to his file, Jones could do anything with computers and electronics, and now he was adding communications equipment to his profile.

Keeble received the signal that it was time for him and his men to get on board the aircraft. They stood as the tailgate of the C-130 dropped. There were two sticks of men and they were divided, five of them in each line. When paratroopers jump from a C-130, they exit from both sides of the airplane. Parker was the last man in one of the lines of five. Keeble would serve as jump master of the stick with Parker in it.

As the plane rumbled down the runway, there was nothing said between the men. They stared straight ahead. Five on one side of the plane and five on the other, all near paratroop doors. Nerves, anxiety, and thoughts of how they had gotten here so quickly floated through their minds. Fifteen minutes of flying passed when Keeble gave the six-minute warning. The aircraft descended to the drop altitude of twelve hundred feet and one hundred fifty miles per hour and the paratroop doors were opened. A few minutes passed before Keeble gave his next command.

"Stand up!" Keeble shouted and the men stood up. "Hook up!" They hooked their static line to the cables that lined the inside of the C-130. "Check static line." The men shook their static lines to make sure they were connected to the cable. "Check equipment." They all made sure that all of the equipment was secured. "Stand in the door!"

Jackson was the first man on Keeble's side and Big Lev was the first man on the other side. A switch ignited for the big man when the doors were opened and he felt the rush of the wind race to his body. The jump master on his side had to hold him back, he was so anxious to get out the door. Keeble saw Jackson shaking so badly his knees were almost knocking. The plane circled the drop zone a couple of times, which allowed Jackson to calm down a little. Lev almost got bored standing in the door watching the ground go by.

The green ready light lit up. "Go!" Keeble yelled and he saw Lev put his knees in the breeze. Jackson's slight hesitation earned him a push in the back to get him going.

One after the other, the men popped out of their respective doors until Parker came up. He wouldn't approach the door. Keeble stepped as far forward to him as he could and grabbed him.

"Let's go; let's go!!" Keeble yelled.

Parker started to fight Keeble's hands and for half a second, it seemed as if he was going to try to push Keeble out to prevent himself from exiting the plane. Keeble steadied himself and started to shove Parker out the door until he looked into the young man's eyes. If the eyes are the windows to the soul, then Parker's soul would not answer this call. Instead of shoving him out the door, Keeble waited for him to step forward. When the ready light turned red, Parker's time was up and Keeble set him back down.

"No worries, son. We'll take you up on the next one. You'll be fine."

Falling through the air and counting one thousand, two thousand, and halfway through counting three thousand, Lev felt his canopy deploy as it trapped air while it expanded. Adrenaline rushed through his body and he got high off of it. He looked up and saw the full canopy. As he descended, he saw Jones and called out to him.

"Jones! Jones! Hey! I just jumped outta the fucking airplane!" Lev couldn't contain himself until he got a look at Jones.

As Jones turned his head to get a look at where the screaming dumb ass was, Lev could see that his nerves were shot. Lev was so high off of his first jump, it never crossed his mind that not everyone was enjoying the experience as much as he was.

On the ground, the men gathered their equipment, carried their chutes to the checkpoint, and congratulated each other on their first jumps. Then they noticed that there were only nine of them at the checkpoint.

"Anybody seen Parker?" Winston asked. "Garrett, he was behind you, right?"

"I don't think he made it out. I never saw him behind me."

When the plane went up for the second jump in the afternoon, the men were more relaxed, but nowhere near comfortable with jumping from an aircraft while in flight. Parker didn't make it as far as the load-in for the C-130. As the tailgate lifted to a close, Parker's time with Unit 416 came to a close as well.

The men were taken aback at the sight of Keeble in tactical combat gear. He would again serve as jump master, but this time instead of riding back down and landing with the plane, he would follow the last man in his stick out the door.

"You ready for this, Sarge?" Lev asked as the plane flew over the drop zone.

"Always," Keeble responded. "You got it, don't you?"

"Got what?"

"That fever. It starts real early; you're a junkie."

"Hell, nah, Sarge. I ain't no . . ." Big Lev wasn't sure where the sarge was going.

"A jumping junkie is what I'm talking about."

"Man, go 'head with that," Winston mumbled, but it drew Keeble's attention.

Keeble started to address Winston but instead decided to issue his jump commands to the men. When the last man on his stick hit the door, Keeble hooked his static line to the cable and stood in the door with both of his hands touching the outside of the door. He took in the moment, letting the wind, the thrust, and the sun hit his face. He popped out of the plane and placed each hand on the side of his reserve while he waited for his chute to open. It was a hell of a rush; there was nothing else in the world like it.

Keeble did not make their next jump with them; he left them in the hands of the Ranger instructors. He was scheduled to have a conference with Colonel Jameson to update him on the progress of Unit 416. There was also transfer paperwork that needed to be completed on Ford and Parker. Rodriguez would handle the logistics of returning Parker to his unit.

An instructor from the Airborne Training School subbed for Keeble on the last jump of the day. It was five o'clock somewhere and the instructor had been celebrating it for some time. He was unsteady on his feet as the aircraft slowed for the jump. When the doors opened and the fresh air hit his face, he could feel himself instantly sober up and felt his judgment was sound. As the warning light turned from red to green, the men on the opposite side of the plane began to exit the paratroop door. The instructor was slow to respond, but he finally started to send the men out of his door. Wind gusts picked up steam as Winston approached the door. As he hopped out of the aircraft, he saw the warning light switch from green back to red. The instructor never saw the light change color; instead he called for Hines to exit the plane. The plane banked, tossing the instructor off balance. He grabbed Hines as he tried to steady himself and pushed him toward the door, causing Hines to trip and bang his Kevlar helmet into the side of the plane. The swirling wind sucked him out of the aircraft and the lack of a proper exit didn't allow him to gain enough distance from the plane. Instead, Hines bounced against the side of the aircraft before his static released his chute from the plane. His limp body descended toward the ground and crashed to the surface of the drop zone.

Keeble finished the paperwork on Ford and Parker before settling in for the conference call with Jameson. Keeble let the colonel know that the attrition rate was less than 20 percent when he was approached by one of the Ranger instructors. They had received a call from the drop zone. Hines had broken his leg during his landing and was medevac'd from the area. Keeble was down another man. Keeble gave Jameson the news that another man had been lost as a result of the incident. Jameson's reply was that Unit 416 now had a 33 percent attrition rate and he hung up the phone. Keeble sat back in his chair for a second and looked at the phone. There was another set of transfer orders that he needed to prepare. In the span of eight hours, the group had dropped to eight.

21

"They are already four men down?" Harlow shook his head. "It's not even a week and they are already down four."

"Keep your voice down," Goldberg warned. At the moment, he was more concerned with the line he had in Heath Lake. The sun had just set and it was the perfect time for them to enjoy some bass fishing.

"It's nothing to worry about, Erick. It's better than I would have expected at this point. I thought we would have lost that on the first day. We knew going in that all of them weren't going to make it." Jameson shifted in the boat.

Their weekly meeting provided a chance for a little rest and relaxation. They couldn't point out who had come up with the plan to go fishing in Georgia. The idea seemed to hit all of them at the same time, but they did agree that it was the thing to do. Even Harlow, who always seemed to be on pins and needles lately, preferred to be on the lake with his childhood buddies.

"As the training continues to intensify, we'll start seeing what we have in these men," Jameson said as the boat shifted in the current. "Oh, hell."

"Shh. You're both killing the fishing," Goldberg said.

"If it was up to me, we wouldn't be in this boat; we'd be standing at the edge of the lake casting these lines," Jameson retorted.

"I don't get it." Goldberg looked at Jameson. "How can a guy who flies around in a tin can with wings, and occasionally jumps out of one of them, be so uncomfortable on a boat?"

"I joined the army, not the navy. Water is not the surface that I choose to navigate."

"Got one," Harlow said excitedly as he started to work to bring his catch in.

"Tell me about the operation you ran in Nerkh," Jameson said to Goldberg.

"It was an operation run by us but controlled by Special Forces, a good one too. The base was perfect, located thirty miles east of Kabul. We had people on the ground, working the area as well. Shit hit the fan there when the Afghan government began accusing the Special Forces of kidnapping and torturing some of the Afghan citizens as they tried to root out Maasiq. A number of the missing men started showing up again, not alive, but piece by piece. When the base was shut down for good, the Afghan government searched the base and found the remains of some of the men who had gone missing. Special Forces got blamed for it, but I can tell you it wasn't them. It was us. I haven't been able to prove that yet, but I am sure it was us," Goldberg said.

"Why is that?" Jameson listened intently.

"You know Special Forces; they would never leave a mess like that, not that kind of trail. It was too deliberate. Some of the agents we had on the ground went rogue and compromised the operation. To throw the heat off of them, they went about the business of setting up the most likely suspect. Good old

Uncle Sam and his bloodthirsty men of Special Forces. To this day, we still haven't been able to close that loop."

"And Nerkh is where Keeble was injured and a number of his men were killed. The same Anemah Maasiq that killed Harlow's nephew," Jameson added.

"Yep, that one. The attack was blamed on Afghan rebels, but I know there was something more, some help they received from our rogue officers. SF was getting too close to Maasiq and peeling back the cover on what was happening with the rogue officers."

Harlow heard the conversation, but was not willing to join in. At the moment, he had bigger fish to fry. He felt like the fish on the other end was capable of breaking his line. "Are you boys going to keep yapping? It feels like I got a whale on this line."

"Let's see what you have there." Goldberg turned his attention to Harlow.

As he pulled the line, Harlow reeled in the slack. Together they were able to control the fish and pull it in. It wasn't the behemoth of a whale they were looking for, but it was about a three-pound bass.

"I'll be damned. That three-pound whale made you two work up a sweat, didn't it?" Jameson reared back with laughter.

Harlow howled while taking an envelope out of his pocket. Harlow tossed it to the waiting Jameson who did a quick scan of the contents, catching a glimpse of the money inside. It was a little bonus for his superb effort thus far. Jameson howled louder and longer at the moon.

While the moon was shining on the lake in Georgia at 7:15 in the evening, it was 4:45 in the morning in Kabul, Afghanistan, and dawn was more than an hour and a half away. The darkened room was illuminated by the single light of the video camera. It sat on a tripod and was aimed at one man. He was on his knees, his feet tied together and his hands bound behind his back. A black hood covered his head. Two captors stood on opposite sides of him, the one to his left brandishing a bloodstained machete. His crime, whether he was guilty of it or not, was betraying the man known as Anemah Maasiq.

Maasiq sat at the back of the room listening to the man asking for mercy, begging for his life to be spared and pledging his allegiance to Maasiq. But the words held no meaning to Maasiq; he cursed the man in Dari and ordered his men to complete the order that they had been given. The man struggled, trying to free himself from his captors. The captor on the right landed a solid kick on the hood causing the man to slump. The captor on the left raised the weapon with the slightly dull edge. As the blade came down on the neck of the masked man, it didn't make a clean decapitation. The man screamed out in agony, praying for death to come swiftly. It was what Maasiq wanted: suffering all captured on video. Maasiq finally relented, ordering another chop at the neck that sliced through the vertebrae, freeing his head from his body.

Speaking in Dari behind the camera, "This is what happens if you betray Anemah Maasiq!"

22

There was a somber mood among the men as they hiked their way back to their base camp. They had all gathered around Hines before he was medevac'd from the drop zone. They offered encouragement, but knew his time with them was up.

Daisy got to Hines before any of the other men. He contacted the others on the communications equipment but none of the team could make out what he was saying, he stuttered so badly. Lev started to beat box on the communications system. This was his way of calming Daisy. Daisy started to drop a verse about his location and the compound fracture of Hines's left leg. Daisy made a field splint for his leg and made him as comfortable as possible until the others got to him.

"That fucking Keeble should have been here," Jackson said bitterly. "That was a good man we just lost."

"That instructor got him jacked up," Winston said. "He should have never gone out the door after me."

"What are you talking about?" Jackson demanded.

"Red light came on as I went out the door," Winston snapped back.

"That may be, but I saw it all. The thrust and propulsion of the aircraft while banking at a thirty degree angle were contributing factors to the incident, but it was the headwind of eight knots that contributed to the degree of difficulty and negatively impacted our dear friend's landing, thus leading to his compound fracture." Jones had observed the plane after exiting it and had drawn a conclusion.

"W-W-What did y-you just s-s-say?" Daisy asked Jones.

"What the fuck did you just say, you stuttering motherfucker?" Jackson was looking to pick a fight with anyone.

Daisy started toward Jackson and Winston was headed that way as well, but they were both intercepted by Lev.

"Gentlemen, I think at a time like this cooler heads should prevail," Turner offered. "Knowing that Hines was a good friend of yours and seeing him go down is bothering you."

"Fuck that Dr. Phil bullshit," Jackson lashed out.

"Brother, I'm just—"

"Didn't nobody fuck with you when you was toting Mitchell's ass around. I thought you bitches needed a room," Jackson said.

If it was some type of approval or one-upsmanship he was looking for, there was none coming his way. The only thing coming his way was Turner. He took three giant, swift steps toward Jackson and without warning, he swung a roundhouse kick, striking Jackson in the temple. Jackson fell like a rock and was unconscious before his head hit the ground. Turner attacked him like an MMA fighter going in for the kill. He landed a few extra blows on him before Jones, Daisy, and Lev were able to pull him off of Jackson. Winston looked on at the scene with delight; he'd wanted to get after Jackson's ass since he'd met him, but his new buddy, Big Lev, had kept him at bay.

"Apparently you ain't for much chatter before you start throwin' them hands, huh dog?" Winston said, laughing. "Bet that motherfucker will know the next time." He patted Turner on the shoulder.

"He h-h-hit t-t-that b-boy so hard, if h-he remembers it, he'll never f-f-forget it!!" Daisy stuttered.

"Sho' you right," Winston said, giving Daisy a pound. "Nice work, Turner. He been seekin' a beatin' since we got here. But now we got to get this nigga right before we get back to the base camp."

They sat Jackson up in an effort to bring him back to consciousness. He started flailing his arms and throwing punches like a boxer picking up the action after not realizing that he had been knocked out.

"It's a little late for that." Wallace looked at him, shaking his head.

"Motherfucker!!" Jackson yelled at Turner.

"What up?" Turner said calmly. He was three steps ahead of Jackson. He might have only responded to Jackson with two words, but they conveyed that he'd already broken him down and was ready to turn his lights out again.

Keeble was waiting for them with the Ranger instructors as they arrived back at the base camp. He congratulated them on their successful jumps and briefed them on the combat bunkers they had to construct before they shut it down for the night, but he never acknowledged the loss of Hines.

Turner did not hesitate to move out and get started. Others followed suit, but weren't as quick to fall in line. Turner hoped that if he got started quickly, no one would have time to bring up his incident with Jackson. Winston took the longest time to get started. He watched Keeble as he walked away. *That dude couldn't give a damn about us*, he thought.

Winston, Daisy, and Lev worked together to dig out a bunker. Daisy jumped in with them because he knew Lev worked like a machine. If he ever got tired, it wasn't showing. Winston was doing his part but Lev could tell there was something on Winston's mind.

"What is it?" Lev asked him.

"What you mean?" Winston kept working.

"There's something on your mind."

"It's that Keeble, man. I seen that type of nigger before," Winston said, his choice of language caused Daisy to stop digging.

"What you talkin' about?" Lev caught Daisy's response, but kept the conversation moving.

"That's a turncoat nigger if I ever seen one. I'm bout tired of this shit," Winston said without any regard for Daisy's presence.

"What you mean about turncoat? How you mean?" Lev asked. For some reason, he had a way of getting Winston to talk.

"I had a teacher when I was a junior in high school. Lombard. He was a history teacher and I was all-city in Compton, running back in football and point guard in basketball. Anyway, he took a shine to a nigga, you know, no fruity shit or nothing like that. Talked my head off about my grades and writing my own ticket. Long story short, he won me over and I trusted that dude. But the first time I got burned for running dope, it was because that ma'fucker rolled me. That teacher fucked up my shot at college in balling and shit. That's when I started banging them streets even harder. Keeble's just like Lombard, propping you up to knock you down."

"I feel where ya comin' from, but I don't think that's his game at all, dog. Keeble, I'm talkin' about, not that Lombard. Keeble's got a job to do and I think he's doin' it. I don't know what to make of him, but I gonna damn sho' get everything I can from him. I had some coaches when I was at A&M who rode the shit out of me. It wasn't 'til I got kicked out of there when I realized they was trying to make me better. Honestly, I think Keeble picked something up off of you that first day."

"The fuck you talking about?" Winston was lost.

"Every group has a leader; our group has a leader. Sometimes the leader doesn't even know he's the leader." Lev let that comment settle on Winston. "You been tryin' to show somethin' to Keeble since he knocked yo' ass out."

"Hey, man, that . . ." Winston stopped digging. Daisy started to dig harder.

"Just listen a minute. You talkin' 'bout havin' enough of this shit, quittin' maybe. But all you been doin' since you got here is competin'. Showin' what you made of. Keeble is here to train us. I think he sees the same thing I see. This group, it's about the men who are here and the ones who can survive the training. I will, and I know I have a leader." Big Lev finished and listened to the silence.

"Man, fuck your big-country Texas ass."

"Yeah, but you heard me. And fuck you too," Big Lev said with a smile across his face.

"T-T-That w-was sp-sp-special," Daisy added.

"Fuck you," Winston and Lev said in unison and Daisy gave them his crooked smile.

They, along with the other men, finished out their bunkers, grabbed some chow, and began to settle in for the next couple of hours, knowing that it would not be long before the start of the next training day.

Turner grabbed his Bible to read a few passages before turning in. He was seeking some words of comfort and guidance. He resisted the urge to find Jackson and apologize to him for jumping on him. More than anything, he was disappointed in himself for letting Jackson's words get to him. This was the kind of mistake that could get him sent back home and that was the last place he wanted to be. He had made a practice of thinking things through and carefully assessing situations before responding since he had left Little Rock. The knee-jerk reaction to Jackson told him that he still had a ways to go.

Shots rang out through the base camp. The men that had started to find some rest found it to be very short lived as chaos ensued. The Ranger instructors were conducting a raid on their bunkers. The men grabbed their weapons and started firing their weapons at anything that moved. Most of the rounds were at each other. Keeble watched from his observation point and thanked God that the rounds weren't live. As quickly as the attack came, it ended. The men looked around at the damage that could have been caused if the rounds had been live. No one had to tell them that there was a lot of work to be done. They could see that for themselves.

23

"You men have to understand that this exercise is nothing at all like what you went through the other night. The ammo being used by the instructors is live. You must stay low to the ground," Keeble warned.

Quite a bit of time had passed since their day had started and the sun still wasn't up. It was 0430 and they were about to conduct live action battle drills. It would be the first time they would put some of their training into practice with live ammunition. They would signal each other to move under the attack of enemy fire while advancing their position on an enemy bunker.

"Just another day at the crib," Winston joked as the men prepared for the exercise.

Jones was leading the men for this exercise and Daisy was his second in command. To his credit, he was looking forward to it. He had spent the previous hour briefing Daisy on how they would proceed and Daisy responded to everything by rapping about it; it was driving Jones crazy. But as the time approached for the training exercise to begin, Jones had a laser focus that rubbed off on Daisy; the level of his concentration was elevated. As Jones gave instructions to the men, directing who would lead, what hand signals would be used, how to flank one another, and who was bringing up the rear, he was morphing from the man who could outthink the entire group into a man who could lead the entire group.

Big Lev and Garrett were Jones's chosen two to bring up the rear. Jones felt good with the big man covering his back and gave the signal to move out. The team worked well together advancing on their objective. The first few rounds did little to alarm anyone; all the men stayed low and paid attention to Jones's signals. Daisy caught a glimpse of Jones in action; he chuckled at the sight of the smile on Jones's face. Jones was having the time of his life leading the other men, and without some type of electronic device in his hands.

That was, until a mortar round exploded and the firing of live weapons intensified. The predawn hours were hammered with flashes of light and hues of red and yellow. The sudden ambush was a shock for all of the men, but Jones kept moving them forward, signaling them to stay down.

Garrett lost his composure. He'd been in shoot-outs before, but this ambush took him out of the training environment they were in and back to his neighborhood where he was shot and his cousin was killed. Garrett jumped up just like he did then in an effort to get out of the house.

Lev saw the look in Garrett's eyes change. Lev knew Garrett wasn't there with them anymore. He grabbed at Garrett's leg as he stood up and started to run, but he was too slow.

"Garrett! Get your ass down!" Lev hollered.

Garret was already in a mad sprint, standing straight up and running for the door that would take him out of the house he thought he was in. Lev sprang to his feet to chase him down. He ran as low as he could, but the big man was as big a target as Garrett was. Lev caught him within a couple of seconds and wrestled him to the ground. Garrett fought back against Lev, trying to get to his feet and get the hell out of there. Lev restrained him like a six-year-old child so he wouldn't get the both of them killed by the crossfire.

When the live fire exercise was completed, the men were gathered for a debriefing where Jones was commended for his leadership under the circumstances and for continuing to pursue the objective. Garrett, however, was removed by the Rangers. When Rodriguez arrived with additional supplies for the men, he left for the day with Garrett and a set of transfer orders.

With each passing day, the men grew more accustomed to losing people along the way. They took on the next assignment, operation, or exercise and kept it moving. They were on a reconnaissance mission and it was Jackson's turn to lead. The men were spread out over rough terrain.

Jackson took four men with him, but dispatched Turner and Wallace to the Black Hawk helicopter that would serve as their transport from the rendezvous point. Jackson personally wanted to keep Turner as far away from him as he could. It was an assignment that couldn't make Turner any happier. It was a chance for him to get airborne in a UH-60 and he didn't argue.

He was in the warrant officer's ear about the Black Hawk from the time they arrived. Turner could not shut his mouth when it came to discussing every aspect of the helicopter. He convinced the warrant officer that he had done everything to a Black Hawk except fly it.

Under Jackson's leadership, the recon mission was doomed from the start. It was an area recon where they were to hike a distance of eight miles, fend off ambushes from their instructors, and identify their enemy stronghold. Once they located the target, Jackson was to call in air support. This exercise, like all the others, was trailed by Keeble and the instructors.

Jackson, dehydrated and sleep deprived, started the hike heading east instead of west. They'd traveled two klicks before Jones called his attention to it. He lost contact with his air support and arrived at the rendezvous point over an hour late. Once he finally reestablished contact with Turner, he gave him the wrong coordinates for both the extraction point and the enemy location.

"That's wrong," Winston said, upon hearing the errant coordinates. Winston rushed to Jackson to show him the correct location and review the map with him.

"You're not fucking up my operation!" Jackson yelled.

"Keep it down." Winston tried to calm him.

"Jackson, he's right," Jones said. "You misread a seven for nine and by my estimation, you will cause the air support to miss the target by more than a kilometer."

"This is my goddamn show!! This is my goddamn show! You're tryin' to fuck me."

"Calm the fuck down!" Winston said.

The more Winston and Jones attempted to calm him, the more animated Jackson became. The only person who was fucking the recon mission was Jackson. He never heard Lev coming at him. Lev barreled into him with a shoulder block that took him off his feet and knocked him out cold.

"That motherfucker might have a concussion," Winston said, looking at Lev standing over him.

"Once a person loses consciousness, they have already suffered a concussion. The length of time in which they are unresponsive can tell us to what degree an individual has been impacted by said concussive blow. This being the second time he has found himself in this state, and if I were using the Glasgow Coma Scale, I would rate his status as a seven, which would be moderately severe." Jones looked around at the men who were lost by his diatribe. "His shit is fucked up." Sometimes layman's terms worked best.

Winston got on the communications system and re-sent the correct coordinates for the airstrike and the rendezvous point as Jackson was coming to. Jackson realized that the operation was no longer his but he never uttered a single word. He stood up, dropped his weapon, and removed his tactical gear. The men watched him as he stepped over his gear. Wallace wouldn't look at him as he walked past him. Right there in the middle of the exercise, he abandoned his men on the battlefield. He would keep walking until he came to Keeble. Drained mentally, physically spent, and with no desire to go on, Jackson looked at Keeble as a tear slowly rolled down his face.

"That's it, Sarge; I'm done," Jackson said, trying to hold onto his dignity.

Darby had broken another one of the men.

After the aerial strike by the Black Hawk, the remaining men salvaged what they could of the mission and hunkered down at the rendezvous point to wait for extraction. There were several passes by the Black Hawk and the flight path was erratic. They looked up in the sky and watched as the helicopter banked awkwardly, dipping before it regained control.

"Wallace, Turner? What the hell is going on up there?" Winston radioed.

Turner couldn't answer; he was preoccupied at the moment, having the time of his life. Wallace was petrified, not able to believe what was happening.

"That crazy son of a bitch talked the pilot into letting him take the controls of the helicopter," Wallace said. He was barely maintaining his composure.

"The helicopter!? Who?" Winston barked into the radio.

"Fucking Turner!! He's about to kill us!" Wallace was in a state of panic.

"B-B-Bullshit," Daisy said, laughing.

"Tell that idiot to get his ass down here right now!" Winston radioed to Wallace. He looked at the rest of the men on the ground with him. "Keeble's gonna have my ass for this fucked-up drill."

"Better you than me," Big Lev said and roared with laughter, as did the others.

"That shit ain't funny," Winston said, but he laughed about it too.

Keeble left Jackson in the hands of one of the instructors and caught up to the unit at the extraction point. They were gathering their gear and loading into the helicopter. They were tripping off of Turner's latest adventure when Keeble joined them. The smiles began to fade and the chatter slowed down when they noticed Keeble approaching the clearing where the Black Hawk sat. There was a collective thought that permeated the group. *Oh shit.*

Keeble stared at all of the remaining men. They had started with twelve, came to Darby with eleven, and with the most recent loss of Jackson, they were down to six. And the bullshit that Turner pulled today could easily have them down to zero and the warrant officer kicked out of the army. They all stood silent, waiting for the hammer to fall. Keeble walked slowly toward Turner.

"It was my fault," Winston said in an effort to cover for Turner.

"Did I call your name? Did I look at you?" Keeble directed

his comment to Winston but never took his eyes off of Turner. "You keep your pie hole shut." Then Keeble narrowed his focus to Turner. A smile crept across his face. "You were flying the fucking Hawk!" Keeble slapped Turner on his shoulder.

"Yeah, I did," Turner said, free of tension, and it relieved everyone else as well.

"That's out-fucking-standing, soldier." Keeble was impressed. Apparently Turner's penchant for flying was a tidbit of information that Jameson didn't put in Turner's file. He wondered if there were other secrets missed in the men's files.

Training continued at Darby with preparation for their next phase. Their final day at Darby would have them participate in a fifteen-mile foot march to the infamous Darby Queen. It was widely regarded as one of the army's toughest obstacle courses. It was a two-mile course filled with twenty-three obstacles. Keeble might have termed this a "fun day," but after so many consecutive nights of three and a half hours of sleep, the men failed to see where the fun was in this little adventure until he joined them on the course.

All of the men approached the course with the leisurely fun that was intended, everyone except Winston. Once he realized that Keeble was in, he attacked the course just like he'd always done. Keeble took up the challenge and ran with him but made sure he stayed behind. He watched as Winston reached the first obstacle, a rope crawl over a forty-five-foot water pit. This had quickly turned into a two-man competition. Winston muscled his way through the crawl and Keeble chuckled to himself, remembering doing the same thing. Keeble was very fluid and smooth in his motions through the rope crawl, closing the gap on Winston. Keeble let him continue to run in the lead at the start of the course. Winston pushed himself harder every time Keeble closed in on him. He could hear Keeble talking shit to him, telling him the old man was coming every time he got close to him.

Keeble was right beside Winston as they approached a huge climbing wall. Keeble looked at Winston and gave him a look that said, "let's get it." It was Winston's chance to see how fluid Keeble was in his climbing. Winston expended a lot more energy muscling his way up. But the whole time, Keeble kept telling Winston to push himself through.

Lev and the rest of the guys signaled each other. They short-cut the course to get to the finish line. They were more interested in seeing how this turned out than running the course themselves.

Winston could not believe that Keeble was in front of him telling him to keep pushing; this old man should be a distant memory, not in front of him talking shit. As they descended on the rope netting, Winston was losing more ground to Keeble, who to Winston, looked to be getting faster. Winston thought of freeing himself of the netting to get down faster.

"Don't even think about it!" Keeble shouted, looking up at him from the ground. "I ain't losing you on this."

Winston heeded the warning until he was about fifteen feet above the ground. Keeble watched as he came to the ground, thinking, *this freaking idiot just wouldn't listen.* But then he found himself smiling when he saw Winston perfectly execute a parachute landing fall. The training was paying off. Winston rolled to his feet and took off for the worm pit and Keeble followed suit.

As Keeble was crawling under barbed wire, it snagged his bootleg, exposing his surgically repaired right leg. Winston saw it with his peripheral vision, but his brain wasn't making sense of visual images; it was trying to get him to push his fatigued body through the course.

With fifty yards to sprint to the finish, Keeble turned on the afterburners to increase his lead over Winston. He slowed at thirty yards, and then stopped at twenty yards. He looked back to Winston. "You've come too far, Winston. Goddamnit! You finish."

Winston churned out the distance, passing Keeble in the process. Keeble fell in behind him and crossed the finish line second. Winston fell to his knees in exhaustion. Seconds later Winston threw up what few contents he had in his body before he began to dry heave.

"Ah, Sarge, you got him," Big Lev said, walking away and not looking back.

"I got him. Just toss me some water and give us a few," Keeble said.

Wallace tossed a canteen toward them. Keeble went over and grabbed it, then came back and kneeled beside Winston. Once he was sure that Winston was finished, he handed him the canteen. Winston wiped the sweat from his brow, took in some water, then spit.

"Why'd you do that, Sarge? Let me win?"

"Because your time's coming, and you'll keep pushing." He paused for a second. "You're a lot like I used to be. There's a light that has to stay lit. We're going to take you to some dark places, most of them within yourselves. You've got to have a light to follow. You . . . you have to stay lit."

Winston wasn't sure what that all meant at the moment, but he took it in anyway. "Sarge, your leg? What's that about, how can you run like that?"

"It happened in Afghanistan. That's another conversation, and I refused to believe it when they told me I would never be able to run again. Keep it to yourself, for now anyway."

"Roger that, Sarge." He wasn't going to tell anyone that he was getting his ass handed to him by an old dude with a bad leg.

He exchanged a look with Winston. Winston met his eyes without a blink; he was letting Keeble know that no matter what came at him and the men of Unit 416, they would be ready to keep fighting through it.

24

Camp Merrill would be the next training destination for the remaining members of Unit 416. Camp Merrill was located in Dahlonega, Georgia. It was a remote region of Georgia where the mountain phase of their training would be conducted. It was a distance of nearly one hundred and ninety miles from Darby.

Instead of reporting immediately to Merrill, Keeble bought them some time because the training would continue soon enough. The added time would give them a chance at their first hot shower since they had left the B-6 barracks and a new set of uniforms.

A normal class of Ranger candidates would be transported to Merrill by Black Hawk, but Keeble and Rodriguez would be transporting them by Hummer. It would take the men nearly four hours on I-85N for them to reach the mountains of Dahlonega. Keeble offered an apology to the men for not having a suggestion for what they should do with their time while traveling, three men to each vehicle with plenty of space, but he was sure they would figure something out before they hit the ground running at Camp Merrill.

The unit was told to fall out with forty-five minutes before their departure from Darby. They wasted no time in hightailing it to the showers. Keeble headed off to his shower area and Rodriguez followed him.

"Forty-five minutes? We're going to hustle up I-85 now," Rodriguez said as he checked his watch.

"Won't be the first time doing that." Keeble smiled.

"So, Tessa got a call from Rita. She was wondering what happened to you."

"Shit, I haven't had time to think about her since the training schedule was accelerated."

"Yeah, and now I get to pass a hundred and one messages." Rodriguez was fishing for more information.

"Seems like there's some interest." Keeble flirted with the idea.

"I'd say so, homes."

"There's nothing I can do about it now," Keeble said as he looked toward the area where the men were showering. "I'm like to do something about it, but now isn't the time."

"I understand." Rodriguez nodded. Keeble was a soldier first. "But I doubt that Tessa will," Rodriguez joked and even drew a laugh from Keeble. "Hey, I have a real question for you though." Rodriguez became serious.

"What's up?" Keeble asked.

"The people behind this, they're sinking some serious dinero. These hombres get new everything everywhere they go. What gives?" Rodriguez felt that his need to know had grown.

"Those men are busting their asses for it too." Keeble would have liked nothing more than to give Rodriguez some specifics, but he didn't have all the details either. "All I can tell you is that they're being prepared to deploy in Central Asia."

Rodriguez waited to see if any better information was coming. It wasn't. They had arrived at Keeble's shower area and he was already stripping off his gear. Keeble gave Rodriguez the scoop on the race between Winston and himself on the obstacle course.

Meanwhile, in the shower area, Daisy started to rap about the beauty of a hot shower and getting the hell out of Darby. Lev fell in line with him and provided a beat. Daisy was able to work Turner and his high-flying hijinks into the rap and Wallace held up his hand to give Turner a high five. Turner considered the implications before reluctantly returning the high five. Winston bounced his head to the beat, enjoying the downtime.

"Shut up! That is not music," Jones yelled. He could listen to some rap, but loved R&B and hated that he hadn't brought the communications equipment in with him to drown Daisy out. "You all continue to indulge his infantile behavior." Jones was fighting a losing battle.

The rapping continued until the men finished their showers. Feeling good about himself, Daisy streaked around before grabbing a towel.

"Somebody help that white boy find a towel!" Jones hollered behind him as he came out of the shower.

"I don't think he's trying to find one. White boy trying to show he can hang with the brothers!" They laughed harder.

"Pervert!" Jones added.

"S-sounds like you got sh-shortcomings!" Daisy yelled back as he took another lap around them and they erupted with laughs.

"That's ugly, and you know God don't like ugly." Turner went biblical on him.

"Might be ugly, b-b-but we can all see it's true!" Daisy pointed at Jones.

All eyes were on Jones. They were waiting to hear the intellectual respond with a display of words that would take them five minutes to figure out how bad of a verbal assault he'd put on Daisy.

"Fuck you!" was the only retort Jones could muster.

"Boo your ass!" Lev said. He was enjoying the humor but also making sure that nothing got out of hand.

It wasn't an altercation that he would have to worry about. Jones was more likely to create an implant device to attack Daisy's vocal cords to get him to stop rapping. Having had their fun and gotten cleaned up, they began to filter out of the shower area. Winston and Lev were the last to clear the area.

"What's up with you and Keeble?" Lev asked.

"What you talkin' 'bout, big man?" Winston wondered.

"Looks like he was giving you more than water back at the Darby Queen," Big Lev said to Winston as they lingered behind in the shower area.

"Keeble talked about what we had in front of us," Winston responded.

"That son of a gun's a heck of a lot tougher than you thought, ain't he?" Lev dug at him.

"Hell, nah. See, if I had been eatin' regular, 'cause you know wit' my schedule and if I got me eight hours of sleep, then I woulda—"

"You still woulda got your ass handed to ya. You saw how that man was running the course. That ma'fucka coulda ran the two miles to the course to race ya. Hell, we could see he was talkin' shit to you when you started fallin' behind," Lev ragged him.

"He wasn't talking shit to me; he was encouraging me." *Damn,*

Winston thought, *did that sound as weak coming out of his mouth as it did in his head?*

"Sounded like he was talkin' shit to me. Man, he could have really put it on you if he wanted to. And the bad thing is, I think you were running faster today than when we were on the other course."

"Man, I thought I was killing him. Every time I thought I put some distance between us, I kept hearing him coming. What's worse is that he kept telling me he was right there." Winston shook his head. "That brother is blood raw in shape!"

"You ain't lyin', and I ain't seen that brother asleep yet. Like I said, bro, we sho'nuff gonna learn a lot from that man," Lev said with the confidence of a man who already knew there was plenty more ahead of them.

"I'm beginning to feel you on that, for real." He gave Lev a pound; he still had his reservations about Keeble, but was at least willing to give him a chance now.

"W-what the fuck are you two d-doing? You two want to get left?" Daisy asked, trying to hurry them along.

In the allotted forty-five minutes the men were given, they were showered, in clean uniforms, and ready for the company move to Camp Merrill. Lev, Daisy, and Jones in the Hummer with Rodriguez, and Turner, Wallace, and Winston loaded into Keeble's vehicle. Their tactical equipment and weapons were flown ahead by Black Hawk to Merrill and would be waiting for them when they arrived.

The men in Keeble's Hummer took immediate advantage of the four-hour road trip. Their heads were down by the time the vehicle cranked up. It was a little different in the back of Rodriguez's vehicle though. Lev was snoring; Jones was barely hanging on; but Daisy, oddly enough, wasn't ready to shut it down just yet.

"Jones! We g-good?" Daisy woke him.

"Until you start rapping again. But we're good," Jones grunted.

"Cool," Daisy said.

"So what is it with you and the affinity you have for rhythm and rhyme music?" Jones asked, but he received a hesitant stare from Daisy. "Why do you like—?"

"Rap," Daisy interrupted. "It w-was how I c-c-could survive on the s-streets in the Bronx. It kept people f-from talking about m-m-my st-stutter," Daisy explained.

"Wow. That's too bad. I mean it's wonderful that you rap; too bad you got picked on for the stutter. People would antagonize me for being smart and into computers." Jones reflected on his thoughts. "Everybody gets picked on for something. How did you get swept into the rap euphoria?" Jones paused, wondering if he needed to clarify his statement.

"I g-got these movies th-that I love. R-Rudy Ray M-Moore d-did a rap about the signifying monkey."

"*Dolemite*?! What do you know about *Dolemite*?"

"That's my shit!" Daisy was so excited, he lost his stutter.

"Shit! *Dolemite, Foxy Brown, Cleopatra Jones, Shaft* . . ." Jones got excited.

"*Hammer, Car Wash, Big Bad Mama!*" Daisy went tit for tat with him on blaxploitation movies.

"Blaxploitation at its finest. What about B-movies?" Jones asked.

"Can't watch enough of them!" Daisy blurted.

Jones was in nerd heaven. They spent the next twenty minutes grilling each other on their love of the genre. It went on and on until they disturbed the big man.

"You two need to shut the fuck up before I give you a shaft!" Lev grumbled.

With only a few hours with a chance at some rest, Jones and Daisy decided to grab some but the two of them could go all the way to Merrill and back to Darby and not run out of movies to discuss.

25

The mountain phase of the training began with an introduction to the 5th Ranger Battalion. And true to Keeble's word, training began as soon as they hit the ground. They were ushered to a site where the instruction began fast and heavy regarding combat patrol operations in a mountainous environment, military mountaineering tasks, and mobility training. The fatigue and stress levels they'd experienced at Darby would soon be a cakewalk compared to what lay ahead of them in these mountains located in the middle of nowhere, miles from any real civilization.

One positive working in their favor: they arrived in the mountains in early May. Two or three months earlier and they would have been dealing with hypothermia and the threat of frostbite at night. A month and a half later and poison ivy would have become an everyday issue. Environmental conditions in the mountains would always be a challenge, but this time of year would be the best, if you could call it that.

After three hours of verbal instruction, their mountaineering training began. They were taught to tie every kind of knot you could imagine; manrope knots, granny knots, wall and crown knots, overhand knots, reef knots, two half-hitches, and more. That was followed by learning climbing fundamentals and techniques, mountain evacuations, and rappelling from the sides of mountains.

Wallace was the first of the men to ascend the face of the mountain on a sixty-foot climb. This was damn sure not a rock-climbing wall at the gym. There were no colored pegs or grips to get your hands and feet onto. Keeble and the instructors set themselves up atop the mountain face. They offered him the security of a harness, but Wallace didn't want one. Wallace welcomed the challenge; he'd been trained in parkour and knew he would have an advantage over the other men.

Loaded with ropes, a hammer, and stakes, he got under way. The men watched his every move; there was a combination of strength and grace on display that impressed them. Every five feet he would pound a stake into the mountain. Keeble and the Rangers were even doing a double take. Not that they hadn't seen that type of skill before, but seeing it so soon from someone from this group was impressive. Keeble's only thought was that this dude had been holding back.

Once he reached the top of the climb, he tied his rope to the sturdiest tree he could find nearest to the mountain's edge. He secured the rope with a bowline knot and tossed it down the face of the mountain. If he wasn't going to use a harness, he was making sure the rest of the boys would not use one either.

Daisy was the next man up following the path that Wallace had set for them. Lev was the last man to make the climb. Because of his size, he clutched the rope and made a grab at every other stake; the big man had no grace. It was sheer power and muscle he used to get up there as quickly as possible.

When it was time to work on evacuations and rescues, Jones

drew the unenviable task of rappelling down the side of the mountain with Lev as his casualty. Jones strapped into a harness and secured the big man before he started his descent. The strain of descending with Lev was evident on Jones's face from the time they got started. But you had to give Jones credit for manning up. There was only fifteen feet left to the bottom when Jones missed his next grab at the rope and the rapid descent turned into a free fall.

"Incoming!" Turner yelled as the men scattered.

Jones tried to land on his feet, but the weight of Lev across his body knocked him off his feet and square onto his back. Lev was treated to the sound of oxygen being forcibly removed from another human being's lungs. Lev moved off of him as quickly as he could to check on him as the other men rushed to help.

Jones groaned in obvious pain. Lev feared that he might have broken some of Jones's ribs. Winston cleared everyone back to give Jones some air to breathe when he rolled over, smiled goofier than anything they had seen from Daisy, and started to laugh as he struggled to catch his breath.

"That was a fucking trip!" Jones said as he gasped for air.

The instructors did a quick check to make sure that he was okay and nothing was happening with him internally. Once they were satisfied, the men were back on top of the mountain rappelling again. Jones did his best to make sure that when he was paired with someone again, it was Daisy.

The training was constant and nonstop, learning how to construct suspension traverses and rope bridges so they would be able to negotiate obstacles like bodies of water. The Rangers worked in rotating shifts around the clock, but for Unit 416, one day blurred into the next. The only interruptions to the instructions were the surprise combat operations that would be thrust upon them and the patrolling they executed while they were en route to the next training site.

For four days, they operated under these conditions with very little food and even less sleep. They ate from the nourishment that the mountain provided in the form of plants and berries. Occasionally, a site might have some MREs, but they almost never came across six of the prepackaged meals—usually four, maybe five meals if they were lucky that they would split amongst one another. The most they came across at one site was six and you would have thought they were dining in a five-star restaurant for the evening.

They slept in shifts; three men would sleep for two hours while the others kept guard of their perimeter; then they would change shifts. And the men of the 5th Ranger Battalion kept a watchful eye on them so they couldn't get any additional shut-eye. If there was anyone slipping, there would be another surprise raid on the camp coming their way.

Throughout the training, Keeble stayed close. He knew firsthand the mental and physical fatigue they were experiencing, as well as the psychological stress they were under. Soon they would be at their breaking point, but he also knew if they didn't falter, didn't succumb to the situation, that they would have a breakthrough.

Turner had a moment on their third night in the mountains. The unit had just finished a climb to the top of Yonah Mountain where they would conduct a field training exercise in the wee hours of the morning. They set up camp after nineteen exhausting hours of training and Turner, Lev, and Wallace drew first watch. They moved out to their respective spots on the perimeter where they would keep watch for enemy trespassers for the next two hours. Fatigued and nearly delusional, Turner was sleepwalking toward his area on the perimeter.

"What are you doing?" Keeble asked.

"Following the trail," Turner responded. He imagined following a trail home. But there was no trail to be found.

"You were supposed to pick up your spot on the perimeter. You passed it fifty meters ago." Keeble snapped him out of his sleep.

"Oh, okay." Turner's response was slow; he still wasn't fully awake.

Somehow he made it back to his spot and settled in to guard his assigned area. It wasn't long before he was struggling to stay awake. He saw something or someone moving; now he was wide awake and ready for action. There was a figure coming down the mountain to his vantage point and he immediately thought it was an ambush until he saw civilian clothes. *How in the fuck did a civilian get up here?* he thought to himself.

"Tyrin Turner. Look at you; ain't you somebody?" the civilian said.

"Oh, fuck," Turner said, as if he'd seen a ghost. "Dennis Thompson? What the fuck are you doing here?"

"That's no way for a religious man to talk," Dennis chided him. Dennis was one of his gang brothers back in Little Rock.

Turner's mind took him off the top of Yonah Mountain and onto a street corner in Little Rock. Turner had a blunt in his mouth, and he was taking a long, deep pull from it.

"Let me hit that shit," Dennis said.

Turner handed him the blunt. They were so high they never paid attention to the car approaching them with the headlights off. When the lights came on, they were momentarily blinded and that's when the shots rang out. Turner was grazed in his shoulder as he dove for cover, but Dennis was hit three times in the torso. It was the attempted revenge killing that had led to his time in the penitentiary.

"You ain't never known me as a religious man." Turner was now back on top of Yonah Mountain and he now knew there was no way Dennis was on the mountain with him. He'd watched him get buried; he was one of the pallbearers. However he continued the conversation.

"No, but I see you, bruh. Reppin' this army shit now, huh? You left the hood in the hood."

"If I didn't get out when I did, I never woulda; feel me?" Turner said.

"Oh, I feel you."

"And I flew a helicopter too!" Turner exclaimed.

"You said you was gonna fly someday." Dennis laughed. As he stopped laughing, he looked at Turner. "And you got saved, huh?" Dennis seemed skeptical.

"Yeah, you know, it helped me make peace with who I used to be and what I used to do. But I think it's time for me to go home," Turner confessed to his deceased friend. Something in him had snapped.

"Go home. I mean we all got to make peace sometime. But what are you talking about? Go home." Then Dennis leaned closer to Turner. "Let me tell you something. Be righteous in your religious convictions, but you can't go back home. Don't you never forget about that motherfucker that you was on the streets. 'Cause that motherfucker, man! That motherfucker was smart as hell and he's gonna keep you alive with this shit you doin' now."

"Turn. Turn! You straight?" Lev heard Turner talking and came to check on him. His eyes were wide open, but he was in a daze.

"What, Dennis? I mean, Lev. I'm good. I'm good." Turner shook his head to get rid of the cobwebs, but he couldn't shake them. He was half asleep and half awake.

"Who's Dennis?" Lev asked him.

"I'm done, man. I'm going home!" Turner yelled.

"Shut the fuck up, man." Lev snatched him.

"I want to go home," Turner repeated.

Lev slapped the shit out of him and shook him. "I said shut the fuck up." Lev waited for Turner to calm down. "I think you fell off for a minute."

"Yeah, I think. I mean, yeah, I guess." Turner was still lost between worlds.

Lev reached into his BDUs, pulling out a cookie he'd saved from an MRE. He knew they were all suffering from a lack of food and rest. It wasn't much, but it was all he had and he knew that Turner needed it more than he did.

"You good now?" Lev double-checked as he handed him the cookie.

"I'm good. Thanks, man. I was trippin'. Go on back. I'm straight." Turner assured Lev he was fine and sent him back to his post.

"Hang in there, brother. We got one hour left on patrol."

One hour left meant that an hour was already gone and Turner had no idea where the time had gone. Talking with Dennis, someone who wasn't even alive, was another one of the blurs that his day bled into. He couldn't explain it and didn't know who he could talk to about it. He ate the cookie and took some time to think it through. Maybe it was his subconscious reaching out to him through Dennis at a moment when he was about to give in, reminding him that with all he was learning and everything that he used to be, this wasn't his time to give up. He thanked God that Lev got to him when he did.

Keeble observed all of this from a distance. He wasn't sure what Turner was experiencing, but he knew what he was going through. He'd seen it happen before, even had his own moment in these mountains some years ago. It was a rite of passage; there was little doubt in his mind that more of the Unit 416 men would reach a similar impasse in these mountains.

The unit spent their last hours on Yonah Mountain applying the skills they'd learned on the lower part of the mountain. The instructors drilled them on different climbs and rappelling techniques before sending them out on a recon mission where all of their newly acquired skills were put to use. Turner attacked the mountain and the mission with a renewed vigor.

"Say he was doing what?" Winston asked Lev.

"He was talking to himself. I couldn't make out what he was saying, but he was laughing, crying, and cussing."

"Reverend Turn was cussing?"

"Man, that shit went on for an hour and it kept getting worse. Man, I couldn't take it. And when I got to him, he was out in left field somewhere; it was like he didn't know what was going on." Lev shook his head.

"Shit, it did that nigger some good though. You see how he moving now. That brother is on some oohwee today," Winston said as he checked Turner out.

"I was worried about him before we crashed, but that man was ready to go for the day before I crawled out of my sleeping bag. He was standing beside my bag and told me, 'Good looking out' and he was ready to roll," Lev said.

"And he hasn't stopped yet. I like that; we all gotta keep it one hundred with him," Winston said with a little determination.

"We all, huh? Brother, if I ain't know any betta, I might think you startin' to see this as a team," Lev said with a wink and he held up his fist.

"Man, if you don't get your ass up that mountain . . ."

Winston gave Lev a quick pound and the two of them fell in

line with the other men in pursuit of their objective. The question was, could the men continue to carry on? These soldiers needed to be able to move farther, faster, and fight harder than any other soldier. These mountains were helping to determine if that was in them.

26

Over the next two weeks in the mountain terrains' unforgiving environment, they would perform many combat operations and take turns planning and leading the various missions. Some of them were during the day; some occurred at night. The missions were against the Ranger instructors with conventional and unconventional warfare tactics and equipment. The field training exercises varied in length, anywhere from two days to as many as nine days with constant attacks and ambushes while they pursued their enemy objectives.

Keeble watched his weary men as they moved cross-country over the Tennessee Valley Divide and the mountains of Georgia, lugged heavy equipment, fought with courage, and bravely fended off ambushes against them and the vehicles they were sometimes transported in. He grew prouder of the men with each passing day, seeing what was growing and building inside of them. They were so caught up in their day-to-day battles with fatigue, hunger, and sleep deprivation, Keeble didn't think they could see the change happening, but he could. They picked each other up, pushed each other, and demanded the best of each other.

All of the missions were led by different men; Unit 416 would descend upon them in different ways, utilizing tactics that were learned during their Darby and Merrill phases of training. There was cross-country movement, parachuting into small drop zones, there were air assaults into small mountainside landing zones. There were times when some of the men might buckle, but they never wavered in their commitment to the unit and what they were now becoming to one another. They would pick one another up when necessary. More times than not it was Winston who was doing most of the picking up. Keeble was concerned about who would pick Winston up when he needed it, though.

Winston's breaking point came on the last day of training in the mountain phase. It was during a ten-mile march across the Tennessee Valley Divide. He'd gone almost sixty hours with no sleep. Jones had blown a call on a mission and made a tactical error that in a real-life situation would have cost all of the Unit 416 men their lives. Keeble knew the error belonged to Jones, but Winston took the fall for the mistake in an effort to shield Jones. That was two bad calls made on the last two operations that Jones had led. Winston knew the heat was on Jones and there was no way he was willing to let that level of intelligence come this far with the unit and fail. The punishment was no sleep until the completion of the mountain phase.

Winston sent Lev out as the lead on the march across the divide and he would bring up the rear. Keeble watched him as he fell in behind them. Two miles into the rough terrain with all of Winston's gear loaded on him, Keeble saw a look he'd never seen on Winston before. He was tired. He'd endured more hours with no sleep than any other man among them. He was hungry, and even though he was marching with the men, he was lost and alone.

"Talk to me, Winston," Keeble said as he rushed up behind him. Winston shook his head as he struggled for words. He continued to march, but his legs became shaky. Another twenty meters and he dropped to a knee.

"I just need a minute, Sarge," Winston said, but he knew a minute wasn't going to do a thing for him. He started to remove his gear.

"What are you doing? Hey! Goddamnit! What are you doing!? Don't you do that!" Keeble pleaded.

"That's it, Sarge." The last two and a half days of churning on no sleep had finally pushed him to his edge and the fall was looking better than the struggle to stay aboveboard.

"That's your team on this march, not mine. They don't belong to me anymore. They belong to you. Don't do this to them. Don't do this to yourself."

"Sarge, I got no more to give."

"Yeah, you do. You got the same thing inside you that I got in me. What they thought about me is what they think about you. That's why you're here. Now get to the business of finishing it."

"I ain't got no more."

"Bullshit! You took on more for them than you should have. You took Jones's deal so he wouldn't get dropped; you and I both know that. So don't tell me what you don't have to give."

"I can't . . ."

"I'll show you what fucking can't is!" Keeble ripped at his right boot, getting it off as fast as he could, pulling up his pant leg and exposing his severely damaged right leg.

Winston was shocked by the extent of the damage to Keeble's surgically repaired right leg. He remembered catching a glimpse of it on the obstacle course, but had no idea it was this bad. How Keeble was able to move the way he did was mind-blowing to Winston.

"They tried to tell me in the hospital that I couldn't keep my leg. I couldn't ever walk right again, and I couldn't run and I couldn't jump out of planes anymore. Well, you know what I said? Fuck them and what they believe I can't do. And don't you tell me what you can't do! Take a second and get your shit together. You have greatness to pursue. So buck the fuck up, get up, ruck up, and go get that shit that's waiting for you!!"

"Yes, Sergeant!" Winston rose to his feet and continued his march.

With each passing mile, Winston gained a little more steam, pushing harder, and toward the end of the march, Keeble thought his leg must really look fucked up, because Winston was practically running to get away from him.

The end of the march concluded their training in the mountains. They were scheduled to immediately board a bus to a nearby airfield to conduct an airborne operation that would parachute them into Florida and their next phase of training. Keeble had other plans though.

BISHKEK, KYRGYZSTAN

Two semitrucks traveled over the dirt roads to their destination. They were carrying a large shipment of military weapons making their move under the cover of night. With only twelve miles left until they reached the arms depot, the drivers and their crews felt confident they would make another successful delivery without incident.

As the vehicles climbed the crest of a hill leading into the mountains, they never saw the men lying in wait under the sand-colored tarp. They did see the flash of red light when the explosion occurred one hundred meters in front of them. Before they could react to what was in front of them, another explosion occurred two hundred meters behind them.

The four-man crew from each truck rushed to get out of the vehicles and into their positions to protect their precious cargo. Each man was equipped with night vision goggles for just such an attack. As they scrambled, they heard a sharp yell, which caused them to turn in that direction and the white-hot flash of light seared their vision through the goggles.

The attackers sprang from their tarps, eighteen of them in total, all dressed in black from head to toe. There were nine of them on each truck and they were on the crews before they could make out their hands in front of their faces. Each driver was held at bay with a gun pointed at them. It took seconds for the other eight men to disarm and neutralize the security crew. The crew was hog-tied with zip ties before they moved to the vehicles and disarmed the tracking system. There was no doubt these men were well-prepared for this attack. The men in black climbed into the rear of the vehicles while the gunmen climbed into the cab with the drivers. Minutes later, the two trucks were rolling along in a new direction, never to be heard from again.

27

Goldberg scheduled the meeting at his office in Langley, Virginia. It was an opportunity for him to get Jameson, Harlow, and one of his agents together in the same place. He and Harlow were the first to meet and were having a glass of Pulteney Scotch when Jameson arrived. It didn't take a lot of arm-twisting to convince Jameson to join them in a glass. Jameson and Harlow talked while Goldberg began to work on his computer.

"Do you have the number of men left?" Harlow stared into his Scotch.

"Not yet, but we will soon enough." Jameson checked his watch. "Keeble is due to report within the next hour."

"There's too much invested; there should have been better information on these men. I can't afford to waste time or money." Harlow's patience was growing thin.

"It wasn't my decision to change the training schedule. We had all the surveillance equipment set up to monitor their first month before they took on the training in Darby," Jameson responded.

"And we don't know a damn thing about them since they went to Darby!" Harlow growled.

"You knew that going in. We were to get updates only every two weeks, more if we were lucky. Today happens to be one of those lucky days," Jameson answered calmly, with his eyes on Harlow.

"I think we all should enjoy the Scotch," Goldberg said as he closed his laptop. "Erick, this was the part of the plan that we knew we couldn't control. We have to let Lawrence do his job," Goldberg said to Harlow before changing his focus to Jameson, "and it is a job that you are being compensated well to do." Goldberg took on the role of peacekeeper.

There was a knock at the door.

"Come in," Goldberg said quickly and the door opened immediately. "Gentlemen, I want you to meet Ray Griffin, chief of base in Uzbekistan."

Griffin shook each of their hands. Harlow took one look at him and disliked him immediately. Griffin was thirty-two and looked like he could be mistaken for a *GQ* cover model that spent plenty of time tanning on South Beach.

"Ray was under my command in South Asia; he was extremely close to our operation in Nerkh, Afghanistan. This is Chief Erick Harlow, Central Asia, and Colonel—soon to be General—Lawrence Jameson."

"It is an honor and a privilege to meet you both. Sorry to hear about the mission at the Afghan border." Ray was already on top of the situation.

"Thank you," Harlow replied sternly.

"I wanted you both to meet him. He's headed to Uzbekistan in a few days. He will be our new field operations commander there. He'll be our liaison to Unit 416 once they are on the ground there."

"We are already laying the groundwork for their arrival. Once we have all the information on the men we will be working with, we can really gain some traction." Griffin nodded. "I look forward to working with you gentlemen and Unit 416. I remember Keeble from Nerkh. Our time overlapped for about two months. Didn't know him personally, but I got reports on him daily. Things got pretty messy there when allegations were made regarding torture and murder of the locals there. But Keeble was completely solid on mission."

"How will this impact the team that is already on the ground?" Harlow squinted as he looked at Ray.

"It won't. I have some people who are going in with me. Their focus will be Unit 416. We'll work closely with the agents who are already there. If you will excuse me, as you can imagine, there are a number of things I need to finish before I leave."

"Thanks for stopping in," Goldberg said as Griffin left the office.

"I like him." Harlow stewed. "He looks like the guy that's screwing my ex."

"Everybody looks like the guy that was screwing your ex." Goldberg glanced over at Jameson. "She was fucking everybody."

"She was not!" Harlow rebutted. "She wasn't fucking me." Harlow even laughed at his own statement.

"We still have concerns." Goldberg changed the subject. "There are moles in our current operation. Griffin is not a concern for me. He will be working with the existing agents but also outside of their scope. What we are doing with Unit 416 will be Griffin's responsibility."

Jameson's ringing cell phone interrupted the conversation. He looked at the phone's caller ID and recognized Keeble's number. He signaled Goldberg and Harlow to let them know this was the call they had been expecting. He answered the phone by putting it on speaker.

"Good afternoon, Sergeant Keeble."

"Good afternoon, sir," Keeble responded.

"Look, I know you don't have a lot of time. The men are coming out of the mountains, correct?"

"Yes, sir."

"And what do the numbers look like?" Jameson asked while Goldberg and Harlow leaned in.

"We're still six strong," Keeble responded.

"Six, excellent. How are they looking?" Jameson had set a maximum attrition rate of six; it was his personal number to ensure the success of the mission ahead. It was also a number he hadn't shared with the CIA boys.

"They're solid, sir."

"Very good. It's imperative that you do everything possible to get these men through." He gave Goldberg and Harlow a reassuring nod. "So your men will be airborne to Florida in the next half hour?"

"Actually, sir, there will be a six-hour delay before we depart for Florida," Keeble said.

"Six-hour delay? Why?" Jameson wondered. "There was already a time delay when they left Darby. This is unacceptable," Jameson stated firmly.

"I understand that, sir, but it is necessa—"

"Sergeant Keeble, you'd better have those men on that plane in ten minutes or you can turn in your uniform with theirs." Jameson gave a look of confidence to Harlow and Goldberg. Sometimes you have to let the men know who's in charge.

"Sir." Keeble paused. "You're more than welcome to this uniform and theirs too, if you want them."

With that statement, the other end of the line went dead. Jameson was stunned.

"Hello, Sergeant?" Jameson said as the three of them in the office stared blankly at each other.

"Did he just quit? He didn't fucking quit, did he? Call him back!" Harlow panicked first.

"Better call him," Goldberg said. With all the cash that he was flowing Jameson's way, they damn sure weren't willing to start this operation over again.

Jameson dialed the number.

"Hello?" Keeble answered like the call could be coming from anybody.

"Sergeant Keeble, I think there was a problem with the line."

"No problem, sir. I hung up. I'll have the equipment shipped back to Benning," Keeble said.

"No, that's not necessary. We just need to get those men to Florida so—"

"Sir, in less than ten days I will have in front of you and anybody else who cares to know, six men, six soldiers that will be Ranger trained, verified, and certified to carry out any operation that you put in front of them. If you don't want that timeline to be jeopardized, it would be in your best interest to grant a six-hour delay." Keeble finished his statement and waited. There was some vibe he was getting from Jameson. It was a hunch, but he couldn't shake the feeling that there was a lot more going on with these people he was working for than he had been told.

The three men looked from one to the other, not quite knowing how to respond, but they were all calculating the money in their heads. Harlow nodded, followed by Goldberg; Jameson shrugged his shoulders and bent closer to the phone.

"Permission granted," Jameson half mumbled.

"Thank you, sir," Keeble replied.

"I want to let you kno—" Jameson started to speak but was interrupted by the dial tone. If he'd had the ability to make himself disappear, he would have.

"Looks like you got him where you want him," Goldberg said sarcastically.

"We have a few days left to grind this out and I need to see every one of you finish this. Do I make myself clear?" Keeble said to the men as they stood in the chow line.

"Yes, Sergeant," the men responded in unison. They were all weak from all of the physical and mental duress they'd been under, but they still responded together. The men watched him as he left, understanding that somehow or another, he had bought them a valuable commodity—time.

Eight hours later, they parachuted into Camp James E. Rudder where training in the Florida phase would be conducted. The instruction began immediately with the 6th Ranger Battalion. Combat arms functional skill, waterborne operations, stream crossings, and many of the missions they would perform would be in a swamp environment, pushing the limits of their physical and mental abilities. Each one of them would continue to plan and lead a variety of missions and combat operations against well-trained, sophisticated enemies.

Each man was dropped into different parts of the swamp. This environment proved to be the most challenging to Wallace. The swamp would change from shallow to deep at the drop of a hat. He could climb anything and bounce from one surface to another, but his best swimming stroke was the dog paddle.

They had eighteen minutes to connect with a small boat at a rendezvous point that would deliver them to their campsite. If any of the men didn't make it to the small boat, they would be dropped from the program. Not only was their ability to swim being tested, but so were their navigational skills.

Lev had gotten within minutes of the rendezvous point when he spotted Wallace standing in the swamp, pointing his compass in every direction, saying the damn thing didn't work. Lev went two minutes out of the way to get to Wallace.

"Follow me," he told Wallace.

Shallow water had given way to a deep drop. Lev heard the flailing behind him and knew what the problem was. He reached back, grabbed Wallace, and pulled him up with him. Once they were in shallow water again, he took all of Wallace's equipment and put it on his back.

"I got your stuff. Just stay close. If the swamp gets deep, grab on tight and I'll pull ya."

The boat was cranking up when Lev and Wallace reached the clearing. The two of them broke out in an all-out sprint to reach it. Lugging his equipment and Wallace's, Lev was leading the sprint. The other four members of Unit 416 were on the boat yelling at them to get on board. As they dove for the boat, Wallace made it in, but the weight of the equipment caused Lev to fall just short of the boat. He got one hand on the lip of the boat as it started to back away. Lev's grip was slipping when Winston grabbed ahold of his hand. Winston had started reeling him in when he slipped. Daisy grabbed him, Turner grabbed Daisy, Jones grabbed Turner, and Wallace grabbed Jones. They finally gained enough leverage to pull the big man and the equipment he was carrying into the boat.

The blur of days and training that began for Unit 416 at Darby, crashed into the mountain phase and was continuing here in Florida. The six hours Keeble had carved out for them were a godsend because during this phase of training, sleep, when it did come, was in a two-hour block, three if they were lucky, at the end of a twenty-two-hour training day.

One of the most important training sessions was how to deal with reptiles in the swamp and more importantly to Lev, snakes. Throughout all of their training, he demonstrated a "can do" or "fuck it" attitude. Whatever he encountered, he constantly told himself, "I can do it or fuck it, I'm gonna do it anyway." But he did have one fear that so far had been kept hidden. He was petrified of snakes and his body became rigid at the mention of them. Daisy picked up on the change in Lev and stuck close to him. Daisy asked question after question about the snakes and reptiles. By the time Daisy finished his questions, the men felt like they had information on every possible piece of wildlife that they might encounter here in the swamp or anywhere. And even though nobody called attention to it, they all noticed that Daisy was stuttering less and less. The responsibility of leading men on missions and patrols impacted them in ways they didn't fully understand yet.

As the training was coming to an end, they were hungry— down to one meal a day and mostly surviving off of what nature provided. They'd lost weight and their bodies were physically spent, but they were still driven to battle through whatever Florida had in store for them.

Their final mission was a seven-day field training exercise. They would alternate the leadership roles on a daily basis, and on occasions, the leadership role would change in a matter of hours. The conditions were fast-paced, stressful, and challenged all of the knowledge each man had acquired over the previous days of training at Darby, Merrill, and Rudder, and it was all under the watchful eyes of the Ranger instructors. They executed raids, ambushes, and conducted urban assaults in an effort to complete missions assigned to them. Keeble was conducting his own evaluations of the men, making notes of their weaknesses while highlighting their strengths. As the days passed, he bristled with pride as he took fewer and fewer notes of their shortcomings.

Their final assignment was to take down an island stronghold, a makeshift drug cartel. The mission was set to take place in a remote area of the swamp. They were given intelligence of the perimeter and the expected number of targets they would encounter. They had the option of choosing who would lead them on the final mission. The decision to have Winston lead them was unanimous.

Early in the morning, they descended on the river. Using a tactical rubber military boat that could seat a nine-man crew, they paddled undetected upriver to their landing site. The river could carry them only so far before it was necessary for them to enter the swamp. The waist-deep water was unpredictable and treacherous at times, but it was the best way for them to access the stronghold undetected. They reached a point in the swamp where there was a river to cross and they took it two men at a time. Winston and Wallace went first and secured the other bank. Once they had the okay, Lev and Jones followed before Daisy and Turner brought up the rear.

According to Winston's calculations, they were halfway through their mission. The objective had twenty-four targets that needed to be neutralized before they could capture the cartel leader. Because it was still a training mission, Unit 416 and its enemy targets were equipped with electronic sensors that would go off once an individual was neutralized.

As the men broke apart from one another to surround the stronghold, Winston advised them to sit tight until they were able to account for the targets. Fifteen minutes of waiting and they successfully identified nineteen targets. Dawn was approaching and they would soon lose their cover. Winston radioed the Ranger instructors and requested air support for the targeted area and the request was granted.

Within minutes, the aircraft was approaching and the sound of ammunition started to fill the early morning air. The sounds of that chaos created a fervor of activity within the stronghold. Seconds later, all twenty-four men exposed their position and Unit 416 began picking them off like flies. Winston felt a rush of adrenaline as they gave and took fire before he thought that this was too easy.

Twenty of the targets' devices had gone off before he told Daisy to continue working the targets while the rest of the men pushed back out in search of an enemy approach from the rear. Daisy picked off two more targets at long range. Jones and Turner picked off one each as they pushed back from their locations. Lev and Wallace each discovered ambush sites that the instructors were setting on the east and west of the perimeter. Lev physically attacked the instructor he encountered to neutralize him. Wallace sped up, trying to get to an area where he would gain a better vantage point. But instead of getting in better position, his foot was trapped, causing his knee to bend awkwardly in the opposite direction. He was in pain, but he picked up his weapon and opened fire on them. They returned fire, but it was too little too late. Lev and Wallace were able to neutralize them before they brought any harm to the unit. They radioed in that all anticipated threats had been removed. Hearing that, Winston attacked the hut that was their primary objective and commanded the inhabitant to come out with his arms raised.

Keeble came out with his hands raised. Winston still had his weapon raised, his right eye peering through the sight with his left eye closed. When he saw Keeble through the lens, he lifted his head and opened his other eye.

"Sarge?" Winston was confused.

"Good call on the push back. Another thirty seconds and they would have lit all your asses up."

"You got anybody else set up out there?" Winston asked, not trusting that the operation was complete.

"Mission complete. Bring your men in."

Winston radioed all of his men to come in. Keeble was joined by the instructors of the 6th Ranger Battalion. They stood in front of Winston, Lev, Jones, Turner, Daisy, and a limping Wallace and presented them with an honorary black-and-gold Ranger tab. It was a replica of the tab that Rangers earn by completing this course. Keeble was no less proud of them, their commitment, and their discipline than he was of the Rangers standing next to him. Keeble and the Rangers standing in front of them saluted the men of Unit 416. Unit 416 returned the salutes. Once Keeble and the Rangers rendered their salute and stood at parade rest, Keeble recited the following words taken from the Ranger Creed, but modified for Unit 416:

"There are hazards of this profession; I will always endeavor to uphold the prestige, honor, and high esprit de corps of my unit.

"Acknowledging the fact that I am a more elite soldier who arrives at the cutting edge of battle by land, sea, or air, I accept the fact that as a member of this unit, my country expects me to move further, faster, and fight harder than any other soldier.

"Never shall I fail my comrades. I will always keep myself mentally alert, physically strong, and morally straight and I will shoulder more than my share of the task, whatever it may be, one hundred percent and then some.

"Gallantly will I show the world that I am a specially selected and well-trained soldier. My courtesy to superior officers, neatness of dress, and care of equipment shall set the example for others to follow.

"Energetically will I meet the enemies of my country. I shall defeat them on the field of battle for I am better trained and will fight with all my might. Surrender is not a word I know. I will never leave a fallen comrade to fall into the hands of the enemy and under no circumstances will I ever embarrass my country.

"Readily will I display the intestinal fortitude required to fight on to my objective and complete the mission, though I be the lone survivor."

Keeble snapped to attention as sharply and crisply as he had ever done in his military career and he alone saluted these men, his men of Unit 416. His men responded in kind, but Keeble couldn't help but notice that grin of Daisy's creeping across his face. Somehow, it was still the same, but not a damn thing about it was goofy.

28

It would be a couple of days before Unit 416 returned to Fort Benning. They would spend those days in Florida cleaning their weapons and equipment in a community center. It would be a chance to go to the Post Exchange, eat food on a regular basis, watch television, and use a telephone if there was someone they needed to call and use it for something other than a firing command. But more important than anything else to them, they would have the opportunity to sleep uninterrupted. It was a few days of decompression that was well deserved; it would go a long way toward reacclimating them to life outside the mountains and swamp.

Wallace was grateful to get the few days before departure; it would allow him to get some much needed rest for his knee. Unfortunately the rest would do him little good. When the company medic examined it, he didn't waste any time in having him shipped over to the hospital. The medic informed Keeble that there was a lot of damage to his left knee. Once the MRI was completed, Wallace's worst possible fears were confirmed. He had torn both his ACL and MCL on the last night of training and would not be allowed to travel back to Benning with the rest of Unit 416. He would stay behind, have surgery on his knee, then be shipped back to Benning a week later.

When they returned to Benning, they did not receive the same treatment as other soldiers graduating from Ranger School. There was no elaborate ceremony at Victory Pond where their Ranger tab was pinned on their left shoulder. Their ceremony of recognition occurred in private, with each other in the swamp lands of Camp Rudder. Their achievement would go unnoticed, just like their unit would. But it made no difference to these five men, because man to man, they could look each other in the eye, knowing what each of them had gone through individually and collectively and knowing for themselves that no one could ever take what they had achieved away from them. Their only regret was that Wallace wasn't there with them; they knew that he had earned the same respect they had.

Instead, they returned to their B-6 barracks the same way they'd left, in Hummers driven by Keeble and Rodriguez. They gathered in formation, where Rodriguez advised them that there was still some downtime before their training resumed. The focus of this leg of training would be counterterrorism and counternarcotics.

"Hey, Sergeant Rod, you all have seen my file, haven't ya?" Winston said. "I not gonna need that counternarcotics training." Everybody laughed, including Keeble and Rodriguez. "I can lead a couple of those classes if you need me to, though."

There was a level of comfort that all the men felt with one another and Keeble. There was a deeper regard and respect for him. They fully understood what it took for him to earn the patches on his shoulder because they had earned one similar to one of his.

"Man, I wouldn't take that class if you paid me to," chided Big Lev, who thanks to the previous month was just as tall but minus a few pounds.

"All right; that's enough. Fall out!" Rodriguez ordered.

"I never thought I would be this happy to get back to the inside of this building," Turner said as he burst into the barracks. "Holy crap!" Turner stopped in his tracks; his jaw almost hit the floor.

"What's the problem?" Daisy said without a stutter as he ran into his back. Then he saw it too.

The barracks had been reconfigured. The big open bay that had been lined with bunks, lockers, and foot lockers, and had housed twelve men, had been divided into six rooms. Rodriguez's space remained intact, but everything else was changed. There was a room for each one of them with a removable nameplate in case they wanted to trade rooms.

"Holy shit is more like it!" Jones said as he got a look for himself.

Before Rodriguez followed after them, he called out to Keeble, "It's been a few days; time to make a call. I kinda let the cat out of the bag and Rita knows you were due back."

A call to Rita would be the first thing on Keeble's priority list as he made his way to the A-10 barracks. He had done well to suppress any thoughts of her while he prepared his men. Completing his mission and compartmentalizing his emotions were not a problem for him; he'd spent fourteen years of his military career doing that, but now was the time for some personal business. Then Keeble would get to the next two priorities, the two military-related ones. The first priority was to find out anything and everything he could about Jameson and this operation; he owed that to his men. The second was to prepare a progress report for Jameson and his associates in the next couple of days. He had been successful at avoiding him since they completed their training at Merrill, although Keeble was sure that Jameson knew the moment training ended. Jameson and his far-reaching eyes never let Keeble or his men get too far out of his sight line.

Keeble set his gear down after passing through the first door. He paused and listened. "I should have known," he said. As he passed through the second door, making a call to Rita just got pushed to the bottom of the priority list. "Do you need my report or are you going to give it to me, sir?" he asked in the direction of the conference table where Jameson, Harlow, and Goldberg sat.

"The men look well. Looks like the rest did wonders for them," Jameson said, looking at a monitor of them checking out their new digs.

"A couple more days and they'll be ready to move to the next phase of training," Keeble said.

"They don't have a next phase of training," Harlow interrupted hastily. "I need these men on the ground in Uzbekistan ASAP."

"I'm sorry, Mr. Harlow," Keeble said. "They just finished Ranger School, an abbreviated one at that."

"Hoo-fucking-ray! I needed these men on the ground as of yesterday and I can't believe I conceded to giving them a weekend!" Harlow glared at both Jameson and Goldberg.

"There is training that is necessary for them. They need to understand the culture and language of where any mission would send them and you're talking about dropping them on foreign soil right away?" Keeble was furious, but maintained his composure.

"The situation has forced our hand," Goldberg began to explain, but Harlow jumped in.

"Fuck that! We are funding this operation, soldier. What

we want is what we want. These men fit the profile that we need. They are thugs and criminals that I provided the training for. It's time to get them where they can make something of themselves. Those boys wouldn't even get a second chance like this on the street. They should be kissing my ass; I gave them a chance of a lifetime!"

This idiot has a God complex, Keeble thought. *He doesn't give a fuck about any of these men. Yeah, they made some mistakes in their lives, but that doesn't mean they don't deserve an opportunity at re-demption and it sure doesn't mean that their lives should be tossed around on his whims.*

"Colonel?" Keeble asked. With one word he was asking if the colonel was just going to sit there. Was he, a black man, going to sit there and let this white man pontificate about these men like he was a godsend and their lives were meant to serve his purpose?

"Training for them will continue in-country, but they have one weekend before we mobilize and activate our assets. And I want to remind you, some of us have our careers on the line here."

And some of you just have money on the line; Jameson was not the man of honor Keeble had thought he was. Keeble would bet everything he owned that Jameson had been bought and paid for. And then it hit him. They never had any intention of spending the next six months training his men. They wanted them when they thought they were ready, not when Keeble knew they would be ready.

"Sergeant, we need you to inform the men that their train-ing schedule has changed and they have been assigned their first mission," Goldberg explained.

"No, you won't, Sergeant. Call the men to formation; I will explain it to them," Jameson said.

Keeble had Rodriguez bring the men back out to formation. Keeble formally introduced Colonel Jameson to the remaining men of Unit 416. He was not aware they had already met this man. They, however, had no problem remembering the man who had hand-delivered their orders transferring them to Unit 416. Keeble then took his place behind Colonel Jameson, Chief Harlow, and Chief Goldberg. This was Jameson's show and he was going to let him have it.

"Let me begin by complimenting you men on surviving some of the most difficult training the army has to offer. I could not be prouder of you men standing in front of me. And I want to introduce you to the men who have made that training possible. This is Erick Harlow and Marv Goldberg." Jameson waited a few seconds as Unit 416 cheered them. "And they have made the decision, because of the excellence you have shown, to assign you to your first mission. You will depart in a couple of days for Uzbekistan for a joint operation with the CIA and the Army Special Operations. As of this moment, you have one weekend of leave. There are open tickets at the airport with each of your names on them. Go home; go to Vegas; go wherever you want, but you must be back here on Monday. At that time, you will be briefed on the specifics of your mission and any and all contractual obligations will be executed and funded pending your mission departure. If there are any questions, we will discuss them next week prior to your departure. For now, enjoy yourselves. Fall out."

Jameson's mention of the mission did little to curb the men's enthusiasm. They had made it through and were ready to embark on their first mission. They all seemed to grasp the concept that money was coming their way. There were lots of smiles and handshakes with Jameson, Harlow, and Goldberg. A celebration of a job well done, rewarded with time off before being assigned to a mission with Special Ops and the CIA. Keeble, stern faced, nodded at them, and then marched back to A-10. His mind raced through the words *executed* and *funded*. The three stooges had trapped them by using their past against them and had kept them engaged with the promise of money. And they had used Keeble to sell them on honor, respect, and pride. Worst of all, the stooges had hijacked him with his commitment to duty and country. He looked back at his happy men, trying to find a skeptic among them and then he spotted Jones. Jones shook hands and gave a courtesy smile or two. He looked at Keeble, and then to the men they were standing in the midst of. Jones could see that there were wheels turning in Keeble's mind just like they were churning in his, thoughts that might be worth sharing.

Jameson, Harlow, and Goldberg thanked the men for their commitment and the great things they would do. It was time for them to do whatever it was they wanted.

Bags were being packed in a hurry. There was a rush of excitement. What should they do with their money and where should they go? Hell, they were all sitting on tickets that could send them anywhere in the world they wanted to go as long as they were back by Monday.

"You goin' back to Compton?" Lev asked Winston.

"Shit, ain't nothing or nobody left for me in Compton, bro. No girl; Moms is gone; ain't never met my pops; and I damn sure ain't leave no shorties back there. That don't even seem like home no more," Winston said.

"Well, I'm catching the next thing smokin' to Terrell, Texas. Be back in God's country. Smell that country air and get my hands on some barbecue." Lev could taste the food.

"That sounds gooder than a ma'fucka to me." Winston was tasting the grub too.

"Only thing stoppin' you is you, dog."

"Shoot, I'm going back to the Rock; get me some of my momma's home cooking. I haven't been back home and slept in that ole twin bed of mine in two years," Turner said.

"I'm going to see my aunt and uncle in the Boogie Down," Daisy said, with no stutter.

"They'll be very impressed with your verbal elocution," Jones said. "They'll love the way you speak."

"I'm sure they will. What about you? You headin' back to Chi-town?" Daisy asked.

"Shit, yeah, he is. That smart ass ni . . ." Winston stopped himself. "That negro won't be takin' a plane either. Probably done created a way to teleport his ass back to Chicago!"

As they continued to talk about what their plans for the weekend would bring, they began to realize what was on the other side of the weekend. The new skill sets they'd acquired at Darby, in the mountains of Dahlonega, and in the swamps of Florida would soon be put to the test in a live combat situation. That reality set a somber mood for the men. .

"Brothers, I have to be honest with you." Turner looked at every man in the room, including Daisy, when he said, "I can't go back to Little Rock. I guess I'm like Winston when it comes to Compton. My mama's there, but it's not home for me no more. I don't have time for those brothers I used to bang with. None of them ever picked me up when I needed it."

"That's the street for you, man. When ya in it, you think those fools got you, but soon as you get pushed to the side, they done forgot you," Winston reflected. "If I never see Compton again, the way I'm feelin' right now, it would be too soon."

"I used to fear going back home, of what might happen to me if some of those old boys ran up on me. Now my fear is what I would do to them." Turner looked at the men around him. There was something different about them, himself included, and he wasn't willing to waste what he'd become on the people he used to know.

"Big man, Terrell and that barbecue sounds like a winner to

me, but I ain't gonna make that run with ya," Winston said to Lev.

"Shit, you know I was thinkin' the same thing. Ain't nothin' really there for me in Terrell. And people have been known to fuck up some barbecue." Lev looked at Daisy. "What about you, Jack?"

"It would be good to see my aunt and uncle. It's been a long time . . ." Daisy paused. He looked at his Unit 416; he looked down for a second, nodded his head, then looked back at the men. "But I ain't never had no brothers before. I'm with you all."

"Well, all right then," Jones added. "But you know your people won't get to hear you serenade them with your oratory skills," he joked.

"I'll leave them a voice mail." Daisy laughed.

"So, we all agree; we're staying put?" Winston watched each man as they nodded their agreement. "From here on out, whatever we're doing, we're doing it together."

Winston looked at each man, and then finally they all said in unison, "Together."

29

Keeble waited until the three stooges were gone before he took to his command center. He typed "Jameson, Lawrence, Colonel, U.S. Army" into the search engine. He wasn't sure what he was looking for, but hoped to find something that would help him piece together this puzzle. The search turned up basic information, years of service, honors, tours, and current duty location— nothing of substance. Keeble sat back in the chair thinking. This is the command center that they'd put together and he was probably being monitored right now. They were constantly one step ahead of him.

He caught a glance on the surveillance monitor of the five men heading toward A-10. He scribbled some notes on a piece of paper before going to meet them at the front door.

"You men aren't gone yet?" Keeble asked as he opened the door.

"No, Sarge; we decided not to go anywhere. We're staying here for the weekend," Winston answered.

"Come in; I'm sure we have a lot to talk about." Keeble opened the door for them. He shook each of their hands as they walked in. When Jones walked past him, Keeble shook his hands with both of his and the paper he'd scribbled on was passed to Jones.

As they entered the barracks, they were shocked at all of the equipment at Keeble's disposal. No one was more intrigued than Jones; monitors and computers were his kind of playground. He took note of the name that was typed on the computer monitor. Keeble took the men on a guided tour of the A-10 barracks and then let the men roam around and the conversations took on a life of their own. There was an understanding that chatter was needed.

"You're pretty good with computers, aren't you?" Keeble quietly asked Jones.

Jones was almost insulted by the question. "'Pretty good,' Sarge?" Insinuating that Keeble needed to get a look at him in action, Keeble waved him to the computer. "You don't mind if I take a look at your system, do you?" Jones hit a couple of keystrokes on the keyboard, did a few quick searches, pocketed the scribbled note, and got up from the command center. "This is something else to see. I wish I had all day to experiment with these systems. My appetite is whetted."

The Unit 416 men shot the shit with the man who'd been their instructor a few days ago and was now about to release them to the mission that the CIA had in store for them. The men told Keeble there was a financial incentive for the men who had completed the training and were being assigned their first mission. The conversations were open but guarded. They followed Keeble's lead. Once they saw all of the surveillance equipment, everyone understood that they were all being watched. Keeble walked out with them when they headed back to B-6.

"I need someone to steal the identity; do you have anyone?" Keeble asked Jones while the other men talked.

"I happen to have a little expertise in that area," Jones confided.

"Wasn't in your file, but I thought you might."

A half hour later, Keeble met up with Jones at the recreation room of Jones's previous unit. It was the location that Keeble had scribbled on the piece of paper. They were huddled in the corner near the pool table with Jones's laptop fired up and already hard at work running multiple downloads. Keeble had his monitoring iPad with him and a Best Buy bag that contained his newly purchased iPad. He casually passed the iPads to Jones. While his laptop continued to run its download, Jones connected the new iPad to his USB port and simultaneously downloaded the files being scanned to the new iPad while he tinkered with the configurations on the old iPad.

"How could you tell?"

"You couldn't see it, Sarge, but there was lag between the keystroke and the image appearing on the screen," Jones said. They were clearly in his wheelhouse. "They're on top of every move you've made and every move we've made since we've been here."

"From there to Rudder and everywhere in between. How long before you get his identity?"

"Almost done. I had to set a mouse first to get into their server. The system is going to chase it. Every time it catches it, it will replicate so the system will pick it up as a virus. Once the system is compromised, I can back-door information on Lawrence Jameson . . . wait for it . . . wait for it, and voilà! There it is, Sarge."

Keeble looked at the monitor. Information about Jameson was beginning to populate the screen. Keeble knew the CIA was dropping money left and right on this operation. When he found out Rodriguez was pocketing an extra three grand a month for next to nothing, he was sure Jameson had his hand in the cookie jar as well; he just needed proof of it.

"I need all the information you can get on any bank accounts tied to him—foreign and domestic."

"Already ahead of you, Sarge." Jones isolated the information to banking statements. "Motherfucker!! The army pays like that?"

"No, not the army." Keeble saw it too. Jameson's name was linked to multiple offshore accounts in the Cayman Islands and two domestic ones. One of the offshore accounts showed three large wire transfers over the last eight months of one hundred thousand dollars each.

"CIA is floating that kind of money, Sarge?"

"Believe it or not, yeah. The Hummers, dedicated training, and all the new equipment doesn't come cheap. They are paying Jameson very well for his part in this. I see why he's keeping a close eye on his investment and everybody involved with it," Keeble said.

"So how do you want to proceed?" Jones asked.

"We're going to keep access to Jameson's accounts; it's going to be used as leverage when the time is right."

The download on Jones's computer and to the new iPad was complete, but the old pad was proving to be a challenge. However, Jones loved a computer challenge. "Bingo. I got it." Jones passed the other pad back to Keeble. "You now have the ability to project any image of the compound you need at any time. You can be on the compound and they'll never be able to find you." Jones paused, not knowing how to ask the next question.

"Good work, Jones. This unit is lucky to have you on board," Keeble said. "You are a magician when it comes to these computers."

"Everybody has a thing; this is mine," Jones said and then there was another pause.

"The mission is to Uzbekistan," Keeble started. "I don't

have all the details yet, but it will be very dangerous. The CIA has leaks they can't figure out how to plug; Unit 416 is their new plug and they are ready to stick it in."

"Truth, Sarge, are we ready?" Jones asked.

"That's the question that's always going to be asked. It's asked of all of us. There is a higher calling that each of you men have and you will answer that call. Being ready means you already know the outcome. You are prepared for anything that comes your way. The Ranger Creed tells you so." Keeble turned to face him.

Jones looked Keeble in the eye; he gave Keeble the same steely look that he'd received from him.

"My man." Keeble gave him a fist bump. "Did you see the last transfers to Jameson's accounts? They occurred after the training started."

Jones nodded his head. "What does that mean?"

"I don't know yet. Could be nothing; more likely to be something. I've got the weekend to find out. So all of you men decided to stay around for the weekend? You didn't want to get back to Chicago?"

"I was considering it; we all were considering going home except Winston. He wanted no part of Compton. He actually gave more consideration to joining Lev in Terrell. I don't know what you do in Terrell, Texas, except watch paint dry. We, all of us, decided it was more important to stick together."

A broad smile came across Keeble's face. He stuck his fist up to give Jones another pound. Keeble considered his next step for the men. "Tell the men to make plans to leave the compound, schedule flights back home. Give Jameson and them a show. When the last man has cleared out, I want everyone back in two hours."

30

Jameson took Harlow up on the offer of the private jet. Instead of flying back to Bragg, he decided to accompany his old friends to D.C. Although he preferred flying in C-130s, it would be very easy to get used to the plush seats that reclined and the smooth flight without the sounds of the propellers churning through the air. The in-flight amenities were also a plus. All three men were nursing a Scotch. Harlow was on number two and was deep in thought.

Goldberg and Jameson discussed the logistics of the transport of the men to Uzbekistan and the readiness of Griffin once the men arrived. Goldberg's bigger question was whether the men were completely ready. Jameson assured him that he had no question regarding the men they were getting. They would do whatever it took to survive and he had no doubt that Keeble had pushed them to their limit in preparation for their mission. Harlow sipped his drink, stared at the two of them, and occasionally looked out the window.

"You don't have anything to add?" Goldberg asked Harlow.

Harlow drained his second Scotch, prepared another one,

and stared back out of his window. Somewhere over North Carolina he decided to enter the conversation.

"What do you want me to add?" Harlow never took his eyes off the window. "I'm tired of losing people around me."

"Don't worry about that girl; if she won't be back somebody else will." Goldberg smiled, trying to lighten the mood.

"I wish this was that simple. This is not about a woman or ex-wives, none of that bullshit." Harlow continued to stare out the window.

"I know. But you can't keep taking it to heart. You know that will kill you faster than a bullet," Goldberg responded.

It was time to address the elephant in the room. Jameson had given Harlow his space. After all, he was the one writing the checks for the operation, but it was time for him to get off the pot he'd been stewing on.

"What are you taking to heart?" Jameson looked at Harlow staring out of the window.

Winston and Lev made arrangements to fly to Texas. Daisy and Turner scheduled flights to New York and Little Rock. Jones was going to take a road trip to Atlanta and agreed to be everyone's driver for the day. Once everyone was packed to leave, they piled into Jones's Kia Optima with Lev riding shotgun.

Jones dropped them off at the airport, parked his car, then rented a car from Enterprise for the next three days. He paid with a credit card so there was a record of him being there. When he left the counter, he left the keys there as well.

Each man picked up his respective tickets at the kiosk for his airline and headed for the terminal. When boarding was announced, each got in line, had their tickets scanned, but not a single one of them boarded their plane. One by one they returned to Jones's car.

Keeble worked on setting up the dummy feed that Jones had configured for him. He looked at the monitor while he connected the iPad. But he was still seeing the live feed. *Jones made this sound so easy*, he thought. One thing he knew for sure, he didn't have the same gift for computers that Jones did. It wasn't until he read Jones's instructions for the fifth time that he was able to bring in the images of the dummy feed. He could still track the live action on the new iPad that Jones had tied into the system.

He put the system on the live feed, and then set the timer for four minutes to switch over to the dummy feed. Keeble grabbed his bags and the keys to the Wrangler that Rodriguez had left for him. Keeble drove away from the barracks with both pads next to him. He could see the Jeep on the pads as it drove away. Three miles later, he turned to head back. The live feed on his pad picked up the vehicle but the other pad that was connected to the system was projecting the dummy feed and never picked up a thing as he came back.

Not sure how long it would be before the men arrived, Keeble wanted to call Rita but had no idea of what to say. There was nothing he needed to say at the moment that couldn't wait a couple of days. He was still responsible for these men, even if it was for only one more weekend. The men deciding to stay together instead of running off in different directions for a weekend spoke volumes to the level of commitment the men had for one another.

Forty-five minutes later, Keeble saw Jones heading back to the barracks with a carload. As he checked the dummy feed, there was no evidence of the vehicle approaching. Jones pulled up to the A-10 barracks and Keeble opened the door to let them in.

"What now, Sarge?" Winston asked.

"We have some work to do," Keeble responded. "Jones, tell them what's happening with the system."

Jones gave them a crash course on the reconfiguration of the computer system and what they had done to create a block so that anything they did was unheard and undetected. After that overview, Keeble told them about the money that was at stake and what Jones had uncovered in Jameson's personal account history. It was something that he was still sorting through. Right now, they needed to dismantle some of the existing cameras and audio equipment at the mess hall and the B-6 barracks, then reinstall them along the trails in the rear of the A-10 barracks.

Daisy, Turner, and Winston handled the disconnects while Lev, Jones, and Keeble handled the reinstalls. Jones showed them what to be careful of while disconnecting. Lev hauled all the equipment to the areas where he, Keeble, and Jones would do the reinstall. The men worked fast and well as a cohesive unit. As they stepped away from the training of Darby, Merrill, and Rudder, they were able to see the well-oiled unit that they had become.

Once they finished, Jones did a check of the system to make sure the monitors were properly connected. They gathered in A-10 and waited until Jones completed his work.

"Can anybody here cook?" Lev wondered.

"It's feedin' time and the big man is hungry," Winston said.

"For real though, who can cook?" Turner asked. "I refuse to eat an MRE if I don't have to."

"Daisy? Jones? Anybody?" Winston looked at all the men shaking their heads.

"Nobody gonna ask me?" Keeble asked, without a hint of a smile.

"You can burn?" Winston couldn't take him seriously.

"You'll see." Keeble shrugged.

"We're good, Sarge. Come and take a look," Jones said.

Jones was clicking on different video images of the paths that led to the rear of A-10. Keeble stood beside him. Jones isolated the image on the screen to one camera; he clicked again and used the camera to zoom in and out. He smiled as he clicked again to manipulate the camera; now he was using the camera to pan left and right.

"Now you're just showing off," Daisy said, laughing.

All of them gathered around the console to get a peek. They gathered up whatever they needed and moved their group to the mess hall.

True to his word, Keeble could indeed burn. As the aroma drifted out into the mess hall, they were looking forward to seeing if the taste would match the smell. The men all sat together listening to Jones and Daisy discuss the positives of blaxploitation and B-movies. Big Lev, Turner, and Winston hung on their every word. Keeble looked at the men, a group smaller than what they'd started out with but bonded together, with genuine respect for one another.

"What you thinking about, Sarge?" Winston snapped Keeble out of his thoughts.

"Just wondering if I forgot something for the chicken," Keeble said.

"So, you know about the money, huh?" Winston asked and Keeble nodded. "How much you in this for?"

"Nothing."

"Come on; for real?" Winston asked again.

"This ain't about money for me. Never was, never will be. I'm a soldier; it's what I have been and what I will be. This training was a way for me to stay connected to what I love."

"That's what's up. When I got recruited to this, it was about the money and they said they could clear my record. But now it ain't so much about that . . ." He cleared his throat. "Looking good on them birds." Winston looked down at the stove. He could feel Keeble watching him as he fidgeted back and forth. "I

ain't used to this, but I like it, never felt connected to people . . .
never had a . . ." He looked over his shoulder to the men at the
table. "Thanks for gettin' me through that night at Merrill."

Keeble didn't know what to say. The word *thanks* wasn't an
easy one to get across Winston's lips. Keeble simply nodded; he
understood. "Get this chicken over to the table. Didn't know you
were volunteering, did you?"

"It's all good." Winston grabbed the chicken and rushed it
over to the guys. "Get it while it's hot!"

As they sat down with their plates of food ready to dig in,
Turner stood up, putting a stop to everything.

"Let us pray." Turner waited for them to bow their heads.
He shot a look at Winston because if anybody was going to be
resistant, it was him, but his head was already bowed. "I want to
thank you, Lord, for the food we are about to receive as nourishment for our bodies. I want to thank you, Father, for the opportunity to share it with these men seated at this table. They are
good men, proud and strong. I pray your blessings over each and
every one of them. In Jesus name I do pray. Amen."

"Thanks, brother," Daisy said.

"And here's to Wallace. The brother that made it through
but didn't make it to," Winston said as he raised a beer.

"To Wallace," they replied as they all raised a beer to him.

"When we leave here and depart for this mission, we are
leaving a brother behind, a brother who has earned his place
with us. He was one of our sticks that has been broken," Jones
said as he looked at Keeble and the four other men. "We are all
sticks and when you put us together, we become a bundle. Do you
know what a bundle is?" Jones gave them a second to consider
their response before answering his rhetorical question. "A bundle is unbreakable."

Jones's words would settle on the men. There was strength

in numbers and the five of them were from different places, different backgrounds, and different upbringings but united by the understanding of a higher purpose. Keeble took the message in as well. The sense of purpose, the unity was something that he would miss. With the men departing in a few days, his purpose for Unit 416 would be complete and then what would be left for him?

On Saturday, Keeble scheduled a meeting with Colonel Jameson for 1200 hours. He knew Unit 416's training, although sound and thorough, was not yet complete. The meeting with Jameson was to address those concerns without the presence of Harlow, Goldberg, and the unit itself.

Jameson drove the back roads to the secret entrance for the A-10 barracks. Knowing the roads were unmonitored by the compound layout, Jameson figured that he would have the drop on Keeble. What he wasn't aware of was the work Unit 416 had done to reconfigure the monitoring sites of the compound. Keeble watched every turn Jameson made en route to the compound. For the last day, Jameson, the CIA, and anyone else that monitored the Unit 416 movement on the compound saw little to no action. The dummy signal feed Jones arranged saw to that. And when they had finished their work, Jones would switch back to a live feed so the system would pick up any action that did occur.

When Jameson entered the corridor to begin his walk to the elevators, Keeble switched the system to the live feed to see where the men were. They were huddled in the barracks watching old black-and-white movies, right where he'd left them. He clicked back to the dummy feed before he took his place at the center seat of the conference table and waited for the secret elevator doors to open.

As Jameson came off of the elevator, he made his way to the

conference table. The room was darker than he remembered, but the bigger surprise was seeing Keeble sitting in his chair at the center of the table. It was an hour before they were due to meet and he knew he hadn't seen Keeble there when he checked the compound.

"Sergeant Keeble? I didn't expect to see you here so early." Jameson attempted to regroup.

"Somehow, I expected you to be early, sir." Keeble stood and saluted the colonel and Jameson hesitantly returned the salute. "Please have a seat, sir." Jameson looked at his customary seat, waiting for Keeble to switch places with him. "On that side of the table, sir."

Jameson did not take kindly to the suggestion and sat down begrudgingly. "You have my attention, Sergeant, and my patience is already wearing thin. Let me remind you that you started to wear on it when the men moved to the Dahlonega and Florida phases for training." Jameson paused; he was already irritated and carefully eyeing Keeble. "Where are the men?"

"Beg your pardon, sir?" Keeble responded.

"The men. Where are they?"

For Jameson to ask that question, Keeble knew Jameson and the CIA were having the men followed, or at the very least, they were keeping tabs on them.

"I assume they are spread all over the country enjoying the weekend before heading to Uzbekistan. Weren't you the ones providing the tickets for them to go anywhere? As I recall, there wasn't a care as to where they went."

"I am aware that there were flights scheduled and boarded, but there is no record of their arrivals," Jameson said.

"Imagine that. Seems like you were tracking them. Obviously, there was some concern as to where they went." Keeble knew he had him wondering.

"I don't have time to play games, Sergeant." Jameson attempted to take control of the meeting. "Now, why am I here?"

"I am going to make this real quick and easy for you, sir. The men depart for Uzbekistan in two days for a mission that they do not have clear details on. And this is because the CIA is ready to put them in play."

"Are we going to cover any new ground here, Sergeant?" Jameson cut in. He was still trying to take control of the situation as it unraveled in front of him.

"Communications and culture in foreign countries has been introduced to these men, but not emphasized in their training. That was another month away in their originally scheduled training. Also, this group's number has dropped from six men to five."

"Again, all details that I am aware of. Those five men will deploy in two days." Jameson pointed to the monitor as he started to stand. "I want them back here! Wherever they have to come from."

"Just a minute, sir." Keeble made it known that it was not time for him to depart yet. "I am volunteering my services to take this mission on with my men."

Jameson sat down again. His ideal number for this unit was six, but he was incredulous that after all the conversations he'd had with Keeble, he now had the audacity to volunteer his services.

"May I remind you, Sergeant, that your services were retained and you have been allowed to remain an active member of this man's army to train the Unit 416 candidates."

"I do understand my role and the capacity in which I function. But may I remind you, sir, that I am well versed in the languages and culture that exist in Uzbekistan and my Unit 416 will benefit greatly from the expertise I can provide them." Keeble stood firm on his points.

"It's not going to happen, Keeble. You're wasting your time." Jameson might have actually considered this, but he would be damned if Keeble was going to tell him what he was going to do.

"How much is it worth to you, sir?" Keeble asked.

"Beg your pardon? You don't have that kind of money," Jameson said arrogantly as he headed to the elevator.

Keeble opened up a file on his iPad that popped up on every monitor in the A-10 barracks. It was records and bank transactions to Jameson's accounts, foreign and domestic over the last six months. There were highlights of the extreme activity over the last couple of months. "Like I said, sir, how much is it worth to you?"

"What the . . . ? How did you get . . . ?" The images stopped him in his tracks.

"I don't think the question is how I got access to this information. The question is why are you getting this? And it doesn't appear to be coming from a military LES. My Uncle Sam would be interested in learning how you were able to accumulate more than three hundred thousand dollars in the last four months. And if he's not, I am sure that the newspapers from here to Langley would find it interesting reading."

"Wait, wait, wait a minute. What do you want? You want a piece?" Jameson was scrambling for a way out.

"Fuck that money, sir. I have access to all your accounts. If I wanted money, I could take every penny that you have. I don't give a damn about that money or the side deal you cut to get it; I do give a damn about my men. If you're sending them, I'm going with them." Keeble was pushing Jameson into a corner.

"I need these men to be successful, but I don't have the authority to make . . ."

"You made Unit 416 happen, didn't you, sir? You and I both know that what's happening here ain't regular army. So, I don't give a fuck how you get it done, just get it done. I am your sixth man, sir."

Now Keeble stood up from his chair, indicating the meeting had drawn to its conclusion. "It would be a shame if those men weren't here Monday." As he eyed Jameson, he slowly turned his head and nodded to the elevator. "I believe you can find your way out, sir."

31

Preparation for departure began early on Monday morning. There was no PT this morning, just time to finish packing their gear before breakfast. Keeble and Rodriguez were there to make sure there weren't any details missed. Everything came to them. Doctors performed physical exams, dentists updated their records; they were poked, prodded, and vaccinated. As a statement of unity, Keeble took part in everything they went through, but he couldn't get Rodriguez to do the same. They also discovered that snakes weren't the only thing that gave Lev the jitters. Needles were pretty high on his list as well.

By lunchtime, the five remaining members of Unit 416 were prepped and waiting for their departure. Keeble let them know that he had to take care of some last-minute things and left them in the capable hands of Sergeant Rodriguez, who took the men to the mess hall for the meal that was laid out for them.

"And the verdict is?" Keeble said as he entered the A-10 barracks.

Jameson was waiting for Keeble in his command center. He thought he was sneaking in early. Keeble knew the minute Jameson arrived; he'd intentionally left his equipment there. Jameson could see the live feed and the dummy feed running simultaneously.

"How did you do it?" Jameson asked.

"I didn't," Keeble said. Then he pointed at the monitor, a live feed of Unit 416 in the mess hall. "My team did it."

Jameson nodded his head. "Impressive. These men will do well."

"We can skip all that bullshit, sir. What's the answer?"

"Sergeant, believe it or not, you can be replaced or erased . . . I believe in the success of these men and our purpose in Uzbekistan. Understand, if this narrative is being rewritten, I am the author of that document." Jameson looked at Keeble; he wanted it understood that he was in charge.

Harlow and Goldberg joined the men in the mess hall for their departing meal. There was ham, turkey, filet mignon, chicken—grilled and fried, and too many vegetables to name with any number of beverages to wash it all down. Harlow's slush fund really set out a spread for the men.

Goldberg made a point to speak with each man individually. He made small talk about the training or the weather, whatever it took to show the men he was concerned about them and grateful for their commitment to the program. Harlow was far less talkative. His interaction consisted of a handshake, a brief thank-you, and handing them a confirmation that thirty thousand dollars had been deposited directly into their respective accounts. It was five thousand more than the amount they were guaranteed for the successful completion of the ASMU training. Goldberg called it a bonus for a job well done, but it was easy for the Unit 416 members to discern why they'd received the additional money. Wallace was missing; he was in Georgia waiting to have his knee put back together and his money had been divided evenly among them. Two months ago, each one of these men would have taken the money with nary a thought behind it. But today, they were different because of what they had gone through together. There was even consideration for the ones they had lost along the way, but particularly for Wallace, who had earned his money with them but was tripped up at the finish line. It wasn't just stuffed into their pockets with an "I got mine" attitude. Somehow the money didn't matter so much. There was an understanding that they'd fought like hell to get to this point and they were better men for it. But their greater concern was what they were going to do from here.

Harlow asked the men to gather around him. It was time to fill them in on the scope of their mission. Their purpose would be disrupting the arms cartels in Central Asia and stop them from getting weapons into the hands of terrorists. Harlow told them that individual targets might change but they would be responsible for saving countless American lives. Their primary CIA contact on the ground would be the chief of base by the name of Ray Griffin. He and his forward team were already hard at work on their behalf. He wished them Godspeed.

Turner asked his brothers to join him in a moment of silence. Goldberg and Harlow took that opportunity to make their way out of the mess hall. Rodriguez stayed with them but let them have that moment to themselves. Turner followed that moment up with a heartfelt prayer.

Turner prayed like a Southern Baptist preacher with a full congregation that he hadn't seen in a month of Sundays. The prayer was long and covered more topics than it needed to. Lev snuck a peek at Winston, who had a smirk on his face. They both were beginning to pray for Turner to stop when Jameson and

Keeble entered the mess hall. Their prayers were answered with the closing of Turner's prayer.

"Officer on deck!" Daisy shouted and the men snapped to attention, sharp, crisp, and with a lot of pop.

"At ease," Jameson started. "There has been a change to your mission. After you lost your last man, I have carefully reevaluated your current status, the amended training schedule, and the immediate need on the part of the CIA. I have pulled a few strings to get Master Sergeant Keeble reassigned to the ASMU 416. I did ask him if he would consider this a few days ago and he has accepted this opportunity to serve with you. As you might know, Sergeant Keeble is well-versed in Middle Eastern languages and culture and will be a tremendous asset for the team."

Jones and Unit 416 exchanged subtle looks with each other; they knew this dude was on the take. Keeble had agreed to let Jameson save face, but if he kept bloviating like he was some sort of messiah, he would risk Jones unloading some money from his accounts just because he wouldn't shut the fuck up.

"Do you have anything that you would like to add, Keeble?"

"I think you've said enough, sir. Thank you," Keeble said curtly, which drew smiles around the room.

The only person who wasn't smiling was Rodriguez. Keeble had given him no heads-up of any kind. He'd thought the reason that Keeble was keeping to himself had more to do with his military career, or the men taking on the assignment in Uzbekistan, not because he was planning to go with them. That one came out of nowhere and blindsided him.

Jameson asked the men to gather around him, which allowed Rodriguez to corner Keeble. Keeble saw him coming. He knew that game of a hundred questions was about to begin, but he couldn't get to an exit quickly enough to avoid Rodriguez.

"Kee, you couldn't let me know? Give me a little warning, ese?"

"I didn't have any idea about how this was going to play out," Keeble said.

"That's why you never made a play for Rita? You knew you were leaving?" Rodriguez was pressing for answers because he knew his wife was still playing matchmaker at home and she would have a ton of questions about Keeble.

"Truth, bro, I haven't had the time. This is who I am and this is what I do. Being in the field with them, having that purpose made me feel more alive than I had in eighteen months." He paused for a second. "Tell her I don't know about tomorrow or what it will bring, but this is what I had to do today." That was the end of that discussion. "Me and my boys got to roll." He shook hands with Rodriguez. "Good luck to you and Tessa with the baby. It'll be here by the time we get back."

"Probably, unless you all get back in a week and a half," Rodriguez said as he left the mess hall and headed back to the B-6 barracks. There was still work left to do and he was still being paid. Harlow had given him confirmation of a direct deposit made to his account. He was compensated for all ten months he'd been scheduled to pull night duty with the men.

"Not likely . . ." Keeble's voice tailed off behind him.

"So you takin' the mission on with us, huh, Sarge?" Winston called to Keeble.

"The old dog just can't sit on the steps," Lev said.

"Welcome to the G-thang, baby!" Daisy sang.

"Hey, fellas." Jones looked at them and then to Keeble. "We just got a big stick added to our bundle." The group nodded. They understood that their group, formidable as they believed it to be, in an instant had become that much stronger.

There was one person who was not nodding. Turner had his head bowed and his eyes closed.

"Turn . . . Is he . . . ?" Winston started to ask.

"Let him work his thing, bruh. We can use all of that and then some," Lev said.

"Forty-five minutes, men, and the Hummer's rolling." Keeble let them know that the countdown was on.

At 1400 hours, the Hummer was loaded with men, weapons, and equipment and headed for Lawson Army Airfield. Keeble drove with Jones up front as his wingman and everyone else rode in the back.

"I wish I could have seen the expression on his face when he walked in there," Jones said.

"Hell, you're the genius that made it happen; I figured you'd have that up on YouTube by now!" Daisy yelled from the back of the Hummer.

" 'I have carefully reevaluated your current status,' " Lev imitated Jameson. "I was 'bout to tell him to get that horse crap out of here."

"There are times when you have to pick your battle," Turner interrupted. "That was one of them. If Sarge didn't allow Jameson to feel that he was still in control, we wouldn't have him here with us."

"I couldn't have said it better," Keeble said.

"When did you decide to get down with us?" Winston asked.

"Right after I busted your nose." Keeble laughed and everyone erupted, even Winston.

"Oh, okay, so we're going back to that, huh?" Winston was still chuckling.

"On the real, watching you men becoming one, that's what I

missed being a part of. It reminded me, that kind of brotherhood—
that's the shit worth sacrificing for."

"Amen, brother," Turner added.

When they reached the airfield, they stopped briefly at the
gate before Keeble was given the directions to the hangar they
would be departing from. They drove onto the tarmac until they
arrived at the hangar where an Airbus A400M was waiting with
its tailgate down. Keeble drove the Hummer into the Airbus.
There the vehicle was secured for takeoff by an eight-man crew.
They asked the men to sit tight while they unloaded all of the
military equipment from the Hummer and secured it for the
flight as well.

Fifteen minutes later, the efficient crew finished their load
in, introduced themselves to Unit 416, and announced that they
accompanied this particular Airbus on all of its flights and would
be with them for the duration of the flight. They would take care
of them on the other end as well. As the aircraft began to rum-
ble to life, they told them to settle in and enjoy the flight; it would
be a long one.

32

Sixteen hours later, the plane touched down at Karshi-Khanabad Air Base in Uzbekistan. The airport was also known as K2 and they'd received special permission to land there. The air base had been operated by the U.S. military from 2001 to 2005, but closed due to strained relations between the military and the Uzbek government. They were greeted by CIA field officers. The load crew moved with precision, unloading the Hummer and their equipment and moving it to a large transfer truck. The Unit 416 men were put into three cars and taken to a secured location where their briefing would be conducted.

Two hours of driving later, they arrived at a seemingly deserted location. But once they entered a tunnel, it was easy to see this was an up-to-date, state-of-the-art facility. It immediately reminded Unit 416, particularly Keeble, of the setup back at Benning.

As the men emerged from their respective vehicles, they exchanged looks with one another, each knowing that training was done and it was time to get to work. They were ushered into a conference room where a young man who looked to be in his midthirties greeted them. There was something familiar about him to Keeble. He'd seen so many faces during his military career, he couldn't put his finger on it.

"Gentlemen, the pleasure is mine. My name is Ray Griffin; I am the chief of base and operations commander in Uzbekistan." He shook hands with them. "Unit 416 was recruited and trained because, as a group, you men possessed a necessary skill set to infiltrate the underground here in Uzbekistan and blend in. The ultimate goal is to stop Iran from funneling chemical weapons through here from Russia. The first step in our infiltration plan is to use your access to U.S. army-issued weapons as bait. Once you gain access to the Afghan arms cartel with the promise of being able to deliver those stolen weapons, it is our hope that you'll be able to gain information about the shipment of chemical weapons, which are targeted for use against U.S. soldiers. From what we have been able to gather from all our intel, there will be an attempt to bring those weapons to the U.S. shores. The Army Special Operations and the CIA sent in a joint team to track down the chemical weapons, but the plan was foiled, because their men could not blend in with the criminal underground and were never trusted. Several members of that team lost their lives."

Griffin went on to explain to them that two weeks ago, the U.S. military arms depot in Kyrgyzstan was scheduled to receive a shipment of eighteen hundred M16A2 rifles and fifteen hundred FN SCARs. The M16s had a U.S. street value of $2.7 million and the SCARs were worth nearly $4 million. The shipment never made it. It was stolen by a band of masked men and seemingly vanished into thin air. Reports showed evidence that the raid was conducted by an eighteen-man crew, all cloaked in black from head to toe, complete with gloves and ski masks.

"In actuality, the heist was secretly conducted by a team I put together, but that information is never to leave this room," Griffin cautioned. "Unit 416 is being set up as the possessors of the missing weapons, and your criminal records, as impressive as they are, have been enhanced, portraying you as ruthless drug dealers, vicious killers, and brilliant scam artists."

Griffin paused. If he was waiting for any of the men to blink, he had the wrong group. The men of Unit 416 listened to him intently; occasionally they would exchange an approving look with one another.

"Iran is a large consumer of the weapons that the Afghan arms cartel has to offer and they are willing to pay top dollar. The cartel itself is not as concerned about the weapons as they are their poppy fields. The money they will make from the sale of arms to Iran is poured back into their fields to harvest more opium," Griffin concluded.

Griffin further cautioned the men that any and all contact with their unit would run through him. If there was anything they needed, he would do his best to make sure they had it. Although they were working jointly with the existing operation on the ground, Unit 416 was his team. This was an unofficial mission they were conducting and if they were caught, the CIA, Special Operations, and the U.S. government would all disavow them. There was a heavy silence that filled the room as the weight of those words fell on the men of Unit 416. In the event they failed, nobody was willing to claim them.

They followed Griffin to the war room where Keeble and his Unit 416 were introduced to the CIA officers and the Special Operations team there on the ground. All six of the men were the epitome of sharp, trained, trim, and fit soldiers: an image that would make any military man proud and would be a welcomed sight in any room they entered. That is, anywhere but here; the reception was anything but a warm one. If the officers bothered to shake hands with them, it was done so with a half-hearted effort before their attention was turned back to whatever work had consumed them prior to their interruption.

"What's up with your welcome wagon?" Winston asked Griffin. To him, the indifference was a sign of disrespect.

"Tensions are high among all of the men right now." Griffin lowered his voice. "We have several operations that have been conducted with some degrees of success but that have ultimately ended in failure. Folks are aware that I am doing things differently and don't always include them. Some of them aren't ready to let go of the reins."

"Not to worry, Mr. Griffin. Unit 416 is ready to serve," Winston offered loudly and confidently. Everyone, including Keeble, stood firm with him on that point. It wasn't meant to belittle any of the previous efforts, but he was announcing their presence and their eagerness for this opportunity.

But that was not the way it was received in the room. "Great; we got some damn criminals with a hero complex," a CIA officer grumbled. The comment was meant to remain under his breath, but Michael Ayers wasn't known for tact. Although he now spent all of his time behind a desk, he was once one of the most brutal operations officers the CIA had to offer and he'd served the CIA and the region for too long to put up with this type of change.

"Ayers!" Griffin's tone suggested that he needed to shut his mouth.

"What was that?" Keeble asked as he stepped in front of Winston. Apparently the team in place didn't get the memo that Unit 416 would be working with Griffin. The pissing contest had started.

There was a comment that Ayers wanted to make, but this

was a time when he used his diplomatic filter. "I have been operating in this sector for a long time; we can handle it," Ayers said
with a "thank you but fuck you" smile.

"Seems to me like somebody thought it was time for a
change," Winston said. He could read a fuck-you smile a mile
away and he did not appreciate it.

"See, I told you we would have to put up with bullshit when
you bring a bunch of two-bit thugs in here," Ayers said to Griffin. "And you want us to sit back and let them do whatever it is
you brought them here to do?!"

"Seems to me like you got some other words that would be
more comfortable comin' out of your mouth, boss," Big Lev said
to Ayers.

"Yeah, you—" Ayers started as the CIA and Ops guys started
to join him.

"Ayers!" Griffin interrupted.

"What, sir? You don't think we know what you're doing?
You just got here and you're bringing this to us. We worked too
hard in this region to let you parade this bullshit in front of us."

Griffin was wondering what the fuck he'd said that for. Lev,
Jones, Daisy, and Turner stood with Winston and Keeble, ready
to go toe-to-toe with this asshole.

"That's enough!" Griffin was fed up. He'd been back in
country for a few days; he was trying to organize a mission and
didn't need any of these men rolling around on the floor of his
war room because some of these men were immature, insecure,
and wouldn't have a damn thing to do with Unit 416 anyway.

"Fellas," Keeble said to everyone in the room, "we might
have gotten off on the wrong foot. I would suggest that when
you read the profile of my men, you don't stop on page two or
three. There are a few more pages that have been added and they
are worth reading because these men understand there's a higher

purpose in their life. That's why they're here. We've all got our dancing shoes on, and I ain't ever been one to mind a two-step, but we have some work to do and I'm sure you do too. So, you want to dance or do you want to do your work and we can go about the business of doing ours?"

The men in the room who'd rushed to their respective sides like water crashing ashore began to roll back like the tide returning to the sea. One thing about the tide; it will rise up on the shore again, soon and often.

33

"I understand this is a challenge for you," Griffin started. "You have been the man on the ground here for a number of years and no one is attempting to discredit the tremendous work you have done here. Now, I need you to understand that I expect nothing less than your level best as we continue our efforts to disrupt and destroy these arms cartels."

Ayers bit his tongue at the prospect working with Unit 416. He had been the point man on the ground here and could feel the reins slipping out of his grasp. What was worse is those reins were being handed over to a group of idiots, and for the most part, they hadn't ridden this kind of animal before. Ayers gave Griffin a cold stare. He heard him but didn't listen to a word that was said, and when it registered with him that Griffin was done talking he responded with, "I will do whatever I can to work with them."

Ayers got back to work; there were more pressing things for him to contend with. As Griffin and Unit 416 prepared to leave the facility, Ayers barely looked their way. Once out of eyesight, though, Ayers's eyes lingered in that direction knowing that he would be dealing with their threatening presence soon enough.

Unit 416 moved into quarters in a rural area outside the city of Tashkent, Uzbekistan. It was the largest city in the once Soviet-ruled Uzbekistan. The national language was Uzbek and Keeble was fluent in its language, history, and culture. The city had changed drastically in recent years, with many of the Soviet-era buildings being replaced with new modern ones. It was a city rich in museums as well as monuments left from the Soviet era.

When the men ventured into the city, they dressed in modern clothing; there was no need to blend in with the citizens wearing traditional Uzbek clothing. African-American men in Uzbekistan would find it difficult to blend in there no matter what they wore.

Griffin had two vehicles for them to use for transportation, an SUV and a sedan, and found them an old two-story farmhouse. It had six bedrooms, three bathrooms, and a kitchen with running water and electricity. There was a large room downstairs that was sectioned off into four work areas. A computer center was Jones's primary working space. An operations center was manned by Winston, but Keeble was always close by. The weapons area was Daisy's home, while Turner and Lev had an area where they broke down the logistics of the city and the area where they would be looking for weapons.

Lev and Turner spent two hours in the Museum of Geology. It was located in the center of the city and was the perfect place to be seen. As they walked through the museum, looking at exhibits of rock samples and precious stones, they saw the same face passing by them at each exhibit. They walked out of the museum, waited a few minutes before going back in, and almost bumped into the man who had been following them in the museum. People were watching.

They created an air of suspicion that these could possibly be the men who were in possession of the missing weapons. Griffin was doing his part to ensure that the right attention was being drawn to them.

It was a matter of days before the Uzbekistan arms-dealing Mafia had them on their radar, as did members of the Russian Mafia. Word had gotten to those groups that some interesting Americans were in the city. It had been rumored all over the country for weeks that almost $7 million in U.S. military weapons had disappeared near Qarshi. The arms Mafia was clamoring with anticipation. They knew it would only be a matter of time before somebody would be looking to broker a deal to unload those weapons. The Mafia also knew it could be days, weeks, or months before whoever was in possession of the weapons would make a move, so they were patient. But when it was learned that the interesting Americans were blacks, some of the cartels jumped to the conclusion that these men could not possibly be the offenders; they assumed these men lacked the courage to pull off a caper of that magnitude.

One late evening, the men met for dinner in a restaurant called the Samarqand, where most of the clientele preferred to arrive late, when most of the citizens of Tashkent were off the street. It was where some of the seedier elements of the city could gather in the company of their own.

Keeble ordered dinner for the men. Jones put on his glasses to read the menu before he realized it was written in Uzbek. He set the menu down since it wouldn't do him any good. They'd eaten enough fruits, vegetables, and soups, so tonight they were going to dine on lagman and manty, dishes that were prepared with meat, noodles, and vegetables. Their order was taken by the owner of the restaurant as Keeble ordered in Uzbek. Intrigued by Keeble speaking the native language, he struck up a conversation with Keeble. The owner also spoke English but wasn't comfortably fluent.

The room had ears; there were others who were interested in the conversation at Keeble's table of six. The owner sent the order to the kitchen and sat with Keeble. He ordered wine for the table and engaged all the men in conversation with the English he was able to speak. Keeble would interpret and clarify what was being said to him or what he was trying to communicate to them in English before giving in and speaking Uzbek. When he asked what had brought their group to Tashkent, Keeble could sense the others in the room listening. Keeble told him they wanted to experience the country of Uzbekistan. As the owner left the table to allow the men to eat, he asked the names of his new friends. They all smiled and nodded their heads but did not offer up their names. They simply said thank you. That made the curious ears in the room more interested in finding out who these men were. The owner left a card with his restaurant's name on it.

"Please come back. I know people who know this country well," the owner said in his native language.

Well-fed, with a little wine to boot, the men made their way back to their vehicles to head back to the farmhouse. Turner drove the SUV with Lev and Jones riding with him and Daisy followed them in the car with Winston and Keeble aboard. Four miles outside of the city and traveling the countryside, Winston and Keeble noticed the set of headlights that popped up behind them at the same time; they were a little more than a mile from their turn on the left.

"Sarge, you seein' what I'm seein' back there?" Winston glanced at the passenger-side mirror and the rearview mirror.

"Already ahead of you. Daisy, take the next right," Keeble said without changing his position in the backseat.

As they turned off to the right, Daisy slowed the car down to see if the vehicle would follow them or trail behind the SUV. Keeble reached through the access compartment in the backseat and retrieved a couple of handguns, handing one to Winston and Daisy each while digging out a SCAR for himself. In the rear-view mirror, Winston and Daisy saw the vehicle continue on the road behind the SUV. Daisy whipped the car around and killed the headlights. They picked up the pace to close the distance on the car. When Turner made his left turn toward the farmhouse, the vehicle behind them picked up speed and continued straight along the road. There was a sense among them that maybe they weren't being followed by that car but they knew there was no such thing as being too careful.

The men gathered in their makeshift control center and went to work. Keeble gave Jones the restaurant owner's business card.

"Let's find out who this bastard is, shall we?" Keeble said.

"Give me a second. I want to download these pictures first." Jones was downloading images he'd taken in the restaurant with his Google Glasses. He had a complete layout of the restaurant and all the patrons who were sitting at the nearby tables. "Big man, I am sending you and Turner the layout now," he called out to Lev.

"They are coming up now," Lev said.

Jones went to work and seconds later he was on to something. The speed at which Jones could work his magic on the computers was amazing. "The restaurant is a nice cover; the owner made money working with arms dealers in Uzbekistan but had gotten out of the game over fifteen years ago when a deal went bad with the Afghan drug lord Anemah Maasiq."

Keeble's heart skipped a beat at the mention of the name Maasiq. Outwardly, he squinted his eyes and followed along.

"Some very interesting ties, Jones. Good work. What else do we need to do, Winston?" Keeble asked.

"Send the images of the folks in the restaurant over to the CIA," Winston said.

"Exactly, but make sure the images are sent to Griffin."

"Roger that," Jones said as he hit send.

"If we're checking them, I'm sure somebody out there is checking us," Winston said.

"No doubt. When we first got to this farmhouse, I had Jones put a trace in on all our profiles. If anybody tried to identify us or get info on us, it would register with Jones; tell us what kind of research people were doing on us. By the way, Lev, you have several assault charges against the police on your record now. Your record was by far the softest of all of us," Keeble said.

"All of us? What the fuck is on your record, Sarge?" Winston asked.

"The shit you were doing at twenty-four, I had mastered at sixteen."

"Sergeant Kee?"

"And that's how I was moving it too, by the ki." Keeble gave Winston a look that conveyed to him, "that's why I've always known you." "Jones, what do we have on the traces?"

"We got a couple of hits here and there the last couple of weeks. Casual stuff, but look at this." Jones pushed the image from his monitor to a large screen on the wall. A chart popped up that showed sporadic activity for the last few days to a hailstorm of activity in the last hour.

"These boys just went ape shit on us, fellas," Lev said as he and Turner came in.

"They're trying to find out who we are, huh?" Turner looked at the screen.

"I'd say we're in play now, fellas. Jones, do me a favor; see what Griffin can get from the CIA and Special Ops on Anemah Maasiq. That's the boy we want to play ball with. He's the big fish who can handle the amount of weapons we have in a trade," Keeble said.

"Looks like I got something back from Griffin." Jones was scanning the monitor and it was also showing up on the big screen.

The images of the people in the restaurant popped onto the screen accompanied by a data report on the individuals of note. There were five individuals of particular note. Three were Russian and two were Uzbek. All were lower-level arms dealers who dealt in quantities of one hundred to two hundred thousand dollars. People who would be useful for information, but less likely to be able to deal with the large number of weapons Unit 416 had to move.

A few minutes later, Jones received a profile on Anemah Maasiq. Keeble jumped on the information. He led a massive drug production and trafficking operation that supplied heroin in more than twenty countries, including the United States. Over the last twenty-five years, he had built a drug empire worth more than $250 million, and that was in money they could trace. It was widely speculated that a portion of that money funded the Taliban in Afghanistan.

Keeble walked closer and closer to the large screen until he was face-to-face with Maasiq's image.

"What the fuck, Sarge?" Winston asked.

"This is the bastard who funded the Taliban in Nerkh." Keeble never took his eyes off of the image on the screen; this was the motherfucker he had been chasing for four years.

The rest of Unit 416 watched Keeble as he stood transfixed by the image. He had forgotten about everyone else in the room.

There were a hundred different scenarios running through his mind all at once, and no words he could find for any of them.

"I don't get it; what's with Sarge?" Turner asked.

"Nerkh is where he got injured. It almost cost him his leg and his military career. Maasiq is the reason he's here with us now," Winston said.

A few seconds later, a grainy video began to play on the screen. It was the video of the Tashkent Cartel and Maasiq at the Afghan border. The action of the video was narrated and Keeble recognized Harlow's voice. He introduced the CIA officer who'd set up the meeting, even gave information about his wife and their two young daughters. When the officer was shown being gunned down in broad daylight at the border, the narrator let that action speak for itself.

34

"Are you serious?" Keeble couldn't believe the question that was being asked.

"He would do his best to get us what we need, that's what Griffin said," Turner pointed out. The men had called it a night, but Turner had a question he'd been trying to find the right time to ask.

"Yeah, Turn, but a fucking . . . a freaking helicopter." Keeble laughed when the word *helicopter* came out of his mouth.

"Sarge, with all the money they are putting into this, it's worth asking for. The worst he could say is no."

"And is there any preference on the type of helicopter lessons?"

"I'd like to fly an Apache, but I got a little experience with the Black Hawk, so I'd like to stay there for now."

"For now. Okay." Keeble shook his head; he was still tripping off of the request. "I'll send him a message." Keeble intended to message Griffin in the morning.

Turner stood in the door waiting for Keeble to send the

message. What he'd understood Keeble to mean was that he was sending a message right now. Keeble looked at Turner for a second before sending the message. After a few more seconds, the phone rang.

"Keeble here," he answered. "No, he is very serious."

Turner stepped out of the doorway leaving Keeble to his conversation with Griffin. He already had his answer and was ready to lie down for the night; it was now up to Keeble to arrive at that outcome.

"Get the fuck outta here!" Winston said.

"I'm serious. He left about an hour ago," Daisy said as he came back into the farmhouse. He was out testing his new long-range sniper scope when he'd spotted Turner through the scope.

Life was beginning to stir at the farmhouse but Turner was already long gone. Keeble had gone to Turner's room after getting off the phone with Griffin. While he didn't get a request granted for Turner to take some lessons, he did get some information on a Black Hawk and a possible instructor. Griffin told Keeble he needed to verify a few things, but if a car arrived at 0600 for Turner, then Turner should take the ride with him. The car arrived at 0610 and Turner wasted no time getting to it. As the car pulled away, Keeble was still shaking his head in disbelief.

"Shit, I should have asked for a goddamned pony," Winston joked.

Two hours after Turner had hopped in the car, they were pulling into an open field. The driver wasn't much for talking during the ride, something that suited Turner fine. He spent the time meditating, but staying aware of his surroundings. The driver slowed to a stop; without a word, he motioned with his head indicating to Turner that it was time for him to get out of the car. Turner stood in the middle of the open field and watched the car as it drove away.

As the sound of the car faded in the distance, Turner closed his eyes and embraced the silence. Standing alone in the field gave him a sense of peace. *Always calm before the storm*, he thought. In the distance, he could hear a faint noise that brought a smile to his face. It got louder and louder as it neared him. He could feel the thumping of the blades as they cut through the air. He counted his blessings before he opened his eyes, in time to see the Black Hawk slowing to a hover. Turner's eyes followed the copter until it landed on his left.

"Tyrin Turner!" the pilot yelled and waved him over as he began to shut down the helicopter.

Turner ran as fast as he could to the side of the Black Hawk. The warrant officer quickly introduced himself as he climbed out of the pilot's seat.

"You're the one who wants to fly?" he asked skeptically.

"Yes, sir!" an eager Turner responded.

"Well, we'll start at the beginning." The warrant officer wondered who'd decided to humor this guy.

Turner wasted no time discussing every detail about the exterior of the Black Hawk and its required maintenance. His military MOS was working on these birds. After he covered every imaginable detail on the outside, he detailed information on the interior. The warrant officer was stunned and impressed by Turner's depth of knowledge.

"Son, have you ever flown one of these?"

"A little bit, but I'm still learning." Turner smiled.

"Take that copilot seat over there; let's see if we can get you flying."

The officer took the pilot's seat on the right and strapped in before starting the Black Hawk. Flight lessons were about to begin and Turner couldn't wipe the smile off his face.

"Has anybody seen Griffin?" Ayers demanded as he came in from taking a smoke break. He had seen less and less of Griffin over the past couple of days. Griffin was spending more time in the hole with people that had arrived with him but was a virtual ghost to all the members of the team that had put time in with him.

"Hadn't seen him," one of the men mumbled.

"Bullshit." Ayers spun on his heels and wasted no time heading to the secluded area where he knew he could find Griffin.

Griffin and his team were busy following the number of traces being run on Unit 416. The enhanced criminal backgrounds were serving their purpose. What the traces were turning up were criminal backgrounds on six men that had been kicked out of the army and, oddly enough, had disappeared within the last several weeks.

A knock at the door interrupted their work. Whoever was behind it tried to turn the locked door handle. Griffin went to the door to see who it was. He opened the door slightly to see Ayers on the other side.

"Ayers, what can I do for you?" Griffin asked.

"The Joint Task Force has a slight problem; they need to see you." Ayers tried to get a peek at what was going on in the room.

"Okay; give me a few minutes and I'll be right there." Griffin shut the door. "Make sure those traces keep finding everything they can on our boys. The more dirt they find the better. We have to keep them chasing us."

At the restaurant, the owner treated Keeble and Daisy to lunch and offered them wine to go with it. They accepted the lunch, but Keeble declined the wine. They spoke in English about the city and its rich scientific institutions, the history of Genghis Kahn and crown jewels; if he didn't own a restaurant, he could have been a tour guide.

Once the meal was finished, the language began to shift from English to Uzbek. It allowed the conversation to flow more quickly. Keeble kept Daisy up to speed as much as possible, but it was a conversation that needed to move fast.

"Why do people want to meet me?" Keeble asked.

"There is great speculation as to why you are here. Your name is?" The friendly restaurateur had taken on a decidedly different tone in his native tongue.

"Miles Keeble." Keeble met his temperament. "I am former U.S. military and I needed a new start."

Daisy sensed the mood in the room shift. He kept his eyes moving around all areas of the restaurant. If there was any odd movement at all, he was prepared.

"And your five other friends? Like you, they needed a new start?" The owner's question went unanswered. "As I said, I know many people who might be able to offer you some assistance."

"Thanks for the lunch."

Although the lunch was insignificant in the context of the conversation, it was significant in regard to the doors that would begin to open up for them.

Winston and Lev were having coffee at an outside patio of one of the local shops enjoying the sights of the city and noticing the women as they passed by. If there was a particularly good-looking woman, the two shared a raised eyebrow and a slight nod of the head.

"I see you like these women too," said a fortyish, short, stocky man at the table across from them. He spoke with a thick Russian accent. "Have you checked out the nightlife here? Tashkent women are really something to see then."

Lev and Winston looked at each other and took it under advisement; it could be worth looking into. They recognized the Russian; he was one of the patrons from the restaurant last night. There was no doubt, they were being watched and people were very interested in getting to know them. Their conversation with him was very brief; they excused themselves feeling sure they would see him again.

When they got back to the farmhouse, Jones was right where they'd left him, in front of the computer. He was a creature content in his own habitat. When they heard the sound of a helicopter approaching; they quickly moved to get their hands on a weapon. It sounded like the chopper was too low and coming in too fast. As they positioned themselves for an attack, they saw the helicopter attempting to land in a clearing. The Black Hawk wobbled unsteadily as it touched down and the men could see Turner in the copilot's seat making the unsteady landing. He had a big smile on his face.

Turner hopped out of the cockpit and met the men as they came outside. He looked back and waved at the warrant officer as he took back to the air. The warrant officer gave Turner a thumbs-up. Turner gave him a salute in return, already anxious for his next flight lesson.

"Damn, rev, you put that bird down by yourself, huh?" Winston shook his head.

"A hell of a lot better than the last time," Lev mumbled.

Turner watched the helicopter as it moved farther and farther away. "Something that I was meant to do." He never took his eyes off of the Black Hawk.

35

Jones stayed at the farmhouse while the rest of the men went back into the city for the evening. They would take in some of the nightlife but each one of the men understood this would be about gaining access. They ran into the Russian but Lev and Winston knew that it was far more than a coincidental meeting. Lev introduced Daisy, Keeble, and Turner to their new Russian friend who had already met Winston. In spite of the friendly image he projected, Jones had given them the lowdown on him: he'd been deathly vicious over the course of his life. Thirteen lives had met death at his hands, and of those thirteen deaths, six were American.

The Russian made quick introductions of the three comrades who were with him. Thanks to the work Jones had done behind the scenes, the unit was aware that these men were members of the Mafia and dealt in small arms. None of them were shy about their conversations with members of Unit 416, and Unit 416 did not hesitate to make their new friends aware of their interest in setting up a transfer of goods with the people of Afghanistan.

The Mafia was gathering information on the five men as they spoke. Mafia members were wired and everything that was being said was being recorded, translated, and verified. They were doing everything they could to get the drop on these Americans.

What the Mafia wasn't aware of was that all of their communications were being intercepted by Jones. In turn, his computer was linked to Griffin and his team, sitting behind locked doors at the CIA headquarters. And all of them worked feverishly to validate the identities of these Mafia members.

The Russians invited them to join them as they took in a couple of clubs. They referred to the city as the "Thailand of the Middle East." The first stop was a belly dancing bar, where men stood just off the dance floor and watched scantily clad women as they danced. It was a nice distraction as the Russians began to press for information.

Two of the Russians pulled Winston and Daisy to the side. "What is the business you wish to partake in?" one of them asked with a thick accent. There was no softball in his approach; he came right down the middle with the heat.

Daisy gave a crooked smile, partly because of the girls dancing, but mostly because of the question being asked. The boys were definitely in play. "We have some p-people back home who would like to do business," Daisy began.

"Opiates," Winston cut in; he was ready to play hardball with them.

The Russians smiled; these silly Americans didn't understand how business was done. "There are too many people already doing the same thing here."

"What the fuck makes you think we want to get down on this turf? I don't remember anybody sweatin' you about doin' business here," Daisy said, with no trace of a stutter and a completely different demeanor that Winston had not seen before.

"We have a distribution network set up throughout the United States; you motherfuckers got us twisted if you think we're interested in this area." Winston's edginess dwarfed that of Daisy's.

"I see. What parts of the U.S.?"

Neither Daisy nor Winston spoke Russian or knew their culture, but they knew condescension was universal and it was on full display.

"My man over there," Winston pointed at Turner, "he's from Arkansas. The big man next to him is from Texas. Over there by himself, he has Georgia and the Carolinas on lock." Winston wasn't sure if the Russian caught on to the slang, but he continued. "My man here is from New York and I got California, B." Winston wanted to use the word *bitch* but *B* was good for now.

"My friend, that takes quite a bit of money," the Russian said, looking them over.

"Still on that shit, huh?" Daisy picked up on the salty vibe.

"It ain't always about money. Shit, if you have something that people want to get their hands on, I hear bartering's a system that's gooder than a ma'fucker around here." Winston paused.

"What are you bartering with?" The Russians were now very engrossed in the conversation.

Winston looked at him for a few seconds before speaking slowly. "We have something that many people would be interested in trading for."

The Russians sat silently for a few seconds, speculating on the meaning of Winston's statement. Then both of them arrived at the same conclusion; maybe they'd stumbled onto something.

The Russian sitting with Lev and Turner spoke to them as if he were talking about walking a dog. "You do realize that killing someone is a part of doing business in this region. But sure, it is no problem; we can make the connection for you."

That was all that Lev and Turner needed to hear. They turned up their glasses in a half toast.

"So who do I kill first?" Turner asked. The Russian headed to the bar to get another round for them, giving Lev and Turner an opportunity to talk.

"These people are down fo' sure; they'll make a deal, even if they have to kill some people to get them out of the way," Lev said to Turner.

"They know how much money is at stake for them. The number of Americans and people in the world that are addicted to this shit is staggering. And ninety-five percent of it is produced in Afghanistan. For them it's like having a corner candy store and the whole world is coming to them to get it," Turner said.

"No shit. Ninety-five percent?"

"Fo' sho', and it ain't like crack back in the day; the world is paying attention this time. They recognize how big a problem it is because rich white kids are on that shit and getting fucked up this time. Left and right, they are going down." Turner thought for a second before speaking. "A man could make a lot of money if he was trying get down with them."

Lev listened and considered the point. There was no doubt about it; there was a lot of money sitting there on the table just waiting to be taken. When the Russian arrived with the drinks, Lev was still lost in thought.

"As soon as you finish this one, we are going to another club, yes?" the Russian said as he placed drinks in front of them.

The statement brought Lev out of his head and back into the room. He and Turner picked up their latest round, nodded to the Russian to convey their thanks, and drained the beverage in front of them.

Three clubs later, they all slipped out of a side door and into an alley. Unit 416 was calling it a night, but the Russians were not done; they were ready to keep the party going. As the group of men separated, it was agreed that they would get together again very soon. The unit headed back to their car but they all came to a halt when they heard the sound of skidding tires. Their first thought was that somebody was after them. When they turned in the direction of the sounds, they saw the four Russians they had been with being ambushed. Three cars pinned them in; there was yelling and finger pointing as men emerged from the cars drawing weapons.

To the Russians' credit, they didn't back down as the twelve men approached them. With no time to think about it, the unit gave a quick nod to one another and knew they were in. Shots rang out in warning as the aggressors continued arguing with the Russians. As eight of them began throwing punches, the other four held their guns on the Russians, never paying attention to Unit 416 who came up behind them and moved with precision. Turner, Daisy, Winston, and Lev each took one of the gunmen while Keeble made sure no one else was approaching. Daisy dislodged the gun first before striking his man in the groin; Turner opted for his man's kidneys while Winston went straight upside his man's head. Lev drove through his man at full speed, thrusting him into two of the men swinging at the Russians. Lev was mowing them down like bowling pins. Keeble watched as the unit wasted little time cutting the men down. He would have joined in, but seeing what the other four were doing to the twelve men, it wouldn't be a fair fight. These men's skills were no match for what the unit had learned during the previous month. There were punches, kicks, and throws that neutralized the men. They knocked weapons out of their reach and left them lying in the street before they pulled the Russians up and found the quickest route away from the alley.

The Russians thanked them as they parted ways; there was newfound respect from a couple of them for these foreigners. It wouldn't be long before the Mafia men began speculating that this group of ex-soldiers who were interested in establishing a drug trade might have a lot more to their story. Their fighting skills weren't something they normally encountered; these men, quite possibly, could be connected to the missing shipment of U.S. weapons.

Keeble drove as Daisy, Lev, Turner, and Winston ragged on each other, recapping the ass whooping they'd just put on those men. Keeble was thinking to himself that these men were comfortable falling back into what they knew best. It was a hell of an asset. Everyone they encountered seemed anxious to get to know them better. And that was all part of the plan to get Keeble closer to Maasiq.

Griffin took a look at his watch. It was three in the morning and time for the next person to get his five-hour break. His five-man crew was a thin one but it was a group that he trusted. They worked like he did, nonstop.

As the door was unlocked and his people switched out, Griffin decided he would take a break as well. He'd been pushing for the last thirty hours straight.

"I'll be back at six," he said as he walked out.

Griffin was on his way to his room when the lights in the war room caught his attention. It was three in the morning; he hadn't been told that the room would be in use this morning. Griffin walked quietly to the doorway.

"Ayers?" Griffin startled him.

"Sir? Sorry, I couldn't sleep," Ayers explained, but he was reviewing images from Samarqand, the restaurant located in Tashkent.

"What are you working on?" Griffin started walking toward him.

"It's the missing shipment, sir. I have been trying to wrap my head around it. Trying to make sense of how it was able to happen." Ayers was exasperated. "What are you doing up so late?"

"Same thing; we're all trying to figure that out," Griffin assured him. "I'm going to get a little shut-eye. See you in a couple of hours," he said as he turned to head to his room.

Ayers watched Griffin as he left. He thought about trying to sneak into the room where he kept his private team locked away. There was something going on in there that he needed to be a part of. Once he was sure that Griffin was gone, Ayers started to ease away from his desk and head that way when some information on his computer screen stopped him from leaving.

36

As Unit 416 continued to explore the city and work their contacts to gather information and build trust with them, Keeble did the same. He'd waited a couple of days before he contacted the restaurant owner. Keeble let the owner know that he was interested in moving some valuable equipment in exchange for heroin. When they met at the Samarqand restaurant, the owner pressed him for more details on the equipment. Keeble did not provide the specifics, but he assured him that it was something people had been trying to locate for some time now.

"My friend, how do I know my friends in Afghanistan would be interested in your equipment?" Burkhanov asked skeptically.

Keeble went to the front door of the restaurant. He stood there for a few seconds, stepped away from the door, then stood in front of it for a few more seconds before rejoining Burkhanov at the bar. Less than a minute later, Big Lev walked into the restaurant with a large canvas bag on his shoulder. He walked to the bar and laid the bag in front of Keeble before going back to the door.

Keeble unzipped the bag, peeled it back to expose a brand new FN SCAR. The owner leaned forward to examine it as if it were fine jewelry. The thought of brokering a large weapons deal brought a smile to his face. They were looking to trade arms for opium, not looking to sell arms in small quantities to the Uzbek and Russian Mafia even though they were very useful in fanning the flames of interest.

"There has been talk about some missing U.S. weapons." Burkhanov looked at Keeble.

Keeble knew what he was asking, but he said nothing. He looked into Burkhanov's eyes and stared at him. Burkhanov found the answer he was looking for.

"And the other weapons? Do you have all of them?"

"I couldn't get them all into one bag," Keeble said flatly, with a straight face. It was a joke, but Burkhanov lost the humor in translation. "Do you have someone who might be interested in my product exchange?"

"I have a friend who will be interested. His primary business is opiates, but he sells large quantities of small arms to Iran. Normally Russian weapons, but this will present a fascinating option to him."

Keeble zipped the bag and Lev scooped it off the bar as the two new business partners continued to speak in Burkhanov's native language. Lev disappeared out the door and went back into the city. Two blocks away, the bag was handed to Turner who disappeared into an alley. Keeble engaged the owner in another ten minutes of conversation before leaving the restaurant.

The Russian who'd initially connected with Winston and Lev was more comfortable with Daisy and offered to meet him for a couple of beers. While Daisy drank a few beers, the Russian downed twice as many. He also had a penchant for hard liquor, which he drank between beers. His lips got looser with every shot and after a few too many, he told Daisy that he wasn't like the other ones and he knew the two of them could really get along. Daisy agreed with him. The Russian boasted that some things were about to happen and he was going to be at the center of it.

"Wouldn't you be more comfortable working with someone like me instead of those herps?" The Russian's thick accent was slurred by the alcohol he'd consumed.

"Herps?" Daisy wasn't sure what he was being asked.

"It is how you would say, uh, nigger I believe is the word." He smiled.

Now Daisy got it. He nodded his head and slowly that familiar grin crept across his face. The Russian thought it meant they were speaking the same language. Daisy ordered a couple more rounds and pressed the Russian for more information. The Russian did a few more shots before they left the bar. Daisy walked with him as they stumbled away from the bar. They helped each other until the Russian turned in the direction of his apartment.

"You good?" Daisy called to him.

"We'll talk soon," he slurred as he waved good-bye, not completely sure of what Daisy was asking him.

Daisy watched him as he staggered on toward his apartment. Daisy went about his business in the other direction. As he got farther away, he stopped staggering, walked with more stability, and caught up with Winston.

"What up? Can you hang with a herp?" Winston said as he laughed.

Daisy smiled and shook his head at Winston. "You all heard that too, huh?"

"Funniest shit I heard all day. For a second there, I thought you was gonna give him the lecture I got," Winston said.

"I wanted to fuck that dude up on the spot." Daisy was still simmering.

"We'll see him soon enough," Winston said as he led Daisy to the SUV.

The Russian stumbled through the door into his apartment building. He made his way up the stairs to his third-floor apartment hitting every part of the wall as he made his way up each flight of stairs. There was a time when this would have bothered his neighbors, but he'd lived there long enough that they had grown accustomed to his rumbling up the stairs. As he attempted to use his keys to unlock his door, they kept slipping out of his hands. He was able to get the door opened on his third attempt. He entered his apartment and relocked the door. As he turned around, he never saw the powerful knee that caught him in the stomach; then there was the bright flash of white light that only he could see as he was struck in his head. Lev caught him as his stocky, limp body began to fall.

Lev grabbed his keys, taped his mouth, and zip-tied his hands and feet before wrapping the Russian in a large rug. He eased his way into the hallway, quietly locked the door, and tossed the rug down a garbage chute, hoping the thick Russian wouldn't get stuck on the way down.

Turner waited near the bottom of the chute for the rug to come down. He could hear the body bouncing from side to side in the chute until it landed on top of the garbage. Turner climbed on the pile of rubbish to pull the rug off.

He loaded the rug onto a pushcart. Winston backed the SUV into the alley and waited to pop the tailgate. That would be Turner's cue that Lev was on his way out of the building and it was time to move. Turner kept looking at the SUV, waiting for the tailgate to open when he heard some noise coming from the garbage chute. He turned to see Big Lev landing in the heap of garbage.

"What happened?" Turner whispered.

"There were some people coming up from the second floor. The stinkin'-ass chute was my best way out," Lev said as they pushed the cart toward the SUV.

"Assess, adapt, and move on," Turner said.

Lev scooped the rug up and tossed it into the rear of the SUV; Turner pushed the cart to the side and hopped into the rear passenger seat. Lev shut the gate and got in as Winston put the car in drive and pulled out of the alley.

"You have any trouble taking him down?" Daisy asked Lev.

"Two shots and he was out. Did you drug him?" Lev responded.

"Didn't have to. He drank like a racehorse. I thought Russians were supposed to be able to hold their liquor."

"Jones got in touch with Keeble; he's meeting us at the farmhouse."

Keeble was waiting for them in the barn when they pulled the SUV in. He was dressed in black from head to toe and there was a chair waiting. Lev got out, opened the tailgate, and pulled the rug out. Keeble motioned for the men to remain silent. He pointed to clothes similar to his draped across the stall in the barn. Jones came out of the house dressed all in black. The rest of the unit did the same.

The Russian was taken out of the rug, stripped of his clothing, and tied to the seat before they removed the tape from his mouth. He began to yell and curse in Russian. Keeble nodded in Lev's direction. He wasted little time in throwing a punch at the Russian's face, which led to more cursing. Keeble nodded to Turner this time and he shot a punch right at his mouth, loosening some teeth. Keeble motioned for Winston to place the hood he was holding over the man's head.

"You yell, we punch. You don't yell, we don't punch."

Simple directions that were easy to follow but not for this Russian who started cursing again. Keeble waved his hand and all of the men took turns throwing punches. Lev, then Turner. Winston took two shots at him because he felt like he was one shot behind. Keeble stopped them after all of them had gotten in two shots.

"There are some questions that I am going to ask you— easy, simple questions. Answer them and we have no problems."

He nodded his head quickly, wanting to put an end to the assault.

"I understand that you have information that something big is about to happen," Keeble said.

"Herps!!" the Russian yelled. Whether they were covered head to toe or not, he knew who his captors were.

"You know what he just called you?" Winston asked Keeble.

"So, I'm a nigger?" Keeble asked. He didn't speak a lot of Russian but he was well aware of the word *nigger*.

Keeble had the men take him out of the seat and placed him in the Murga position. It was a torture position he was forced to maintain. If he made any move to alter that position, he was immediately struck by one of the men and forced back into the position.

Information was forthcoming, but as Keeble probed for more information, the Russian became resistant. When Keeble started the process of waterboarding, it wasn't long before they had all the answers they were looking for. The Russian had knowledge of chemical weapons and materials being transported to Afghanistan from Russia. The route they were taking was across the Aral Sea. The sea, on the border of Uzbekistan and Kazakhstan, was all but dried up.

Jones returned to the farmhouse to go to work on the computer to gather more information. Lev once again zip-tied the Russian's hands and feet, and taped his mouth before hog-tying him to the chair with the hood on his head. Lev stayed with him as the rest of the men returned to the farmhouse.

Winston contacted Griffin and gave him the information they were able to extract. Winston also made Griffin aware that the package was still with them. Griffin told them that he and two of his men were on their way to the farmhouse. He had one of his officers sync his system to Jones's when he was on his way out. The officer was able to see what Jones was doing. The fact that it only took Jones a few minutes to break into the Russian logistics system flat-out amazed him. The officer was able to interpret what Jones was finding.

When Griffin arrived, Keeble took him and the two officers out to the barn and a few minutes later, Lev was on his way back to the farmhouse. Keeble brought Griffin up to speed on the groundwork that he'd laid to establish contact with the Afghan drug lord Anemah Maasiq. They were using the scent of the weapons to draw him in, but he needed Jones to work with Griffin's officer to establish a track on Maasiq and the restaurant owner to determine if and when there was contact between the two.

"Some of this work is throwing darts up against the wall, but I hope some of it might stick. Maasiq is a thorn in my side and has been for a couple of years," Griffin admitted.

This drew a curious look from Keeble. "He's a man who has been on my radar for a number of years as well." He tried to say that calmly, but underneath, he was burning up. He wanted to hunt that bastard down and kill him.

"I know." Griffin paused to read Keeble's reaction but he gave little. "I participated in an operation in Nerkh almost two years ago that had me close to nailing him."

Nerkh is why Griffin was familiar to him. There were some questionable activities by the CIA there that had brought scrutiny to the Special Forces unit Keeble was attached to.

"You were new on the ground when the Special Forces operation was coming to an end there. Now I remember you," Keeble said. He'd never met him then but might have crossed paths with him from a distance once, maybe twice. Keeble stared at him, searching his memory to see if there was more to that story that he could immediately recall.

"If we're able to move on that operation, it should be a capture and kill operation." Griffin seemed to want Maasiq just as badly as Keeble.

"No doubt. I can promise you, I'd die trying." There was an understanding between them. "What happens to him?" Keeble motioned toward the barn.

Griffin turned his attention to the Russian and a cold, steely, measured voice came from him. "Take care of him," he instructed his officers. "I want one of your men to go with them," Griffin said to Keeble.

Lev watched the two officers as they released the Russian from the chair but left the ties on his hands and his feet and carried him to the tailgate of the SUV. When and if anyone found him, it wouldn't be all of him in the same place.

A little more than an hour later, Jones and the officer he was working online with had the information they were searching for. They'd determined that a large shipment of chemical weapons would be transported in one week from Chelyabinsk, Russia, to Mazar-i-Sharif, Afghanistan. Chemical weapons that would be tested against U.S. forces before landing in the hands of terrorists. There were four semitrucks and three jeeps scheduled to move in a convoy. They had the route of the shipment, the checkpoints along the way, and the projected time they would encounter each checkpoint.

The men sat down as a unit and examined the route the shipment was scheduled to travel. Keeble had thoughts on multiple points to attack; he was familiar with the topography of the land. But he did not make a suggestion; he wanted to see what the unit would decide. There were several points along the route they discussed, but Turner suggested to Winston that he consider the Kyzylkum Desert. Winston weighed the other options, but agreed with Turner that the desert would provide them with an advantageous opportunity to attack. Jones was able to retrieve satellite images of the desert. The area they decided on was sixty miles north of the city of Zarafshan. Daisy was studying the images looking for the best place to set himself up and provide cover for the men. Griffin watched how quickly Jones gathered information and navigated the computer and found himself wondering if he would be interested in coming to work for the CIA.

Keeble oversaw the planning for the mission, but he allowed the Unit 416 to devise the plan of attack. He was proud of the give-and-take between the men. There were places where they applied their individual strengths and knew when to defer to one another. Winston was the one in charge and made the final call, but Turner was the one who could spot potential problems and offer some insight that would tweak the decision being made. Keeble was pleased that the decisions they ultimately came to were the same ones that he would have advised for this plan of attack. The more they collaborated with each other, the faster they came up with solutions, and it wasn't long before they had a preliminary sketch of their plan of attack.

Keeble realized that the more these men could do to function without him, the better off they would eventually be. In the back of his mind, there was a week and counting before this shipment was ready to move toward Afghanistan. Privately, he hoped that Burkhanov would contact him so he could move forward in the pursuit of Maasiq.

37

The decision to tail Griffin was made in haste. Ayers was working at his computer following up on information regarding the missing weapons. He went to find Griffin to discuss the information, but as he rounded the corner to the locked office that Griffin disappeared to for the majority of his day, Ayers saw Griffin and two men he didn't know hurrying to exit the building. Curiosity got the best of him; this might give him an idea as to what he was doing with that Unit 416, he thought. Ayers hadn't seen hide nor hair of them since they arrived. Feeling he had nothing to lose, Ayers thought, *What the hell, let me see where they take me.* It wasn't the best laid plan and so far it was coming up empty.

Ayers never had the opportunity to see who was in the barn; he was never able to get close enough. There was too much open space and he would have easily been seen in the daytime. He was waiting for nightfall so he could move closer to the barn, but at dusk there was an SUV pulling out of the barn. He had no way of getting closer to the barn nor could he get back to his car in time to follow the SUV.

He suspected the old farmhouse was where Unit 416 was holed up, but he had to get a visual confirmation. As he made his way back to his vehicle he felt he was leaving empty-handed but at least he knew where the farmhouse was. It was now a matter of confirming who was staying there and what they were up to, something he wouldn't be doing if Griffin hadn't kept everyone out of the loop of what he was doing.

"The king has returned," one of the Special Ops guys said when Ayers returned to his desk.

Ayers gave him the finger, staring at him as he walked to his desk. He logged back into his computer so he could work on what he should have been doing instead of traipsing along the countryside.

"Anything new to report on the missing weapons?" Ayers called to the Special Ops corporal.

"No new intel to report," the corporal replied with a fuck-off attitude.

"This damn thing is a needle in the haystack." Ayers's comment didn't draw a reaction. He looked around for a second before walking back to the corporal's desk.

"What?" He looked up at Ayers.

"Do you know anything about a farmhouse outside of Tashkent?" Ayers asked quietly.

"Yeah, there are a lot of them," the corporal responded.

"Any of them belong to us?" Ayers wondered.

"Not that I know of. Why do you ask?"

"Need a little time away; wondered if we had something I could get away to and keep my money in my pocket." Ayers wasn't willing to share information that he wasn't sure of. No need to arouse any suspicions.

"A fucking farmhouse? Man, those missing trucks are really fucking with you."

Ayers gave him the finger again and went back to his desk. Was he the only one that gave a damn about those weapons? It was pointless for him to attempt to get any more work done this day; he was more consumed with Griffin and the farmhouse than anything else.

Lev was in the middle of nowhere, riding shotgun with the officers. Twenty-four miles from Guliston, Uzbekistan, they turned off the main road into an area with a rundown looking warehouse. The location would be nearly impossible to find if you didn't know where you were going. It gave the appearance that no one had been there in years. The driver turned off the headlights on the way in.

Lev helped them as the officers removed the Russian and dragged him into the warehouse. The zip ties had caused his hands and feet to go completely numb and his mouth was still taped. The officers followed the familiar path in the warehouse. Lev noticed the moon; it offered a little light as it shone through broken windows. The narrow hallway led to a room that was lit by a single bulb.

There was one man waiting for their arrival. He stood beside a slanted stainless steel table with surgical equipment at his ready. The stench of death still lingered in the room no matter what chemicals were used or how many times the room was scrubbed down. The Russian started to squirm as he recognized the smell. He attempted to make noise, but the muffled cries for help would go unanswered. Multiple blows to the head would silence him once again. The two officers cut the zip ties before strapping him to the table.

Lev didn't fully know what was about to happen but it didn't seem good. There were no words between the men, no instructions needed for the officers; this was not their first rodeo.

Satisfied that the Russian was secured, the waiting man picked up the syringe filled with succinylcholine and injected the Russian with fluid that paralyzed his muscles but left him awake.

The officers backed Lev out of the room; they would leave the man to his work. Lev now had a thorough understanding of how these officers took care of loose ends. As they left, Lev could hear the surgical saw being tested. The Russian could hear the saw too. Worse than that, he could feel the agonizing pain as the saw cut through his legs, dismembering them. The Russian would feel everything being done to him but the injection prevented him from being able to utter any noises.

Griffin was picked up by the officers. Before he left, he gave the men his word that he would do his best to provide the logistical support for their operation but the men would be on their own out there. When he asked if there was anything else he could do for them in the meantime, Turner didn't miss the opportunity to secure himself another flight lesson. Daisy asked Griffin if he could get a pony for Winston.

"The flight lesson I can do." Then Griffin looked at Winston. "The pony will have to wait." Griffin smiled as he got into the SUV.

They went back into the farmhouse and gathered around to take a look at their plan to intercept the weapons. Jones flashed images of the route the convoy would take and the area of the desert where they would attack from. It was a solid plan.

"That's it. We're about to get our dicks wet," Jones said.

The men laughed; they were stunned by Jones. It was one of the first simple statements that he'd made to them. Whenever he spoke, it would take some type of interpretation to decipher what he was saying.

"Yeah we are; only that's not the plan," Winston said.

"What are you talking about?" Lev was confused; he'd missed a lot and seen even more while he was with Griffin's officer.

"If they didn't come through with you, you always suspect everything about them." Winston looked at Keeble.

"You don't trust Griffin?" Turner asked.

"He's been fine so far, but we need to keep our eyes out. I trust every one of my brothers in this room though," Winston responded.

"The plan we have in front of us is the mouse. In case there are any cats out there, they have something to chase," Keeble added. "Jones, can you pull the route up again?"

"Just a second." Jones had the image up in no time.

"We didn't want to show our hand to Griffin too soon. Kee told me that I was gonna need a good plan, but that it was gonna be a dummy plan," Winston shared.

"Instead of letting the shipment get into the middle of Uzbekistan," Keeble was pointing to the route the shipment would travel, "we might have a better advantage if we attack the shipment here." Keeble pointed to the Aral Sea.

Jones was able to pull up satellite images of the massive dried-up lake bed. The lake bed was littered with old and rusted ships that had been left there more than twenty years ago.

"There are a lot of places where I could set up." Daisy was looking at all the ships. The thought of setting up a sniper location hidden amongst the ships excited him. "I think that's my spot right there." He pointed to an old tugboat elevated above the other ships. It would allow him to provide protection for his team.

"Attacking there will have us on them just after oh-one-hundred," Turner said.

"We can parachute in here." Lev pointed to an area less than half a klick from the dried lake bed. He quickly changed gears and got on board with his men.

"Exactly. If we waited until they reached the desert, it would be just about dawn," Winston added.

"Night is a better cover for all of us, but what about Daisy?" Lev smiled at the joke he was making.

Daisy looked at the other five men then. "Screw you," he said to Lev as they shared a moment of humor. Like Jones had said, they were about to get their dicks wet.

The dummy plan would remain in play; they would not notify Griffin of the change in plans until the last minute. Keeble felt a certain sense of trust toward Griffin—they had a common enemy—but Keeble was also well aware of the possible moles within the CIA. All of the equipment that they would use for the attack would remain the same but the timeline and the destination would be altered. The men all agreed that the best plan of attack would be in the Aral Sea.

Over the next week, they would rework and rehearse every facet of their attack on the Aral Sea. They would run it forward, backward, upside down, and sideways. Every man knew where he was supposed to be at every minute. Each one of them knew where everyone else was supposed to be as well.

"Sir, do you have a few minutes?" Ayers stopped Griffin as he was on his way to the hole. It was what Ayers had nicknamed the locked room, once Griffin was inside; there was no telling when Ayers would catch him again.

Griffin reluctantly stopped. "What is it?"

"I'm making some headway. I have a source that just might be on to something with the missing weapons. A few days ago, one of my informants let me know he had a contact that was on to something. He's waiting for his source to resurface," Ayers said.

Griffin paused for a split second, then said, "Thank you," before heading on his way. He was already connecting the dots; Ayers would be waiting a mighty long time for his source to resurface.

Ayers was pissed. He'd updated Griffin on the progress he was making and the asshole had barely batted an eye. Griffin was consumed with Unit 416 and seemed to have little concern for anything else.

The hovering Black Hawk interrupted Unit 416 as they were running through their scenario for the Aral Sea. There were two days before the operation was scheduled to take place and the only person missing was Turner since he was piloting the Black Hawk. The few short lessons definitely payed off for Turner because he was able to bring the chopper to a smooth and even landing. He took his helmet off and jumped out like a kid that had just had the time of his life. Daisy went to get a closer look at the M60 machine gun that it was equipped with. Within seconds, they were surrounded by all the men.

"How you got to pull this off is amazin' to me!" Winston yelled as the helicopter climbed back into the air.

"Brother, I didn't pull it off. It was the power of prayer and Sergeant Keeble," Turner said.

"It wasn't me; there was no way in hell I thought that Griffin would go for it." Keeble looked at Turner and the smile on his face. "How was it?"

Turner paused, looking up in the air as the helicopter flew away. "For me, being up there, flying, it's like being in heaven, Sarge. I don't know how to explain it; it just gives me a peace, you know?"

The guys let him have that moment to reflect. Winston, however, who was always ready with something slick to say, looked at him and said, "That's cool."

"Let's shut it down for a bit before we run it again," Lev suggested but he was already headed back to the farmhouse.

Lev was headed in to use the bathroom as the rest of them followed in behind him. Jones wasted no time in getting behind the computer as was his custom. He felt like he was missing something anytime he was away from the computer. Jones scrolled through the most recent data and leaned forward to the monitor.

"Oh, shit!" Jones opened the alert. "Sarge! I got a notification. There was contact between Maasiq and the restaurant owner."

Keeble rushed over to see what Jones had found. "No shit!" He was more excited than a kid at Christmas.

Keeble could see that the contact had been established within the last couple of hours. Mentally, he was already trying to carve out that mission for himself. Maasiq was in his sights, within his grasp, and he looked forward to hunting him down. They could revise the Aral Sea mission; the rest of the unit could handle it themselves.

"So what does that mean, Kee?" Winston asked. He could already see Keeble's wheels churning, trying to get his hands on Maasiq.

Keeble met Winston's eyes and that's when Keeble had to pump his brakes. Winston was processing everything that was in Keeble's mind just as fast as he was. But there was something else that Keeble got from Winston. These men were trained and motivated, but had never been in a live combat situation. Even though they were ready, there was no way in hell he was gonna leave them on their own right now.

"It means I need to make Griffin a point of contact with the owner while we take care of the Aral Sea."

Jones let out a big sigh of relief. Daisy gave that smile while Turner offered up a quick prayer of gratitude.

"If you want to go quickly, go alone, but if you want to go far, go together," Jones offered to the group.

"My man," Keeble said to Jones. "We're going far," Keeble said to all of the men. He was the man responsible for leading the training of this group; in many ways he was their leader. That was a job he was grooming Winston for. But they were a team that needed each other and from this point forward, they were all peers, each carrying the same weight for the success of the group.

Keeble checked his phone and saw that he had been contacted by the restaurant owner. He checked the time of the call; it was received shortly after the contact had been established between the owner and Maasiq. He didn't want to call Griffin, but he had no other choice. There was no way for him to get to Maasiq for himself, not without abandoning the men that needed him most. After bringing Griffin up to speed, Griffin wanted to get a meeting set up with the owner of the restaurant; they could meet in Tashkent if necessary.

Keeble returned the call. Burkhanov wanted to meet with Keeble as soon as they could. He smelled money and was ready to get after it. Burkhanov informed Keeble that he'd spoken with his friend and he had something of significance to discuss with him. Keeble advised him that in order to move this further along, there was someone else that he needed to bring with him.

An hour later, Griffin met Keeble in front of Samarqand. He warned Griffin the owner was already a little spooked by having another person present, so it would be best to make him feel like he was in control of the meeting.

"We need to build trust with him. This is a man who can

help me get closer to Maasiq. Since I have a few things going this week in Zarafshan, I need you to stoke the coals," Keeble said.

"We'll keep the fire burning; don't worry about that. If these weapons can get us to Maasiq, I'll make sure to fan the flames." Griffin wanted to get to Maasiq almost as badly as Keeble.

The restaurant was empty when they knocked on the door. It took a few minutes before Burkhanov opened the door. He welcomed them. "Please come in and have a seat. Would you care to join me for lunch?" he offered in broken English. He was apprehensive, but courteous.

"Thank you; we will. This is a very trusted friend of mine that I wanted you to meet," Keeble said fluently in Uzbek.

"A pleasure to meet you. My name is Ron Grayson," Griffin said perfectly in Uzbek.

Griffin hadn't mentioned to Keeble that he also spoke Uzbek, but Keeble had come to expect anything and took it in stride. A background on Ron Grayson was being created, as they spoke, by Griffin's team. The fact that he spoke Uzbek went a long way toward putting Burkhanov at ease.

"I am not as fluent in Uzbek as I would like to be," Griffin explained.

"Not a problem. I appreciate the effort," Burkhanov replied.

"My friend has been able to keep my equipment off the shelf and in safekeeping so to speak. I am sure that you understand that as we get closer to . . . doing what we are looking forward to, our net has to get a little wider to bring things in."

As they shared lunch and a couple of stories, Keeble told Burkhanov that he would be out of town for a few days. He said that was why it was necessary to introduce him to Grayson. If there was anything that would need his immediate attention regarding his friends in Afghanistan, Grayson would be able to address it.

Keeble and Griffin parted ways as they left the restaurant.

Keeble had the sense that he was being followed as he made his way back to his car. That suspicion was confirmed as he caught a glimpse of one of the Russian men he'd met a few nights back attempting to go unnoticed. Keeble continued on his way without giving away his awareness of being watched. About two miles from the farmhouse, Keeble turned onto a deserted road, but stayed close to the main road. He quickly messaged Jones with his location and suspicions.

He opened the hood of the car to take a look at the engine and waited. Minutes later he heard a car as it approached on the road. It began to slow as it drove past him. Keeble was able to make out three occupants all eyeballing him as they drove past the deserted road. He listened as the car slowed to a stop a hundred yards or so down the road; it idled there for a few seconds before it started backing up. Keeble grabbed his weapon from under the hood of the car and headed for the thick brush nearby to get what cover he could find. Fortunately there was a rut he could lie in. He scrambled to cover himself with brush.

Keeble watched the three men as they cautiously got out of their car and approached his. They weren't there to help, they were there to hunt. He watched as all three of them kept their hands near their waistbands. They pulled weapons as they surrounded the car but looked at each other dumbfounded when they realized that Keeble was missing. They spun around, trying to see what direction Keeble had gone in. They knew Keeble couldn't have gotten too far away from them. As they spread out in different directions, Keeble lost sight of two of them. He listened as the footsteps got farther away. But one walked to within ten feet of him and stopped for a second before walking right by him. He stayed completely still, barely breathing as his pulse began to race. Keeble needed to wait fifteen seconds so the men would be farther away from each other before he made a move.

There was the sound of a car approaching fast from the opposite direction. The three men heard it too. Startled by the noise, they started heading back to their car. Keeble tripped the man as he came back across his path. As he crashed to the ground, Keeble was on him. He locked him in a choke and pounded his head into the ground. He could see the other two men scrambling back to their car with their weapons raised ready to fire at the oncoming vehicle. As they took cover between the cars, Keeble fired off a couple of rounds in their direction, drawing their attention back to him. They hesitated to fire because Keeble had stuck their friend in front of him. That hesitation provided enough of a delay that the oncoming vehicle was able to hit its brakes, turn the car, and swerve into their car. The impact of the sideswipe was enough to throw the men into Keeble's car. Daisy popped out of the car, quickly raised his weapon, and fortunately for them fought the urge to squeeze off two hot rounds into them. Lev got out of the driver's side and raised his weapon as well to hold them at bay.

Twenty minutes later, Griffin's men had three more guests to take for a ride to the warehouse in the country. As the men were loaded, Griffin took a look around to survey the damage to the vehicles. He just shook his head. The message was clear; there would be no more trips into town before they took on the mission. No words were exchanged before Griffin went back to his headquarters.

38

"Again!" Winston yelled.

All six men gathered around one another. They were simulating their exit from their aircraft into the lake bed of the Aral Sea.

"Go. How long until we hit ground?" Winston asked quickly.

"Thirteen seconds," Lev answered.

"Then what happens?" Winston demanded.

Every time a question was answered, Winston jumped right on it with a question about the next position they would take up. He was relentless, but knew it would increase their precision. Keeble nodded his head at every challenge Winston offered. To their credit, the entire unit was on top of it. Every one of them understood that this was how they would keep each other alive.

At 1500, they stopped the dry runs to perform their equipment and weapons check. In eleven hours, they would be at the Aral Sea stopping a shipment of chemical weapons from getting into the hands of terrorists. The operation that they had trained for was at hand.

Once Jones finished his weapons and equipment check, he went inside and got on his computer. There was an alert that he opened immediately. It was information on Mazar-i-Sharif, the final destination of the chemical weapons. He called Keeble in to take a look at the information.

Keeble stared at the information on the screen. "Are you sure about that?" He couldn't take his eyes off of the data in front of him.

"One hundred percent, Sarge. What do you want me to do?"

Keeble looked outside to his men. "Get me every bit of information you can on that compound. Don't miss a detail."

"What are you going to do?" Jones thought it might have been better to keep this info to himself.

"I don't know, but I'll figure it out. Good work; and get that shit set up for Griffin."

Jones bypassed the CIA's firewall, broke into their system, and altered the flight times for their drop by four hours. Instead of 0400 they were now scheduled for takeoff at 0000 and their pickup was set for 2200. Griffin would receive a delayed e-mail of the change at 0100.

The dummy attack plan was scheduled to be released to the CIA and Special Ops at 2300. Griffin's private team was aware of the plan to attack at Zarafshan, but the altered plan to attack at the Aral Sea would be a shock to him as well. He was putting the information out to the rest of the team on the ground in Uzbekistan so they could witness firsthand how Unit 416 functioned in a hostile situation.

Once their prep work was complete, the men sat down to a meal together before they would try to get some rest. There was very little conversation among them. As they looked from one man to another, there was a confidence, trust, and loyalty that these men felt for one another. They understood what they were undertaking wasn't about them or the money that enticed them, or the men they used to be. This was about standing with each other and serving their country with honor.

When it was time to get some rest, no one went to their room. They sat with each other. If they could sleep, they did. If they needed to check their equipment again, they did. If they needed to review their attack, they did that too. Turner, however, had the need to pray and before they did their own individual thing, they got on their knees and prayed with him.

Ayers hung up his phone; he was stunned—silent but not surprised. His competence had been challenged and his life threatened. As if it wasn't bad enough to be threatened, the threat was made by his own family member.

His cousin was expecting a shipment to be delivered within the next forty-eight hours and he was questioned as to whether or not the CIA had knowledge of the shipment. And if they had knowledge, what were the plans to stop it? Ayers assured him that he was not aware of any plans in action, nor had there been suspicion of any shipment that his cousin spoke of. Any assurances that Ayers had to offer held little or no value to his cousin at this point. That was largely due to his massive failure a month ago when he'd dropped the ball. The weapons that were hijacked and seemingly disappeared into thin air were his responsibility. Ayers had had a plan in place; he'd had a team set to steal the weapons and hand them over to his cousin, but that plan was foiled by someone hijacking his hijack. His frantic search to find out what had happened to the weapons had more to do with his cousin than U.S. security.

Information over the last month, since the incident, had been very hard for him to come by. Any work or any leads that he

tried to follow led to dead ends or left him hanging on informants' words, waiting for more information. And with Griffin in
charge, he felt like he was spinning his wheels.

Ayers made note of the time. He'd been at home too long
and it was time to get to work. At least there, he'd try to follow
up on his cousin's request. As he locked his door, he looked to
see if there was anything unusual, checked his car before getting in, and then did a quick check of the interior before starting
it. He took a deep breath as he turned the ignition and let it out
as the engine turned over. Ayers did not take the threat to be an
idle one. If he failed his cousin again, he already had plans in
place to take up hiding in Pakistan.

Griffin was in the war room getting a briefing from the CIA
and Special Ops joint team when Ayers arrived. Griffin looked
at his watch.

"Glad to see you could join us today," Griffin said pleasantly.

Ayers looked at him and nodded to him as he headed to his
desk. Anybody that knew Ayers knew what he was thinking: *asshole*.

Griffin knew exactly what Ayers was thinking. *Wait until he
gets a look at Unit 416 tonight*, he thought.

At 2200, the transport arrived at the farmhouse for Unit 416.
They loaded their equipment and themselves in five minutes and
made the forty-minute trip to the airfield. It was just before 2300.
As they hustled onto the C-130, they rigged up their parachutes
and tactical gear. At 2300, Jones got an alert; TRANSMISSION SENT.
Griffin, the CIA, and Special Ops had just been delivered notification of the operation.

"Somebody want to tell me what the hell this is!?" Ayers erupted.

He was in the war room with everyone else. Griffin called

them in and was waiting for the notification. There were surprised looks on almost all the faces in the room; the only ones not surprised were Griffin and the members of his private detail. A shipment of chemical weapons was being intercepted at 0400 in the Kyzylkum Desert, sixty miles north of Zarafshan.

"We have it on good intel that chemical weapons are being transported to Afghanistan. At oh-four-hundred, Unit 416 will be moving to secure it. That's five hours from now. You're all invited to see how they function," Griffin advised.

"Why weren't we informed?" Ayers was faced with a bigger dilemma.

"It is my operation," Griffin said slowly.

Ayers held his tongue. Any comment he made would cause him far more trouble than it was worth. He stormed out of the room, then out of the building and didn't stop until he reached his car. This goddamn Unit 416 and Griffin were doing their best to get him killed. Ayers knew what he had to do; he would have to get rid of that unit before their existence got rid of him. He took a quick look around before pulling the phone from under the front seat and sent a quick message—*Attack 0400 near Zarafshan.* Ayers hit send, grabbed a cigarette from his glove compartment, and smoked it before going back into the building.

Keeble took a look at all of his men as the plane began to taxi down the runway. They gave reassuring nods to each other. There was a steely look in their eyes; not a single man wavered. This was the easy part; the question would be how they would respond when the bullets started to fly.

"How you doin', Sarge?" Lev asked.

All eyes turned to Keeble. It seemed as if everyone wanted to ask that question, but none was willing to be the first. "I'm good. I have an attack plan that is rock solid. More than that, I have a group of men . . . I have a group of brothers that I have never been prouder to take the field of battle with!"

"I am an elite soldier who arrives at the cutting edge of battle by land, sea, or air," Winston said.

"My country expects me to move farther, faster, and fight harder than any other soldier," Daisy said.

"I will show the world that I am a specially selected and well-trained soldier," Jones followed.

"I will always keep myself mentally alert, physically strong, and morally straight," Turner added.

"I will shoulder more than my share of the task whatever it may be, one hundred percent and then some," Lev said proudly.

"Surrender is not a Unit 416 word," Keeble started before they all joined in. "I will never leave a fallen *brother* to fall into the hands of the enemy and under no circumstances will I ever embarrass my country. I will fight on to my objective!"

These men, this band of brothers, knew they were prepared to meet the challenges of the next few hours.

Jones received an alert notification; it was 0100 and an e-mail had been delivered to Griffin. Everything was right on schedule.

Griffin was in his office locked away with his team when he read the notification.

"You sons of bitches!" he said with an approving smile.

"What is it, sir?" an officer asked.

"Was there a change in the pickup time for Unit 416?"

"No, sir," the officer said while keying in information. "Ah, yes, sir, the pickup time, flight time, and drop have all been altered."

"The show is going to start a little earlier than expected. It's fucking brilliant! They're attacking at the Aral Sea." Griffin laughed as he shook his head. "Get me a visual on the Aral Sea and I need it on the screen in the war room and I need it quickly. All of our timelines have moved up by four hours. That means we only have fifty-nine minutes until our boys start rockin' and rollin'." Griffin was looking at his watch.

39

The temperature dropped to eighty-two degrees on the dry grounds of the Aral Sea as night fell upon the abandoned area. There was not a sound to be heard anywhere. That peace was disturbed at 0200 when the sound of a C-130 flying at eight hundred feet churned through the air and disrupted the stillness of the night.

Keeble stood at the exit door as it opened up and gave the men the order to stand up. Jones and Daisy would exit on Keeble's side while Lev, Turner, and Winston would exit from the other side. Keeble gave the order for the first jumpers to stand in the door as he waited for the readiness light to turn green.

"Go!" Keeble yelled as the light went to green.

The six men exited the aircraft from both doors. Six seconds later, all the men were clear of the cargo doors, heads tucked tight, and counting to four. As the parachutes deployed, catching air, they would look up to check their canopy and they could see the C-130 as it began to climb high into the night sky.

It was a full tactical military jump made under the sweet cover of darkness. They would be on the ground in thirteen and a half seconds, long before the C-130 would make it back to its cruising altitude.

The brevity of the time in the air wasn't the only hazard of this tactical jump; they also had to use the toggle knobs on their chutes to dodge the remains of the old rusting ships as they landed. Jones landed on top of one of the vessels. He hurried to clear himself of his chute and tucked it in a corner of the ship. The rest of the unit dumped their parachute equipment at the ship nearest their landing spot.

Once the men reassembled, they put on their night vision goggles and waited for Turner to locate the attack position. He pinpointed the location with his compass and seconds later, he charted the distance. Once he had his bearings, he let them know it was less than one klick to the northeast.

They hightailed it through the dried-out riverbed to their access site, keeping their eyes peeled for a possible ambush. Abandoned ships littered both sides of the pass and they set up a half-mile-wide perimeter. Daisy set up in his chosen vantage point. He was four hundred and fifty meters to the right of the men on an elevated ridge. Keeble, Lev, and Turner were on the ground spread out on opposite sides of the pass while Winston hunkered down on top of one of the abandoned ships. Jones covered the back side; he initiated a radio check with the men once they were in position. It would be their last verbal contact; all other contact between them would be done with hand signals.

Griffin was set up in the war room with a handful of the CIA and Special Ops teams that were hanging around. They had limited visual access to the area; with such short notice it was the best he could get. Members of his team were working to improve the visual. They were able to pick up the men's movements as they got themselves into position.

Ayers was coming back in from another trip to his car when he heard the activity in the war room and went to check it out. Everyone in the room had their eyes on the large monitor. He looked at the grainy image; it almost took his breath away. It looked like an ambush setting up. He checked the time on his watch, even checked the wall clock. There were four hours before there was a scheduled attack.

"What the hell's going on?" Ayers pointed to the monitor. "That's not Zarafshan."

"No, it's the Aral Sea," Griffin replied but kept his eyes on the monitor.

"What the f . . . what are they doing there?" Ayers was panicking but doing a good job of not letting it show. "This is the kind of operation I should have been in charge of."

"Mr. Ayers, are you questioning my judgment?" Griffin took his eyes off of the monitor and moved his focus to Ayers.

"No, sir. Just would like to be kept up to speed."

"Noted, Mr. Ayers. Have a seat. Now this is where we get to find out if they know how to dance," Griffin said, reminding Ayers of his personal invitation. Griffin looked at the rest of the room, daring anyone to make a condescending comment.

Ayers reluctantly took a seat while trying to figure out how to get out of this room without raising suspicion.

Winston used SkyHawk binoculars to keep an eye on Daisy; they were equipped with video capability and night vision technology. Daisy heard the convoy before he spotted it. He put his night vision goggles back on and located the convoy as it made its way to the mouth of the Aral Sea. The lights were off, but the vehicles moved at a good clip, about thirty miles per hour. The approach was from Kazakhstan, just as expected. He flashed a hand signal to Winston who gave the heads-up to the rest of the men. Daisy counted the number in the convoy and something was wrong. There were supposed to be seven vehicles in the convoy but he only counted four vehicles. Two large trucks and a jeep were missing. He signaled Winston to let him know the number wasn't what they'd expected. Daisy scanned the horizon to see if the other three vehicles were trailing farther back. There was nothing else behind them, not a thing out there moving for miles.

Only four vehicles, Winston thought. He considered the possibility of a trap and thought it might be best to abort the mission. For a brief second, he looked to Keeble's vantage point. He was solid and ready to roll. So were all of the men. Assess, adapt, and move on—Winston took a deep breath and signaled Daisy. It was time to lock in.

The convoy slowed as they approached the area where abandoned ships caused their path to narrow. Winston waited for the convoy as it crept closer into their crosshairs. He was patient and calm, and once they were perfectly aligned, he signaled Keeble who nodded, then gave a quick thumbs-up to the men on the ground. They had a three-second countdown before the attack began with Keeble, Lev, and Turner. They fired quickly and accurately, shooting out the tires of the vehicles first, then following that with rapid fire on the vehicles. Objective number one was to eliminate their ability to escape. When the convoy realized they were under attack, the lead jeep attempted to pull into a covering position in front of the trucks. Daisy drew a deep breath and exhaled as he squeezed the trigger. His first shot took out the lead driver before he could get his jeep set. The driver never knew what hit him and the jeep crashed into one of the rusted ships. Three other men jumped out of the jeep returning fire as they ran for cover. Lev got a shot off, striking one of them in the leg while the other two headed in Turner's direction. Turner fired two shots, dropping one but missing the other. Keeble picked up where Turner missed, stopping the second man instantly. Lev jumped to his feet and closed the distance to the man on the ground. Lev never heard the bullets whizzing by him as he pulled out a bowie knife. The wounded man tried to reach for a handgun and fired wildly as Lev dug the knife into his chest.

The jeep covering the rear of the convoy pulled close to the trucks. The four men got out and headed for the trucks. Daisy fired two more shots before they got there. Both kill shots struck the driver of each truck in the head. One of the jeep's occupants got his hands on an automatic weapon and opened fire erratically, accidentally striking one of his own men. Unit 416 took cover. Turner signaled the other men that he was doubling back deeper behind the ships. Daisy waited patiently for his next shot. Jones tried to get a fix on what they were doing. Two men were trying to work their way to the trucks' cabins. As they did, several men were climbing out of the back of the trucks firing AK-47s.

"They're going to try to blow it!" Jones yelled.

"The hell they are!" Winston yelled, exposing himself as he ran across the bow of the ship, squeezing off quick rapid-fire rounds at the men around the trucks.

A man with a machine gun moved to fire at Winston but it opened another clear shot for Jack and he did not fail. Keeble was on the ground picking off one man after the other as they climbed out of the trucks. Daisy was able to pick some of them off as well. The men who were working their way toward the cabin turned their guns on the exposed Winston and started firing on him. Winston was forced to take cover again. Lev was able to get his hands on one of them. He snatched him down from behind and started choking him out. As the man's body started to go limp, Lev pulled the bowie knife across his neck with such force that it nearly decapitated him. The other man, horrified by Lev's brutality, turned to shoot Lev but Turner was able to get a shot off on him before he could squeeze a round off at Lev. The man fell dead beside Lev. He shoved the body of the man he'd killed next to him and took cover. Unit 416 eliminated the targets quickly and efficiently.

"Come out with your hands up!" Keeble ordered; then he issued the same command in Turkic and finally in Russian. With no response, he fired several warning shots, and then issued the commands again while his men maintained their cover. Keeble moved carefully toward the trucks. Suddenly machine gun fire erupted; Keeble and Lev hit the deck in search of cover under the trucks. There was another man in the rear of the truck firing at anything he thought he saw moving. As he moved to reposition himself, Daisy smiled and squeezed off another round. There were no more shots fired.

They cautiously moved in on the trucks while Daisy and Jones kept their eyes on the perimeter. Once they were sure that all threats had been neutralized, they began the recovery part of this mission.

There was one survivor of the convoy but judging by the looks of his wounds, he did not have a whole lot of time left in this life. Lev, Turner, and Winston took inventory while Keeble attempted to communicate with the mortally wounded crewman.

"Hello, comrade," Keeble said in Russian. "We want to help you but you have to help us. Where are the other trucks?"

The man made a motion for Keeble to come closer to him so he could speak. As Keeble leaned in the man attempted to spit in his face but he didn't have enough strength to do that. Lev was walking by when he saw this. He stood in front of them with his bowie knife in his hand. Looking at Keeble, he cleared his throat and shrugged his shoulders.

"All you gotta do is say the word, Sarge," Lev said.

"Hold what you got, big man. He won't be here but a minute," Keeble said but he was also sure the hills had eyes.

After assessing the inventory, they quickly realized this was only half of the payload they were expecting. Jones opened up satellite communications with Special Ops and called for the extraction team. He gave them the coordinates of a clearing one klick to the south, reported the action from the scene, and signed off immediately. Unit 416 gathered their equipment and bailed out of the area headed for their extraction point. They had fourteen minutes before the Black Hawk was due in. It would carry them back to the base camp.

As Griffin watched the satellite feed of the men clearing the area, he was a little disappointed that they hadn't retrieved the full load of chemical materials and that they would have to regroup, but he was impressed with the unit's efficiency and teamwork. He had two other takeaways from watching the group: Levern Smith was fucking brutal, and somehow word must have gotten out on their planned attack in Zarafshan. He turned to the men in the room whose eyes had been locked onto the action on the screen. Ayers was watching him. Griffin smiled in his direction.

"Looks like they can break-dance and you're still doing the two-step. I need my people back in the hole. Everybody else, I need a lock on the remainder of that shipment ASAP and I need you to sit tight right here. We have forty minutes to clear that site and get those chemical weapons out of there. Once it doesn't make that next checkpoint, the Afghans will come looking for them."

Once he had his team back in their secured space he began

to break down their next steps. "How long until we extract them?" Griffin didn't want anyone out there to have any information on the Unit 416 team.

"We have a twelve-minute ETA," one of the men responded.

"Communicate to the Black Hawk crew that I want Jones to fire up his laptop immediately when he's on board, then open up communications so I can talk to him."

"Copy that."

"How far?" Winston asked Turner. Winston had a sense that something was not right. He glanced at Keeble, who appeared to be unfazed, and that settled him.

"Just over half a klick," Turner said as he checked his compass and map. They were making good time and would be at the extraction point in less than ten minutes.

"Hey, stop, stop, stop," Lev said from the front of the group. "You hear that?" he said as he lowered his voice.

Keeble signaled for everyone to switch over to their headsets. Jones pointed toward a line of trees and the men made a move for it. Daisy was putting his night vision goggles back on when he spotted two vehicles headed toward them; they were coming from the direction of the extraction point.

"I see two vehicles headed our way, no lights. Looks like small trucks and they ain't ours," he whispered into his headset as he made his way to the cover.

"I thought we had at least a half hour before they missed their checkpoint." Winston was thinking out loud.

"Our friends back there may have gotten a distress signal out. Probably got them some backup out there." Keeble spoke quietly.

"Spread out in this cover and stay out of sight. We're gonna let this probe get past us. Best not to engage unless we have to; we have a schedule to keep," Winston ordered.

Keeble was thinking that this was the kind of shit that made his life worth living. He was sure they would have to engage them soon enough. If not now, then when the Black Hawk showed up.

They were all crouched, locked, loaded, and keeping still and very quiet, waiting as the vehicles, carrying a total of nine men, drove slowly past them. They would wait for the trucks to pull over the crest of the hill before moving again. The squawk on Jones's sat-com broke the silence; he'd signed off earlier, but had not shut the system down. Jones muffled it as fast as he could, but it was too late. There was yelling from the vehicles and they came to a stop when they picked up the noise.

One after the other, the trucks started to turn around, turning on their headlights. The glare blinded Daisy as he removed his night vision goggles. Winston and Keeble both ordered the men to take the offensive. They started squeezing off rounds at the oncoming trucks, taking out headlights and windshields. The occupants fired back in their direction hoping to hit anything.

The driver of one of the trucks lost control of his vehicle and clipped the rear end of the other truck, tossing some of the men out of the beds of the trucks and causing both trucks to lose control. The clipped truck rolled to its side, dislodging the remaining men. The other truck sped forward toward the trees, running headfirst into them and narrowly missing a partially blinded Daisy. There was no gunfire coming at them. Jones and Turner continued to fire on the rolled truck but no one took shots at the one near Daisy. Instead, Winston, Lev, and Keeble moved in for hand-to-hand combat. One of the men staggered from the truck but had enough wits about him to grab Daisy, putting him in a choke hold as he reached for a knife. Lev launched himself at him, causing him to lose his grip on everything. Lev grabbed the man by his head and violently ripped his head to the right; hearing the neck snap in his hands gave him a rush. Keeble could see the driver was already dead from a gunshot wound and turned his attention to a man who was reaching for his weapon. Keeble locked eyes with him, but only for a second; he refused to see into his soul as he took it from him. Keeble struck him with the heel of his hand, catching the bottom of his nose and driving his nasal passage into his brain. Winston used the truck as leverage to swing around and kick one man into another as they were coming to their feet. Once they were down again, Winston grabbed a knife, jamming it into the back of the one closest to him several times before turning his attention to the other man who was still dazed when Winston grabbed him by the head and began smashing his face into the side of the truck. Blood spurted from his face after his head was thrust into the metal. Winston could feel the bones shattering in his hands as he shoved a few more times for good measure.

Jones and Turner played cleanup on the other truck, firing at anything that was still moving. There was no hand-to-hand combat with them. Instead, one laid down suppressive fire as the other moved closer to where the men had been thrown from the trucks. They would alternate this pattern until they stood over three lifeless bodies. Jones looked down at the death in front of them realizing for the first time that his hands had been the cause of it. It rocked him and he choked hard as he swallowed it in.

"Brother, it was them or us," Turner said to Jones. It was just as much for himself as it was for Jones. He knew he would have to rectify this with his soul, but now was not the time.

"Anybody see anything else?" Winston radioed.

All clear came back from every one of the men. The men gathered back together and once Daisy could see well enough, they rucked up and got the hell out of there. They were cutting it close for making it to the extraction point on time and they damn sure couldn't wait to see if anyone else would be joining them. They double-timed it to a point where they could take cover and wait on the helicopter.

As they heard the Black Hawk approach, Turner popped a flare to mark their spot and the helicopter quickly swooped in. It was a two-meter sprint from their cover to the clearing. Winston gave the order for the men to move out as the bird was hovering to make a landing. Daisy led the way with Turner beside him; Lev covered Jones while Winston and Keeble brought up the rear.

"Aw, shit!" Keeble said as he stepped on some uneven terrain and pain shot through his lower leg. It was only for an instant, but it caused him to stumble before he caught his balance.

Winston grabbed at him to make sure he was steady. "I got you, Sarge." They were twenty yards away from the bird.

Just as they hopped into the Black Hawk, they could see headlights approaching in the distance.

"We got company, boys!" Daisy yelled.

"Let's get the hell out of here!" Winston yelled to the Black Hawk crew as they started taking fire from a distance.

Daisy and Turner returned fire as the Black Hawk began to take off. Keeble took a position on the railing behind Turner to return fire. Lev did the same behind Daisy. Turner hopped on board while Daisy continued to lay down fire. He was so obsessed with shooting that Big Lev had to snatch him into the bird by his LCE. Daisy dangled and continued to fire as the bird took flight, all while Lev struggled to bring him in. Bullets began to whiz by closer and closer. Keeble ordered the Black Hawk crew to start laying down fire as a rocket launcher was fired at them. It narrowly missed as the bird tilted to the left. The pilot had no idea the rocket was coming; he tilted the bird to give Lev some leverage in getting Daisy on board. The crew fired two rockets back and laid down enough machine gun fire to get clear of the area.

The rush of the firefight began to ease as they moved farther away from the area. Jones banged away at his laptop, trying to locate the rest of the shipment. The other men checked each other out to make sure that the unit came out clean. They gave each other a couple of "Atta boys" for their near-perfect execution with their intended targets.

"You good, Kee? How's the leg?" Winston asked.

"It's good. It's just something else to work with. Way to lead out there." Keeble was short on compliments and this was one of them.

"Thanks, Sarge."

"Hey, Sergeant Kee, I got a lock on the weapons," Jones said.

"Let's hear it; don't be shy now," Keeble said.

"The shipment is four hours ahead, headed for the Uzbek and Afghan border. They are approximately four hours from the border."

"Son of a bitch. The CIA give you that intel?" Keeble wondered out loud.

"I don't have a thing from them."

"Get me Griffin on the sat phone."

Within seconds, Jones was able to make contact with Griffin.

"Do you have an update on the balance of the shipment?" Keeble asked.

"My men are still working on that and we will have a revised plan of attack once we get you back on the ground at the compound." Griffin paused for a second; he should have had his people trying to track down the missing vehicles.

"We are scrubbing that plan, Griffin; it is a waste of our time. We are rerouting for Denau, Uzbekistan. We need two armored jeeps and a truck that look like traditional Uzbek vehicles," Keeble said before handing the phone to Jones.

Jones gave Griffin a list of the communications equipment that he needed and the coordinates of where they would meet the vehicles. When Griffin questioned the need for the equipment, Keeble snatched the phone back and said if the equipment was not there when they arrived in two hours, then he could tell him exactly who his mole was.

Unit 416 devised a plan to intercept the remaining weapons at the border of Uzbekistan and Afghanistan. The materials were headed for a compound in Mazar-i-Sharif. Jones had researched the facility yesterday and broke down the specifics of the compound for them. It was eighteen thousand square feet in a wooded area with most of the building underground; it was guarded by twenty-four Taliban rebels, all heavily armed. Keeble also revealed to the men that the compound was under the control of the Afghan drug lord Anemah Maasiq. Every single one of them froze. By now they all knew the name of Anemah Maasiq and what finding him meant to Keeble. He told his men they had the option of letting this mission cool if they wanted to because they would be on their own. But once they intercepted the weapons, he was going after Maasiq. There was very little discussion; they were with Kee. Keeble gave the pilot the order and the copilot entered the destination coordinates.

Griffin contemplated his next move. He looked at the map of Uzbekistan and Afghanistan. Denau was a city lying to the north of the border en route to Mazar-i-Sharif; they were separated by a distance of sixty miles. He quickly surmised that Keeble and his unit were planning to intercept the shipment there.

Griffin went back to the war room to see what progress had been made. He looked at the monitor and the map. Not much had changed since he'd left the room.

"Ayers, what do you have on those materials that were missing?" Griffin asked while still looking at the map. He kept his back to Ayers.

"We're turning up dead ends," Ayers responded as something on the screen drew his attention. "We'll keep digging," he said as he slid his chair away from his desk. Ayers looked as if he'd seen a ghost. He moved closer to his desk and went back to work. He wanted everyone to know that at least he was trying to get things done.

"Hmph. Good enough." Griffin thought, *Jones had already turned something up*. There was definitely a problem with this team on the ground. Griffin would deal with that soon enough, but right now he needed to get back to his own team and get on the horn; he had less than two hours to move hell and high water to get Unit 416 what they needed.

Ayers watched Griffin as he left. Once he was sure that Griffin was gone, he eased out of the war room and went to the bathroom. The message he'd received made him sick to his stomach. It was one thing for him to be threatened; he expected that, especially after what Unit 416 had done. It was another thing entirely for his wife and children to be threatened.

40

Two hours later, Unit 416 was loaded up and traveling the dirt roads of Uzbekistan to head off the convoy of materials at the Afghan border. Keeble didn't know if they would get this far but Griffin had come through for the boys with one truck and two jeeps. Keeble took one jeep alone; Winston took the jeep loaded with the communications equipment and took Jones with him. Turner drove the truck with Lev and Daisy in tow.

Unit 416 searched for any signs of activity as they approached the border. Jones was hard at work on his computer gathering information on the border and the layout of the land. There were about fifteen minutes until the sun was due to rise so they still had the advantage of using the predawn darkness as their cover. Once they were parked, Lev, Turner, and Daisy gathered by Winston's jeep. Jones was gathering some final intel while Keeble did some final checks of the area to make sure the coast was clear. A few minutes later, he joined the men.

"All right, boys, we gotta move fast," Lev said.

"Jones, how ya comin'?" Winston called back to the jeep.

"Got some printouts coming now." Jones got out of the jeep and handed papers to each of the men. He'd laid out attack points and positions where the men could set up and take advantage of the nearby abandoned buildings. There was a little drawback; the best way for them to attack would separate them. The distance between Winston and Keeble would cover almost a mile. The distance was something that brought that familiar smile to Daisy's face.

"Now I really get a chance to put that scope to the test," Daisy explained as he felt everybody focusing on his grin.

Turner gave a brief word of prayer before Keeble dispatched the men to scout out their positions for the ambush. It would be at least another hour before the convoy was expected but they understood that time moved fast and so should they. Communications were to stay open at all times. Keeble would stay closer to the checkpoint at the border until the men were set; then he would move into position. But for now, he found a little covering for his jeep.

Keeble had been waiting about ten minutes for the men to let him know they were set when he heard the sound of a vehicle approaching from the south, it was coming from Afghanistan. It was not at all in the direction that his men were setting up their ambush. It was a modern BMW using only its parking lights, but it was only one vehicle.

"I got a vehicle approaching from the south. No headlights." He took up a position behind the armored jeep.

"You need us to peel back, Sarge?" Winston replied.

"I only make one vehicle." Keeble was looking to see if there were any other vehicles or any movement whatsoever. "I'm good, but keep the lines open."

Keeble held his position, trying to determine what type of threat he was faced with.

The car slowed to a stop as it neared the border. Keeble waited, partially hidden behind the jeep. A man stepped out of the passenger side of the BMW. Keeble immediately recognized Ayers. What was he doing on the ground in Afghanistan?

"Keeble?" Ayers called.

"Ayers?" Keeble maintained his position behind the car.

The guys heard him say the name over the communications system. The name *Ayers* was repeated and Winston asked, "What the fuck?"

"What are you doing here?" Keeble locked Ayers in his sights and prepared to squeeze the trigger.

Ayers raised his hands, making sure that Keeble knew he didn't pose a threat to him.

"I have something I think you would be very interested in." Ayers still had his hands up as he moved very slowly toward the backseat of the car. "We've been after the same thing, you and me."

Ayers reached into the backseat of the car and pulled out a hooded man who was tied up. The bloodstains on his clothing indicated that he'd needed some alternative persuasion to take this ride with Ayers. Ayers stood him up; he didn't want to alarm Keeble so he slowly reached for the man's hood. Ayers snatched the hood off his head, revealing something that shocked Keeble.

"Motherfucker," Keeble said slowly as his blood began to boil. He heard his men ask what was happening.

"I know this is what you want," Ayers snarled. "I've been after it too."

"Anemah Maasiq." Keeble couldn't believe his eyes. He rose up from his position, revealing himself. He locked eyes with Maasiq; he wanted to use his bare hands to squeeze the life out of Maasiq. Instead, he locked Maasiq back into his sights. The answers to his questions would come later.

"I've have spent years tracking this man down. Where're your me—"

Before Ayers finished his sentence, three shots rang out from the driver's side of the BMW. One shot struck Keeble in his right shoulder and the other two hit him cleanly in the upper torso. The impact kicked him back ten feet. It is where Keeble went down and where he stayed. Ayers walked closer to Keeble to get good look at his handiwork.

"Who's dancing now, you son of a bitch?"

"Cousin, we need to go; they'll be back here any second." Maasiq spoke in Dari.

"Nice work." Ayers admired his dirty work. "If you kill the head, the body will die!" He untied Maasiq, put him back into the rear of the car, and jumped in beside him. The driver wasted no time in getting the car turned around before speeding back in the direction from which he came.

Winston heard the three shots ring out. "Kee! Kee!" He called into the mic of his headset, but there was no response. "Sarge, come in." Still there was no response from Keeble.

"What was that?" Lev asked over the radio.

"Hustle back to the border. Leave Jack on the hill locked and loaded to cover me."

Winston reached the border checkpoint first. He saw Keeble lying on the ground, ten feet away from the jeep with blood all around him. Winston rushed to his side; his body was motionless but he was still breathing. He could hear Keeble gurgling, drowning in his own blood.

"I got ya, Sarge. I got ya." Winston quickly scanned Keeble, realizing how much trouble Keeble was in. He moved as fast as he could back to his jeep, grabbed some QuikClot and bandages. When he was back at Keeble's side, he tore off Keeble's equipment, ripped his shirt open, and saw how fast Keeble's blood was escaping his body. Winston patched up every hole he could find with the QuikClot and wrapped the bandages around him.

"Siq . . . Maasiq . . . it was him . . . Ayers." Keeble was gasping and struggling.

"I know; we're going to get him, but you gonna be fine, Sarge! You hear me! You gonna be fine."

Keeble mumbled, no longer able to form words. His strength was fading fast. "Thank you." He smiled, knowing the end was coming. "Your show," were the last audible words he spoke.

"No, don't do this, Sarge. Sarge! You fight, goddamnit!" Winston yelled, tears flooding his face.

"Fellas, we got company. There are six vehicles coming in, two to three men per and they ain't friendlies," Daisy squawked over the radio.

"Fuck, they got Kee, and I don't see those fuckers anywhere," Winston said into his mic. He grabbed Keeble, putting his body into their jeep.

"Jones, I want you to get back to higher ground. Take cover and start laying down fire," Winston instructed as he grabbed his weapons out of the jeep. "On the hop, son; let's move!"

"We'll be there in a second," Lev said. And that's when the bullets started flying.

"Take cover! Ambush!" Winston stayed low and scrambled to Keeble's jeep.

They were firing everything they had. AKs and machine guns forced Winston to stay put in the armored jeep. Lev arrived with the truck and pulled in front of the jeep. Turner fired from the passenger side. Daisy started firing shots from his vantage point. He struck two drivers, causing both cars to careen off the dirt road, overturn in a rut, and take all of its occupants with them. Jones also began returning fire.

"We got some rebels on our hands," Daisy said into the mic.

"They're settin' up a wall with their vehicles. Looks like they want to have a shootout." Daisy was steadily shooting at the bodies near the overturned cars.

"Jack, you see what I see? On your right, sixteen hundred meters," Jones said.

Daisy was too busy exchanging gunfire with the rebels to take a glance off to his right.

"What do you got?" Winston asked while returning fire.

"Two trucks and a jeep. Somebody told these fuckers we would be here," Jones said.

"Keeping us occupied while they took a different route," Winston said.

"That's why they hunkered down," Lev said. "How's your shot, Jack?"

"I'm working to get better," Daisy replied. "I see a grenade launcher." Daisy settled in for a shot. As the grenade launcher took a stand to fire toward the truck, Daisy's round struck the grenade launcher in the shoulder. He fired the round toward his own men instead of at the truck, forcing them to take cover from the explosion.

"Jones, hit these guys with two rockets. Lev, get that M60; Turn, you cover too. When we stop, you move up and we cover you. Roger?"

"Roger," Turner said.

"We're moving in on these bitches! Daisy, keep laying it down. Love what you're doin', bro. Move out!"

Unit 416 closed in on them very quickly. Jones fired the rocket launcher; Daisy picked off anything that stood up while Winston, Lev, and Turner advanced on their position. Winston and Turner stayed low, but every time Lev made a move, he stood up like he was going across the middle for a pass, daring them to shoot him while he was getting off rounds with the M60. They shot at anything that moved. Jones started to send one more rocket, but thought better of it because Unit 416 was too close to their position. There was no return fire from the opposition. From what Jones could tell, the threat had been neutralized. Then the barrage of gunfire started up again; they were baiting the unit to draw them in. Lev, Winston, and Turner grabbed whatever cover they could.

"Hit those fuckers!" Winston radioed.

Jones grabbed the second rocket launcher, and damn the distance, he let it rip. It struck what was left of their barricade and they began to scatter like roaches. Turner, Winston, and Lev followed them on foot, mowing them down as they went.

One of them cut into one of the abandoned buildings. Lev missed him with the machine gun but followed him into the building. As he came through the doorway, Lev was struck in the chest with a two-by-four. If he was a man of average height, he would have been struck in the head. Lev took the shot and started swinging haymakers, landing his second shot, which lifted the rebel off his feet and hurled him into a wall. Quick as a cat, Lev was on top of him, pummeling him. He didn't see the blood as it flowed, couldn't feel the bones breaking under his punishing blows, and he didn't hear the person come in behind him. He never knew that a knife was being raised to stab him. The gunshot broke the trance he was in and he heard the body fall behind him.

Lev looked at the body. He saw the knife near it. When he looked up, he saw Winston with his SCAR in hand. He thanked God his boy had had his back. Winston gave him a hand to get him up. He looked at the damage Lev had done with his bare hands.

"Damn, son." Winston motioned for Lev to pick up the M60 so they could get the hell out of the building.

Daisy and Jones kept a lookout for anything else that ap-

proached while Winston and Lev inched closer to the rebels'
position. Turner laid down a few more rounds every couple of
seconds as he made his way to the position, just in case. They
wanted to move fast. The chemical weapons were getting farther
away from them and closer to Mazar-i-Sharif, but they had to secure their position first.

These rebels were nothing more than a sacrifice, a distraction to allow the chemical weapons to clear the border. Mission
accomplished by the rebels while Unit 416 failed to derail the
convoy.

"Where the hell are they?" Griffin was livid. "How can we not
get a satellite feed at the fucking border!"

"Something in the system keeps locking us out, sir."

"That's horse shit! I need to know what's happening with
my men and my damn equipment!"

Griffin left the hole and headed straight for the war room.
He scanned the room, looking for one thing.

"Where's Ayers?" Griffin asked.

"Isn't he in the hole with you?" one of the Special Ops guys
replied.

"Fuck no. How long has he been gone?"

"Two hours, I guess. He said he was going to the hole when
he came back from the head."

Griffin knew he had screwed up. He went to Ayers's space in
the war room and started searching it. He got one of the men to
get him access to his computer. Within minutes, they were able
to uncover death threats being made to him and his family by
Anemah Maasiq.

The BMW pulled into the guarded compound at Mazar-i-Sharif.
Maasiq issued commands to the men to prepare for the arrival

of the trucks and weapons. He warned them of the possible attacks that would follow before hustling Ayers inside, down three
levels to the most reinforced area of the compound. Maasiq had
two men stand guard while they entered a room.

"You have brought this shame on your family!" Maasiq said
in Dari. "Now I only have half of my weapons."

"At least you have half! And you wouldn't have that if it were
not for me," Ayers responded in Dari. "How dare you threaten
my family?! I am your cousin," Ayers said in English.

"It was the only way to force you to respond! You are Shapur
Maasiq, the son of a king, and it was time that you started to act
like it." Maasiq spoke in English as well.

"I brought you face-to-face with Keeble. He is dead, cousin!
What do you want from me?" Ayers pleaded.

Maasiq contemplated for a moment. "I need you to stay here
and wait for the weapons to arrive. Make sure there is no problem; I must go to Kabul to handle some affairs. I might have a
lead on your missing truckload of M16 weapons." He turned
toward a panel in the room that slid open leading to an underground tunnel. "You have done well, cousin Shapur." It was a ref-
erence to Keeble. "Your family is safe, but you should know, you
would never be able to hide from me, not even in Pakistan."

Maasiq walked through a door into the tunnel. As the door
closed behind Maasiq, the panel slid back into place and he was
gone. Ayers, known to his family as Shapur Maasiq, was visibly
shaken as he was left to handle his cousin's affairs.

41

"Fuck that; let's go get them," Lev said.

"He's right," Turner said. "We don't have anybody backing us up and whatever that is in front of us out there, it's going to be coming after us too."

"We gotta keep pushing; we can't trust anybody but us," Daisy said.

Winston and Jones nodded their heads. They all stood around Keeble's body. Whatever he'd been hit with, it penetrated his body armor; he'd never had a chance to survive no matter what Winston did when he got to him. Winston wanted to follow those bastards into Afghanistan and kill them all.

"Griffin was the only one who Kee talked to and this is how he ended up. We have to do this. We don't have much of a choice; I'm sure that somebody is attempting to set us up for the fall," Lev said.

"You're right. Ayers shows up at the border with the mother-fucker that Kee has been huntin' for years. We can't trust none of them bastards. So screw the CIA, Special Ops, and the fucking Taliban," Winston said.

They covered Keeble's body with a tarp and parked his jeep in one of the abandoned shelters. As the men left, they paid their respects to him. Winston was the last one to leave his side.

"We'll be back for you, Sarge. I promise you that," Winston said, and then he whispered, "I will never leave a fallen comrade to fall into the hands of the enemy."

Lev, Daisy, and Turner took the truck while Winston drove the other jeep with Jones. They picked up the path of the convoy. There was enough to worry about with the bad terrain when they traveled through Uzbekistan, but the big concern as they left the border and ventured into Afghanistan was the possibility of ambushes and IEDs. Jones attempted to hack into the communications' system for the compound in Mazar-i-Sharif.

"They're good." Jones commended them for their ability to block his hacking attempts. He was trying to access their security system so they could arrive at the compound undetected. But that hope soon dissipated when the unit was about two miles out and entering into a wooded area.

Lev almost successfully dodged an IED, but the tail end of the heavily armored truck caught it. Winston and Jones were eighty meters behind them and saw the explosion. The truck was badly damaged, but all of the occupants were okay.

Winston knew they needed to move fast to get to them. "Time to ditch that computer and pick that weapon back up," he said to Jones.

"Already ahead of you." Jones had a different look in his eyes; he was no longer shaken by doing what they'd had to do to survive. He had his SCAR in hand as they pulled up next to the truck.

Lev, Turner, and Daisy were okay but a little rattled. Jones and Winston covered them as they grabbed weapons and gear and got out of the truck. When everybody was set, they moved out into the woods for cover, three to the left side of the road and two to the right. Although they moved fast, it almost wasn't fast enough. They had just made it into the tree line when they heard a vehicle approaching their damaged truck. The ambush team was in two flatbed pickup trucks. They immediately started to open fire on the jeep and the truck. Lev and Jones covered the rear while Winston, Turner, and Daisy covered the front. They kept a lookout for any late arrivals to the party and an eye on one another.

When the rebels realized that the vehicles were empty, they got out of their trucks to take a closer look. Their chatter started to pick up. The unit wasn't sure what they were saying, but they could guess their next move would be trying to locate them in the wooded area. That's when Winston gave the hand signal for them to go on the offensive. The unit engaged them in a fire-fight, initially firing multiple shots to cause them to panic as a couple of them were hit. The rebels had put themselves in a bad position by running to the damaged vehicles. They shot back at anything that moved and wherever they thought the bullets were coming from as they started toward the tree line. Unit 416 was calm under fire, squeezing off one round at a time with pinpoint accuracy, neutralizing the ambush in a matter of seconds.

"We don't have a shot of getting in there with the jeep and that truck's not goin' nowhere. It's footwork from here on out," Winston said, and the men agreed. They were two hundred meters deep into the woods.

"It's less than two miles." Turner was calculating the distance and locking in the coordinates for everyone.

Jones was back on the computer trying to break down the security and communications systems again.

"Any luck with their communications system?" Winston asked.

"Still nothing," Jones responded.

"Don't worry about it. Can you still access CIA and Special Ops?"

"Anytime."

"We might need some fire support to help us get out of here."

"Not a problem. I have been in that system so many times, if I can alter the flight plans, I can arrange the support." Jones assured him that would be a piece of cake.

"We're taking this compound. We're going to lose sight of each other; keep the radios open but the talk to a minimum."

"It should take us no more than thirty minutes to three-sixty the compound," Daisy said. "I will set up a sniper location at the highest point I can find."

"I'll take the north side of the compound; Jones, you take the south. Winston, you and Turn can flip a coin for east and west," Lev said.

"Let's get it," Winston said.

They all checked their watches. "Meet me at the compound in thirty," Turner said.

Lev wasted little time moving out because he had the farthest to go and he was toting the most weapons and Jones's communications equipment. Once he reached the south side of the compound, he dropped Jones's equipment and set a tracking device for it. He was on his way to the north side in no time.

Shortly after Lev headed to the north side, Jones followed the tracking signal to the spot where Lev had left his communications equipment.

Turner was closing in on his positon on the east side when something caught his eye. He pulled out his binoculars to take a second look. There was a helipad on the east side of the compound and what he thought was a Z-20, the Chinese clone of the Black Hawk. He also saw a large parking area and what he believed to be the two trucks they were looking for.

Winston made it to the west side without incident. He'd been there for eight minutes and the unit was approximately four minutes away from reestablishing contact when he heard voices and people moving in the distance. There was another ambush setting up. Quietly, he placed the Magpul silencer onto his SCAR. There were four men walking near his location. He listened for any other voices or footsteps. There were none and the men practically walked right over Winston as he sat perfectly still. He fired four shots in succession. The first man was still trying to figure out what hit him by the time the fourth man was shot. Winston walked up to each one of them and put an additional round in their head for good measure.

"Everybody, lock your silencer onto your SCAR," Winston said into the radio and quickly got off.

Daisy set up his sniper position five hundred meters from the compound. It had just enough elevation to give him a view of the top of the building. His problem, though, was that he'd damaged his microphone on the climb up. He would be able to hear them, but he would not be able to communicate with them.

As they reached the thirty-minute mark, Winston initiated a radio check. Each man responded except for Daisy. He did the check again, but still didn't hear anything from Daisy.

"Jones, can you get a visual?" Winston asked.

Daisy was perched in his spot giving a thumbs-up and signaling a problem with his equipment. Jones confirmed the visual on Daisy and let them know he had an equipment issue. Once everyone was set, the men would begin to close to within one hundred meters of the compound. The only exceptions were Daisy and Jones.

Jones had a layout of the compound on his screen and would give them a description of the layout they would encounter. Their objective was to get to the lower right quadrant of the building. That was the primary parking and storage area and likely where the trucks were. Turner was able to confirm a visual of the two trucks.

The roof of the compound was guarded by four men and Daisy had a visual of all of them. He was also responsible for the men on the ground on the south side of the compound. These men were expecting an attack, so Unit 416 was readying themselves to strike with shock and awe.

Once everyone was in position, Winston gave the order. Daisy started with the men on the ground on the south end, then moved to the rooftop. He was able to pick off the enemy like they were tomato cans. They saw the rebels around them beginning to fall and knew they were under attack, but because of the lack of noise, they did not know where the shots were being fired from. That allowed Winston, Lev, and Turner to attack from their positions on the ground. The guards were looking up, trying to figure out what was happening on the roof. By the time they realized that the attack was on and started to fire their weapons, they were already hit.

Lev, Turner, and Winston met on the south side as they readied themselves to infiltrate the compound. Daisy started to advance toward the compound to reposition himself. He began to open fire again from his new position. They took care of anything on their left or right while Daisy took care of the center. He cleared the pathway for the three of them to gain entry to the compound.

As they forced the door to the compound open, gunfire erupted from the Taliban. The Unit 416 members responded in kind, and all of their movements were in sync. While Winston and Lev continued to lay down fire, Turner tossed in a hand grenade. They pushed forward while covering one another's back, moving methodically to the next lower level. It was there they had to separate as they came into a large, wide space. As they sought cover, Lev was struck in the leg, but was able to duck inside an office to hole up and get himself together.

Instead of finding a place where he could check his wound and get back into the fight, he found himself in a room with three men who had run for cover from the hand grenade explosion. One of them had a weapon and was turning it on Lev, but he was already locked and loaded and got his shit off first. The other two men jumped him, trying to wrestle his SCAR away from him. One of the men grabbed at his wound. Lev rammed the back of his head into the chin of the man behind and flipped the man that had ahold of his SCAR to the ground. Lev dove toward him as he pulled out his bowie knife and brought it down into the man's chest. He grabbed his SCAR and turned in time to see his head-butt victim rushing at him. Lev punched him with an uppercut except he still had the knife in his hand. He ripped upward with such ferocity, you could hear the man's rib cage breaking.

Turner laid down cover fire and watched Winston's back as he made his way to the lower right quadrant of the building. Winston fired at anything that moved in front of him. But it was a blindside block that got him. Turner could not get to him because he had to take cover. Turner was outnumbered by the rebels firing at him and was doing the best he could to hold them off.

Ayers jumped on top of Winston. He knocked the SCAR from his grip, pinned him down, and popped his right ear, disrupting his equilibrium. This made Winston far easier to manhandle. Ayers dragged him into another room where two other men began kicking, punching, and choking him. The attack was brutal; it would have been more merciful to kill him.

Daisy started to make his way into the compound. He'd lost count of the bodies he'd put down, but knew the number was nowhere near the twenty-four they were due to encounter. His next contribution would come inside the compound. He reached the second floor where the Taliban had Turner pinned down and were closing in on the office where Lev was holed up. Daisy fired shots faster than anything he'd ever done on a range. His adrenaline was pumping and drew the attention of the men that had cornered Turner. It was enough of a reprieve for Turner to get himself clear to catch up to Winston.

Winston got worked over by Ayers and the two thugs with him.

"You niggers thought you were something special, didn't you? Griffin comes in here and takes over my operation and treats you fucking criminals like royalty."

"Fuck you, Ayers," Winston said as he strained to see him.

"Fuck you."

"Where's Maasiq?"

"Halfway to Kandahar; who knows? What difference does it make to you?"

"I'm going to kill you, and then I'm going to kill him."

"That's what your dumb-ass sergeant thought too. You don't understand the power of the blood that runs through my veins; it is the same power that runs through Maasiq's veins."

"Power of veins; what the fuck does that mean? You ain't shit, you selling out your country. You ain't shit; you ain't from shit and you ain't never gonna be shit."

"Fuck you, nigger! I am from royalty and so is Anemah Maasiq!"

Jones and the entire unit could hear everything that was being said. The blindside tackle had opened Winston's mic. Jones heard the punishment Winston absorbed, but could not believe the shit Ayers was saying. Once he realized that it was Ayers in the room with Winston, he started recording everything that was happening and being said in that room. This shit was the CIA. He paid no attention as Griffin snuck up on him. He was startled by the touch on his shoulder and knew he was a dead man when he recognized Griffin. Griffin motioned for him to keep quiet.

"There is a way that things are meant to run here in order for a peaceful balance to coexist. We now have too many people interfering with that balance who don't know how this shit is supposed to work."

Griffin was stunned, listening to this man betraying the CIA and his country.

"When you disrupt the balance and screw with my money," Ayers continued, "there is a price to be paid."

"So Keeble was a price to be paid?" Winston asked.

A vicious smirk came over Ayers's face. "The best three shots I ever saw. That ni—"

Before he could get the word out, Winston head-butted Ayers in the nose, shot a knee to one of the men's testicles, and tried to rip the other man's set off with his bare hands, and he left the two men there writhing on the floor in pain. The gunfire continued to erupt inside the compound. Unit 416 was forcing the attack, shooting everything and everybody standing. Lev started firing again as he limped his way out of the office. Winston pulled his knife from the sheath on his boots. He made four quick punctures to Ayers, one to each shoulder and each thigh. As he fell in pain, Winston kicked him between the legs and slapped the shit out of his right ear.

"That's how you bust an eardrum, motherfucker!" Winston said to Ayers before retrieving his SCAR. He emptied a couple of rounds into his attackers before turning his attention back to

Ayers. He wanted nothing more than to shoot him in the face and watch him die. Instead, he struck him in the face with the butt end of his SCAR, then he stuck his knife into each shoulder one more time.

"That's for using the *N* word."

Unit 416 swept the premises in a matter of minutes, annihilating everything along their way to the lower quadrant. Lev, injured leg and all, dragged the wounded Ayers behind him. When Lev, Daisy, and Winston reached the bottom level of the compound, they finally hit pay dirt. Lev climbed into one of the trucks to get a quick evaluation of the contents.

"Bingo!" Lev shouted. The truck was still loaded with chemical materials and he was sure that's what they would find in the other truck. "We got it all, boys, we got the rest of the shipment!"

"Stick his ass in one of those trucks," Winston said to Lev as he climbed out of the truck.

"Gentlemen, you only have about four minutes to get out of there. I just got some information from Griffin. There are over a hundred hostiles headed your way. We got an airstrike coming to head them off, but you don't want to be in the middle of that soup," Jones said as he and Griffin headed back toward the truck and jeep.

"You heard him; let's move! We don't have much time. Where's Turner?" Winston said.

"What's your twenty, rev?" Lev asked.

The engines of the helicopter on the rooftop started to come to life. "Up on the roof. Better get up here quick, fast, and in a hurry if you're riding with me."

"Roger that," Daisy said.

Three minutes later, Turner had the helicopter successfully in the air. They were taking on gunfire and could see the hostiles in the distance. The enemy was closing in pretty fast and could cause them a problem as they touched down in the clearing to pick up Jones and Griffin. But as concern grew for how that would play out, they heard the sound of jet engines approaching. It was like music to their ears. In a few seconds, they would hear the sweet echo of music that only a rocket being fired upon an enemy can make.

Turner set the helicopter down at the Uzbekistan/Afghanistan border. Griffin ordered his private team, the CIA, and the Special Operations unit to meet them there. As the members of Unit 416 climbed out of the helicopter, a number of the men and women of the CIA and Special Operations unit nodded and applauded as they passed by. Unit 416 didn't notice them. Griffin ordered his people to remove Ayers from the helicopter and take him into custody. As two men pulled the battered and bound Ayers from the helicopter, they weren't able to detect that he had loosened his restraints. Ayers head-butted one of the agents and kicked violently at the other in an attempt to get at their weapons. As Unit 416 turned their attention to the commotion, they saw Ayers making a last-ditch effort to maintain his freedom. Before any of them could make a move at Ayers, Daisy's near-automatic-reflex action already had his SCAR up, locked, loaded, and a round squeezed off that struck Ayers in the center of his forehead. All of the people standing around were startled by the sound of the shot ringing out, but the five men of Unit 416 stared at Ayers as his body seized one last time before his soul would begin its rightful dissent into hell.

Satisfied that Ayers had met his justifiable end, the five acknowledged one another before they walked to the shed where they'd left Keeble. His body had already been removed. There were no words exchanged, but as each man's eyes met the others, there was an understanding of what they'd been through last night and the last couple of months and there was no doubt that each man had an understanding of who had helped them to get to where they were, as men, today.

Griffin entered the shed; he took a second to take in the space and the gravity of the moment before he said, "We have taken care of Sergeant Keeble. We recovered his body when we tracked the jeep that he was in. I want to apologize on behalf of the CIA. Master Sergeant Keeble was a hero many times over. I am sorry for your loss."

The men nodded and thanked him.

"That was an incredible shot you took," Griffin said to Daisy. He paused for a second as those words sank in; then he continued. "Just to let you know, we have a lot more work to uncover on Ayers. He is the first cousin of Anemah Maasiq. Their fathers fled Iran in 1979. Maasiq's father fled to Afghanistan, keeping the family name. Ayers's father fled to the United States, changing his name to Ayers. Ayers has been feeding classified confidential information to Maasiq for years. There have been coercion and death threats involved, but suffice it to say that was our mole." Griffin started to leave the men, but there was one last thing he wanted to get off his chest. "I also want to thank you men for the work that you've done, for yourselves and your country. Truth be told, I was hoping that we could work together again sometime down the road."

"You never know, sir. Anemah Maasiq is still out there somewhere looking to get his hands on some U.S. military weapons," Jones said. It was a matter of fact.

EPILOGUE

One month after being flown back home to the United States, Unit 416 gathered for a memorial service for Master Sergeant Miles Keeble at Arlington National Cemetery in Washington, D.C.

Colonel Jameson, Erick Harlow, and Marv Goldberg attended the service. Winston, Big Lev, Jones, Daisy, and Turner served as pallbearers. They were joined by Staff Sergeant Rodriguez and Edward Wallace. The service was an intimate one attended by several close friends.

Keeble was addressed with full military honors. Unit 416's hardened, disciplined soldiers chose to stand at attention during the entire service. They saluted him during the twenty-one-gun salute and again during the playing of taps when the honor guard folded the U.S. flag. Rita Perez requested and was allowed to attend the memorial. Winston was given the honor of presenting the flag to Rita. The moment she lost it almost caused Winston to lose it as well. He reached into his pocket and retrieved Keeble's dog tags to hand them over to her as well. Rita looked at the tags in his open hand, carefully folded his hand around them, and gently pushed them back to him. Winston looked at the tags, then to each of the men. They all gave him a nod; the tags were his to keep. Mike Winston was now the leader of Unit 416. He tried to hold it together but the weight and responsibility of that moment caused Winston to lose it.

After the ceremony, Jameson, Harlow, and Goldberg pulled the men aside. Because of their service and heroism, they had earned the option of serving with any duty assignment of their choosing. They also had the option of leaving the army altogether.

"Sir, we appreciate those options, but we have a destiny of greatness to pursue and we are on that road together," Winston said.

"'Ain't nothin' but a G thang baby,'" Daisy sang.

"So you're staying with the ASMU program?" Jameson smiled.

"Unit 416, sir," they all said in unison.

"Unit 416," Jameson acquiesced.

The men turned to salute Keeble one final time before leaving when they saw his headstone unveiled. It listed his name, rank, and dates of birth and death, but it was the last two lines that drew them in. It read:

MSG KEEBLE

DESTINY FULFILLED